Hot
Under His
Collar

Hot
Under
His Collar

ANDIE J. CHRISTOPHER

JOVE
New York

A JOVE BOOK
Published by Berkley
An imprint of Penguin Random House LLC
penguinrandomhouse.com

Library of Congress Cataloging-in-Publication Data

Names: Christopher, Andie J., author.
Title: Hot under his collar / Andie Christopher.
Description: First Edition. | New York: Jove, 2021.
Identifiers: LCCN 2021003774 (print) | LCCN 2021003775 (ebook) | ISBN 9780593200049
(trade paperback) | ISBN 9780593200056 (ebook)
Classification: LCC PS3603.H7628 H68 2021 (print) | LCC PS3603.H7628 (ebook) |
DDC 813/.6—dc23
LC record available at https://lccn.loc.gov/2021003774
LC ebook record available at https://lccn.loc.gov/2021003775

First Edition: July 2021

Printed in the United States of America
1st Printing

To Great-Grandma Rice,
who would have been torn between
being proud and scandalized

CHAPTER ONE

MOST PEOPLE MADE THE mistake of assuming that Sasha Finerghty was a nice girl. This was understandable because she tried to be *kind* to others, but she'd quit trying to be *nice* about a year ago. Before that, she'd always followed her mother Moira Finerghty's rules for comportment for girls. First, one must always be pleasing to the eye. Keep ugly emotions, dark circles, and pimples well-concealed, and—most important—never do anything that could cause Moira a moment of embarrassment in front of the Ladies Auxiliary Board.

That last one was the kicker. Moira was embarrassed by anything that didn't fit her extremely precise and exacting—yet constantly shifting—standards for behavior. Moira believed that not only was perfection possible, it was the least her daughters could do for her.

Of course, she still looked the part of "one of those nice Finerghty girls." She was all perfectly pressed sheath dresses and Mary Jane heels with no scuffs. And she never told anyone that she had started experimenting with simple carbohydrates, sleeping until noon, and binge-watching *Lucifer* all day.

That would be like a fluffy black kitten going around and telling everyone that she was a ferocious panther. No one would believe her. Even her best friend, Hannah, didn't know the depths of her depravity and thought of Sasha as some sort of stalwart moral compass.

If it was improper, untoward, fun, or her mother would think her lax-in-morals for it, she wanted it. And the list of what her mother thought to be depraved was legion: white after Labor Day, black panties, red panties—anything involving panties, really—dark nail polish, cursing, drinking, smoking pot, and even thinking about having sex outside the confines of a heterosexual marital union blessed by the Holy Church in Rome.

Sasha had come by her taste for the taboo quite honestly—given the propensity of children to rebel against their parents—but had learned to keep it under wraps because it made her life easier.

Forbidden fruit would be Sasha's downfall. And it would come either in the form of mangoes, which would give her anaphylactic shock, or the insane amount of lust she felt every time she laid eyes on Father Patrick Dooley.

It didn't matter if he was all the way across the sanctuary of St. Bartholomew's Catholic Church, and she was working to make sure that flower girls, bridesmaids, and the bride walked down the aisle on cue while simultaneously ensuring that the caterer had shown up at the reception venue.

Every time she saw Patrick Dooley, she went wobbly-kneed and flushed. There was something about the way the candlelight glinted off the strands of his jet-black hair and made his green eyes look almost otherworldly. The lilt of his voice as he said the introductory rites caused her to feel indecent things—as though he were whispering dirty nothings right in her ear.

The first time they'd met, her best friend had prepared her.

"He's a total Father What-a-Waste," Hannah had said.

Sasha hadn't really taken her seriously. "Oooh, I haven't seen one of those in the wild for a very long time."

Hannah had the last laugh when Sasha's throat had dried out and she'd muttered a hello and made a beeline for the bar when introduced to the man. She—who had been a debutante—lost all sense of manners when she met that man.

Father What-a-Waste didn't come close to encapsulating Patrick Dooley. He had vitality coming out of his pores. The way he smiled and looked everyone directly in the eye as though they were the most important people in the world was captivating.

Sasha didn't know why he'd become a priest, and none of their mutual friends had shared. She didn't dare ask, because she didn't want to seem too curious about the man. But she couldn't stop imagining the scenarios. And every time she'd seen a hot priest on screen—not that she'd started seeking them out or anything—she'd superimposed Patrick's face on them in her mind.

She'd never had a thing for a full-on priest before, and it was extremely taboo, even for her. More mortifying than the fact that she had a crush on him was that their friends had noticed her crush, despite her best efforts to hide it. Her best efforts weren't very good, apparently.

It was rather annoying, given that she'd recently decided not to covet unavailable men. Aside from being deeply sinful in this case, it was not going to get her any closer to being married. She'd often tried to tell herself that there really wasn't anything about Father Patrick's hair, or his eyes, or the craggy dimples in his clean-shaven cheeks that was so much more handsome than every other man she'd ever met. But that was a lie. It was that he was the epitome of unobtainable, and the taboo of it gave her a kind of rush she couldn't get from overindulging in reality television and pastries. Definitely not from any of the perfectly blah men she'd met on the three dating apps she was currently juggling like a part-time job.

But she had to learn to ignore it if she wanted to get married and have a family. That was something she wanted that she could actually have. And it didn't matter whether she could summon even a scintilla of the passion aroused by Father Patrick Dooley's wedding homily or the frisson of something she felt whenever he looked at her, even though he barely looked at her.

She only wanted him with the heat of a thousand suns because (a) he was a priest, and therefore she could never have him, and (b) even if he wasn't a priest, he wouldn't acknowledge her existence.

It was just like her first real crush—Jake Sanders in the sixth grade. He was the cutest guy in school, but he persistently ignored her batting her eyelashes and dropping things in front of him. She'd even baked him cookies on his birthday. He'd pointedly thrown them in the trash, and somehow it had only made her want him more.

And her crush on Patrick was eerily reminiscent of her lusty imaginings about her first-year English professor—a Canadian former professional hockey player with a rakish scar from a split lip to show for it. And the way he talked about books by old, dead, cis white men made them seem *almost* interesting at the time.

Patrick made God seem more interesting than all the Catholic schoolteachers, theology professors, elderly Fathers, and relatively nubile seminarians she'd met in her whole life had.

It was a miracle that she made it through the ceremony without interrupting the proceedings with an audible, wistful sigh. She knew she'd made cow eyes at Father Patrick the whole time because Hannah rolled hers as they left the church for the reception venue.

"Thank God he won't be at the reception; otherwise you would combust." Although Hannah had no clue as to the depths of her crush, she'd sussed out that Sasha had a crush on Patrick. Hannah thought it was cute rather than a ticket straight to hell and made jokes about it. Sasha let her do so because getting her to stop would require her to reveal how deeply serious her pants feels for the good priest truly were. She would never survive that sort of humiliation, so she kept her mouth shut.

But she agreed that they were lucky Patrick was not joining the celebration at the reception. They had way too much work to do, what all with making sure no one got gluten who wasn't supposed to get gluten and that the mic cut off before the mother of the groom's toast got way too racy for the mother of the bride.

Some people, including her family, thought Sasha's work was frivolous. But they'd helped her and Hannah with start-up cash because she couldn't very well be idle until she got married and had lots of babies, as every Finerghty woman had done for generations and generations. But Sasha derived great satisfaction from her work. Since they didn't work funerals, Good Time Girls' Events was in the business of harvesting joy. And that had value.

She wished her parents could see that, even though she was glad to be far, far away from them.

Sasha was gathering the favors that several guests had left on the tables when a she felt a tap on her shoulder. She jumped, because most of the guests were bidding the bride and groom farewell out front.

She quickly turned and saw one of the groomsmen smiling down at her. Immediately and problematically, she compared him to Patrick. Where Patrick was dark haired and green eyed, this man was blond haired and brown eyed. He also had the unsettling tan of someone who spent entirely too much time in the outdoors without sunscreen. Where she and Patrick shared the pallor of two people who spent most summer afternoons cloistered inside with a book as Gutenberg intended, this man looked like the sort who pursued beach volleyball or—shudder—hiking.

"Hi, I'm Nathan." He held out his hand, and she looked at it for a long moment before offering her own.

"Sasha." She really didn't know what else to say, but she knew she shouldn't remark on how white and straight his teeth were. The feral part of her wanted to do that. But the lady that her parents raised bit her lip to stay silent.

He apparently thought her lip bite was charming, because his smile got wider.

After another silent beat, she asked, "Did you misplace something?" She often had to gather a plethora of lost-and-found items after wedding receptions with an open bar—umbrellas, purses, one time even a thong from an empty coat closet.

"No, I . . . uh . . . was wondering." As he spoke, Sasha felt a level of dread. He was going to ask her out. This wasn't the first time it had happened while she was on the job, and it wasn't the first time Sasha had craved the protection of Hannah's big, sparkly ring. Between that and a positively wicked death stare, groomsmen and drunken wedding guests always left her alone.

Right now, patiently waiting while Nathan spat out his request for her number so that she could give it to him because she would feel guilty if she didn't, she wished she had half the chutzpah that her best friend did.

"I was wondering if I could get your phone number."

There it went. "Oh, uh . . ." She did this thing—it was automatic—where she looked down coyly and stared at him from beneath her lashes. Her sisters did it too. So had her mother and generations of women before them. "Of course."

Nathan let out a breath when she said that, signaling that he'd been nervous that she might refuse. Sasha would never be so mean as to turn down such a polite query for her phone number. If he turned out to be creepy or boring, she could always block him later. Nathan was perfectly handsome, with a nice smile, just about tall enough—sort of a dreamboat if polite, handsome, blond men who were just about tall enough made her feel anything at all.

His smile got even bigger, and she mirrored it. It wasn't his fault that his earnestness deflated her lady boner like a cold shower or reading entries from the r/relationships subreddit did.

She gave him her phone number and saved his when he texted her.

And she only got a little bit sad when he texted her to set up a date for the following Thursday night.

WHEN FATHER PATRICK DOOLEY joined the priesthood, he'd thought he'd struggle with the vows of poverty, celibacy, and obedience. Especially the celibacy one. But what he didn't anticipate were his struggles with accounting and paperwork. His issues with the vow of celibacy were entirely theoretical, and he could normally avoid the focus of his inappropriate thoughts. His problems with accounting and administrivia were very immediate.

Sitting in hour three of a financial briefing from Sister Cortona, he thought he might just up and quit then. Not because the stout, fifty-something nun wasn't lovely—well, not that anyone who'd ever met her would tell her she was anything less than a shining rose of a bride of Christ—but because he'd much rather be hearing confessions or tending to the sacristy or even flagellating himself with a long run in the summer heat.

Hell, he'd rather be reading to the pre-K class, even though their teacher thought that *Hop on Pop* was way too violent for the three- and four-year-olds. The chaotic energy of small children was never boring.

As Sister Cortona droned on about the level of tithing, for some reason he flashed back on Sasha Finerghty fluffing the bride's veil before she walked down the aisle yesterday. He should definitely not be thinking about how lovely Sasha had looked in a pastel dress that hugged her small waist. Or how her thick, dark ponytail would feel like silk in his hands.

He was getting fidgety, flexing and unflexing his fist.

The light in his office—all somber mahogany paneling and stained-glass windows—was scant. The smell of old frankincense and the mineral tinge of holy water was almost too relaxing, and he was worried that he would nod off on the sister again. She wouldn't hesitate to smack him across the back of the head—hierarchy of the Church be damned—so he did his best to stay awake.

When she paused to take a breath, he asked, "Is this going to get less depressing?"

She looked over the top of her gold wire-rimmed glasses and sheaf of papers that somehow spelled out the fate of all the parish's programs in a language of chicken-scratched numbers that he would never be able to decipher if something—God forbid—happened to Sister Cortona. "I'm afraid not, Father."

Then she did the thing where she somehow flattened and pursed her lips at the same time, and he knew that he would have to double up on his heartburn meds that night or be breathing into a paper bag by the end of the meeting.

He'd expected to feel like he was in the world and not of the world when he'd become the pastor of St. Bartholomew's a few years ago. He'd been almost fresh out of seminary, but the Church was so starved for priests—see the vow of celibacy—that he'd gotten his own parish much sooner than he would have in decades past.

And he was lucky. He was in his neighborhood and could see his family whenever he wanted. Being close to his dad and brother eased just a bit of the loneliness that he could never admit to anyone. The loneliness that he felt whenever he wasn't saying Mass or ministering to someone.

The administrivia and the feeling that he was never quite a part of real life were a complete drag, though. And somehow, the administrivia made his ever-present loneliness worse.

As Sister Cortona started to speak, he forced himself outside his head and back into the gloomy office. "The budget shortfall will force us to shut down the pre-K program—"

If anything could yank his brain back from his maudlin thoughts about how he should be content but wasn't, it was hearing that they would have to shut down the pre-K program.

He'd taken ownership—even the Catholic Church employed consultants who said things like "taking ownership"—of creating the program for low-income children when he'd started at St. Bartholomew's. It was open to all the neighborhood kids, regardless of whether they were members of the parish, with tuition on a sliding scale. And it had been a resounding success. Kids who had spent two years with them were reading earlier and seeing higher math test scores in the first and second grades. The program had done more to burnish the Church's reputation locally and bring parishioners back to services than anything the diocese had done over the past few years.

Decades of scandalous, harmful, traumatizing behavior by priests had thinned out the ranks of the faithful and those who answered the call to minister. Patrick believed that initiatives like the pre-K program, things that actually helped people in the community, could turn the ship around. The fact that people in the neighborhood surrounding St. Bart's now knew a priest who wasn't a total creep was actually getting butts in pews. The pre-K program was a more important part of his ministry than saying Mass.

Losing it would be devastating, and he couldn't let it stand. "How much do we need?"

"We're twenty-five thousand dollars short when it comes to paying for the teacher's salary and the necessary supplies."

"Shit," he said quietly.

"Language, Father." Sister Cortona gave him the same look that Sister Antoninus used to give him and his best friend, Jack, when they threw spitballs during class. It was *withering*.

"We can't lose this program." He was adamant about that. He would do whatever it took to keep the pre-K kids learning. He was so agitated that he stood up and started pacing. "There has to be something that we can do."

"We could start charging a larger fee." When Patrick threw her a look that he hoped was just a little bit as withering as hers about his language, she added, "Just a small amount of a larger fee."

"None of the kids could afford it." Well, virtually none. All the public schools in the neighborhood were Title I schools—low income. The families that sent their kids to the pre-K program needed to save their money for food. If St. Bart's started charging higher tuition, their enrollment would drop almost immediately. "Could we hit up the Dioceses for more money?"

That elicited a snort from the good sister. "You could try, but the archbishop isn't as susceptible to those pretty fuckin' green eyes as the silver hair brigade at daily Mass is."

Patrick ran his hand through his hair, which also elicited a snort from Sister Cortona. He didn't think she actually thought that he was a useless pretty boy, but she liked to deploy any weapons at her disposal to keep him in line. Making derisive noises about his good looks helped her do that. In her mind, she probably thought that grooming his thick black hair at all was unbecoming to a man of the cloth. She took her vow of obedience rather loosely, but she was good with the numbers and could pinch a penny until it bled. Which made her indispensable.

He suddenly had a searing headache and just barely suppressed the urge to bang his head on his desk. The last thing he needed was Sister Cortona telling him that he would ruin his pretty face that way in her perfectly annihilating deadpan voice.

"Could we do a fundraiser?" he asked. That, at least, gave him a concrete, external goal that would keep him from spending too much time in contemplation or trying to have a conversation with God, who never seemed to answer.

"It would have to be a mighty big fundraiser." She did not sound hopeful, but that only motivated Father Patrick. There was something about her faint praise and dry insults that he found very inspirational. If he were in therapy, that would be something that he would look at.

"I'll look into it." He'd save the pre-K program, and he would feel *good* again. Probably. Definitely.

CHAPTER TWO

PATRICK HELPED HIS FATHER behind the bar at Dooley's three nights a week. It was time that Patrick could ill afford away from his duties, but even Sister Cortona looked the other way because he did it in the name of being a dutiful son.

His father didn't thank him, just looked him up and down and said, "I suppose you'll do," every time he walked in the door.

Danny Dooley was a hard, stubborn man from a long line of hard, stubborn men. Patrick's father, grandfather, and great-grandfather had all run Dooley's their entire lives. Patrick's great-grandfather had practically shit every brick of the exterior, the way that Danny told it.

Now that Danny wasn't as hale and energetic as he had been, he couldn't run the place all on his own. And, someday, he wouldn't be able to work behind the bar at all. Patrick tended bar that night while his father went over the books at the end of the bar, near the doors that led to the office.

Even as an adult, Danny liked to keep an eye on his sons when they were in his domain. Didn't matter that they were both adults and Patrick was a functioning adult. It still made him feel deeply cared for that his father wanted to be around him. Even if his father wasn't much of a talker, he never worried about where his paperwork was. He'd never done his own taxes. His father might not have been free with pats on the back or words of affirmation, but he was steady.

Chris had started making noises about them selling and had gone as far as to field a few offers. He didn't want anything to do with running the business now that he was an attorney on the way to making partner at his firm. Uncharitably, Patrick thought that his meteoric rise had a whole lot more to do with his brother's gift for bullshit than it did with his smarts.

Patrick would never be able to take the place over, and Danny had never quite accepted it. His father would have liked to put any connection with the Catholic Church in the ground along with his wife, but Patrick had prevented that by entering the seminary.

All three of the Dooley men were at a permanent impasse when it came to what to do with the family legacy. The prospect for any legacy at all was in severe doubt at the moment. Unless Chris got his head out of his ass—which would take major surgery or a true miracle in Patrick's view—his brother wasn't going to find anyone willing to put up with him beyond a few weeks. And Patrick was obviously not going to be carrying on the family name.

Despite the cloud of uncertainty over the future of Dooley's, it was comforting to be there.

IT WAS INCREDIBLY FOOLISH for Sasha to suggest that she and Nathan meet at Dooley's bar on the South Side of Chicago. She'd known that as soon as she'd hit send on the text. But she'd been annoyed that Nathan left it to her to find a place for them to go even after he'd been the one to ask her out. Besides, Nathan worked for the baseball franchise on the South Side, and Dooley's was convenient to his office.

Sasha was blowing this one tiny thing out of proportion because she didn't *want* to like him. Her friend Bridget had given her the side-eye when she'd complained. Easy to do when one was affianced to the one non-terrible billionaire on the face of the planet.

Even Hannah was giving him a break. "Maybe he was trying to be polite," she'd said with a shrug. A year and a half ago, her best friend would have lit into a soliloquy about how suspicious it was he couldn't make such a simple suggestion, but times had changed. Hannah was deeply in love with her handsome, brilliant, patient, and kind husband.

And Sasha was still alone. And dating. And hating every single second of it.

She didn't hate it enough to not put care into it—especially if Father Patrick happened to be filling in as the bartender. If Patrick was there, maybe she could direct some of the lust he inspired in her at Nathan and try to spark something. And, if Patrick was reading a dusty leather tome all alone in his priestly cell—not that she'd imagined this scenario often at all—then Nathan would benefit from her efforts to look nice.

Winning all around.

When she walked in the bar, her gaze was immediately drawn to the man behind the bar.

Patrick was there, sans collar, with his sleeves rolled and his hairy forearms revealed all the way up to his elbows. *Dear God in heaven, please forgive me.* He was so gorgeous that she lost a step. When he looked up and grimaced at her, she could have been knocked over by a flutter of wings from a butterfly across the planet.

Coming here was a worse idea than she'd thought when making the venue suggestion. She should have listened to her better angels—the ones that she'd tied up and gagged in the recesses of her mind when sending that text.

She didn't know how long she stood there, waiting for her sense to return. But she knew that it hadn't returned when Nathan appeared in front of her out of nowhere.

He even did that thing where he waved a hand in her face. "Are you okay?"

No, she was absolutely not okay. She was deeply *not okay*. She was aflame with desire to lick a priest's forearms while she was supposed to be on a date with another man.

She was not okay, and she'd done this entirely to herself.

But instead of saying all that, she put on her "I'm dying to be your best girl" smile—another Finerghty woman classic—and said, "Just fine." She shook her head and knew that her long, dark hair would fall nicely over her shoulders and her pretty, pink silk blouse. "A long day is all."

Nathan smiled at her, and it was so sweet that she made a valiant attempt to forget about the man standing behind the bar, who was pointedly not looking at her.

This guy was way too nice for her to sort-of-kind-of use him to try to resolve her crush on Father Patrick—which wouldn't work anyway. "Listen, do you want to go someplace else?"

"No way." Nathan looked around the dark bar, with its quiet booths and dark wood and stained-glass beer advertisements. "I love this place." He winked at her, which caused an internal cringe. "Points for picking it out."

Gross. Why did guys always insist on giving points for things? It was as though overcompetitive, hyper-toxic masculinity had to bleed its way into everything. She tried to remember what her therapist had told her about making snap judgments about people and how that limited her. She took a deep breath and imagined that maybe his father hadn't shown him enough affection. If things worked out, she could tell him she hated the points thing later on.

Regardless of him giving her points for something he should have done and the questionable wink, she let Nathan steer her into a corner booth, where she sat with her back to the bar.

Not being able to see Patrick had to help. She would try to give this man with a nice smile and a pressed shirt a chance. He had a good job, wore a nice watch, and he was *right there.* It would be a lot easier to convince herself of the appeal of his availability with her back to Patrick.

Nathan went over to the bar and ordered them drinks. Sasha did her level best not to turn around and scrutinize both men side by side. That would be a terrible idea. And she was mostly successful. She didn't turn around until Nathan put down his card and said, "Keep it open."

He must have thought that this was going to last for longer than one drink. Sasha girded her loins for two hours of small talk, then shook her head. She was just here to get to know him better. A first date was low stakes. She tried to reframe it as something that could be fun. When had she stopped being curious about other people?

Probably around the same time that she'd gone on her thousandth first date. Still, she could pretend. One thing that she would have to keep from her upbringing was faking it until she made it.

When Nathan returned to the table, she put on her best smile and said, "Thank you," even though he hadn't asked her what she wanted. She took a sip of her vodka and soda, and it was strong. Must be Patrick looking out for her.

Must not think of Patrick.

She smiled at Nathan. "So, tell me about your job."

When he started detailing the finer points of ticket sales for a professional baseball team for ten minutes, she blocked out everything else.

PATRICK DIDN'T LIKE THAT Sasha was in his dad's bar. He didn't like that she would be here any night, and he really didn't like that she was here the night he'd happened to agree to fill in for his dad. And he really didn't like that she was here with a date. Generally, he needed to brace to see the woman. Like, before the wedding last Saturday, he'd run an extra two miles in the hopes that he wouldn't react to her. Because he shouldn't even be *thinking* about her.

He knew he couldn't avoid her because she was his best friend's wife's best friend. They were bound to run into each other, unless he avoided his best friend, and that wasn't going to happen.

Sasha got under his skin. There was something about her shiny perfection that irked him. And she was very beautiful and made him think of things that were not helpful for a priest to think of.

When they'd first met a couple years ago, he'd thought he had died and was encountering an angel. Her face was pale and almost cherubic—with a ski-slope nose and a cleft in her chin. She was almost too beautiful to look at straight on.

But now, he thought she was probably a witch sent by some malevolent force to make him question his sanity.

Mostly he got through the whole celibacy thing with vigorous exercise and pretending that he didn't have a dick. Sasha, with her sweet smell that reminded him of the summer during college he'd spent in Greece, silky brown hair, and doe eyes, definitely reminded him that he had a dick. More than any other woman he'd met since Ashley, she reminded him of the deep satisfaction that could come from earthly, carnal love. Every time he saw her, he had to pray that God would remind him of why he'd taken his vows. Christ's love was assured and infinite, and it would never leave him.

Christ's love survived death. And when he was a grieving and heartbroken twenty-one-year-old man, he'd found that so compelling that he'd committed his life to it.

He'd made a life inside it, and he was of service to his community and to God. What he did and who he did it for was important. Joining the priesthood had saved him—he owed his life to the Church.

Seeing Sasha, feeling the things she aroused in him—remembering who he'd been before—made him forget who he was supposed to be now. He couldn't do anything with his attraction, so he tried to block out its source.

He would not waver.

But even with her back to him, it was impossible to ignore her. So he scrubbed the already clean bar that was older than him and had kept his belly full and his feet shod for over thirty-two years. He promised himself he would pour an extra-large draught of the good scotch his brother had given him for Christmas before bed. He might not be able to have a woman to keep him warm, but whiskey was permissible. The peat would scrub his nostrils of the sweet fig scent that Sasha had brought into the bar with her.

He tried desperately to ignore her presence while she was on a date in his bar with a man who looked entirely too appropriate for her.

But Sasha Finerghty made him feel helpless in a way he hadn't felt for a decade. As soon as that slick guy had put his hand on the middle of her back, he'd wanted to leap over the bar and snatch it away.

He had no right to.

He had an obligation not to.

But he still wanted to.

Patrick was saved from unsuccessfully trying not to imagine Sasha's date with a black eye by Jack walking into the bar. At that moment, he wanted to curse his best friend for bringing Sasha into his orbit, and so his greeting was probably a bit sharp. "What are you doing here?"

"Whoa, buddy." Jack held up his hands. "Trouble in the God salt mines?"

Patrick sniffed and grabbed a glass to pour his friend his favorite beer. Jack sat down and glanced over his shoulder. "Or girl trouble?"

"I don't have girl trouble." That was a lie. Sasha was plenty of trouble. And he tried not to lie almost as much as he tried not to imagine how smooth the skin on Sasha's thighs would be or what it would be like to be able to touch her.

"Sure." Jack gave him a smile that said he didn't believe him. Of course he would see it all; they'd known each other since Jack was born about a year after him. Their moms had been best friends, and now they were best friends. More like brothers, really. Jack would know what it looked like when he had a crush, and he wouldn't keep his mouth shut about it. That just wasn't how their friendship worked—and Patrick usually appreciated it. But not now.

"I actually do have church problems that I've been meaning to talk to you about." Patrick's role required him to be a counselor to everyone, but he didn't feel like he had anyone to talk to—other than Sister Cortona. She was more likely to point out more problems when he needed solutions. But Jack could sometimes be a sounding board for him. Patrick hated to ask, but now seemed to be the time.

Jack took a sip of his beer. "Shoot."

"We might have to close up the pre-K program at St. Bart's." Even saying it caused a pang.

"Seriously? Even after all that good publicity about the test scores?"

"Yeah." Patrick let out a sigh and put his head on the bar. "And it's not like the kids at St. Bart's"—who were mostly Black and Brown—"will be welcome at any other Catholic schools nearby."

Jack just snorted in understanding of the subtext of his message. Extremely helpful.

Patrick was about to turn and pour himself a whiskey when Jack said, "Maybe we can help."

Jack was part of a "we" now. And Patrick was happy for him. He never thought he'd feel anything about not being part of a "we." But now, with Sasha across the room—he'd never let her out of his line of vision, even when he was talking to Jack—and his best friend as a smug married, he felt something. Something he wouldn't put a label on.

"That's a big ask, man." He'd just wanted to vent, not heap any obligations on his friend.

"Don't even start, bro." Jack gave him a "you've got to be kidding me" look. "If it weren't for you, I wouldn't be married to Hannah. Let us help."

"It's twenty-five thousand dollars' worth of help." Maybe if he understood the gravity of the problem, Jack would back off. Damn, but Patrick hated depending on anyone else.

Jack just shrugged. "Hannah and Sasha raised that much money for some children's charity last week. In one night."

"I can't afford to pay them."

Jack shook his head. "They'll give you the family discount."

"I can't afford to pay them *anything.*"

"The family discount is free." Jack stood up. "And maybe this beer."

Patrick wasn't quite sure what to say. He was always floored when someone showed him a kindness, even though kindness and charity were sort of his *things*. "It's too much, man."

"No." Jack looked him right in the eyes. "It's not."

Then, his best friend went over and talked to Sasha and her date for long enough that it was clear that Jack didn't like the guy either. Otherwise, he would have left them to enjoy their drinks in peace.

CHAPTER THREE

HOW LONG HAD IT been since Sasha hadn't dreaded answering her mother's calls? It seemed like forever. She had to pick up by the third ring unless she wanted to be interrogated about what she had been doing that kept her from picking up promptly. This time, she answered from her watch before the phone started vibrating in her gym bag.

"What are you doing?" Her mother's question sounded innocuous, but Sasha wasn't new here.

"Walking." The best strategy with Moira Finerghty was to give her as little information as possible. She hoarded information like weapons to be deployed at will.

"Shouldn't you be working?" Even that morsel was too much. Not that her mother would know what it was like to work a job outside of ladies' lunches with her cronies, during which they drank vats of gin and tore down whoever couldn't join them that day. Good times.

"I'm an event planner, Mom. Most of my work is at night." Sasha knew that was a mistake the moment she said it.

"That explains why you can't seem to meet a nice man." There it went. About thirty seconds into her conversation. This might be a record.

Her best option now was a redirect. She sighed. "Did you need something, Mom?"

Because her parents had paid for her condo in Chicago, she owed it to them to pretend she respected them the two times a year she visited and over the phone. It strained more and more every year, but she should be able to pay her own way soon. And then— she allowed herself to fantasize for a brief moment. Then she might never talk to either of her parents and maybe even her sisters again.

"I just called to tell you that Marlena is pregnant." Somehow, her mother managed to share that otherwise happy information with judgment toward Sasha's different choices. Sasha would never, ever talk to her daughter that way if she was lucky enough to have one.

"That's wonderful news," Sasha said, with genuine happiness for her sister. They didn't understand each other, but she wished her sister every joy. "I will call her after my workout class."

She had never been so happy to see the gym where she and Hannah took bootcamp classes three times a week. That kind of suffering she could handle.

"I gotta go, Mom." She opened the glass door, and then raised her voice over the din of the waiting room. She spotted Hannah and pointed at her phone, mouthing, "My mom." Hannah rolled her eyes in sympathy. "I'm at the gym."

"Well, at least you aren't letting yourself get fat," her mom said, and then hung up. Nothing like a little fat-shaming to sign off with. Next time she'd be sure to tell her mother about eating a really decadent dessert, just to spike Moira's blood pressure.

Sasha had actually always loved working out. It was one of the only activities that allowed her to make her mother think she was complying with the patriarchal beauty standards the Finerghty women were bound to by tradition, while simultaneously making her feel strong and capable. It was both compliant and subversive.

Hannah used to joke that Sasha had grown up preparing to be a revolutionary in Gilead but stopped when Sasha told her that it hit far too close to home. That was the great thing about having a friend like Hannah—she would say anything but shut up quick if her honesty was inadvertently hurtful.

Today, however, her best friend was uncharacteristically silent at their workout class. And a little bit green around the gills. This was deeply concerning, because she could usually count on Hannah to get her through a bootcamp workout with the power of her sarcasm.

Without the running commentary, she felt as though she was dragging through the class.

"Are you okay?" Sasha asked during a water break.

Sasha looked at her best friend, and Hannah looked decidedly not okay. Her normally flawless skin was an alarming shade of green.

"Do you need to leave?"

Hannah held up one finger. "I think . . ." That was all she got out before running out the door and straight toward the bathroom. Sasha smiled apologetically at the instructor and gathered both their things.

Although she was concerned about Hannah, she had an inkling of what was going on. Hannah and Jack had gotten married last year, and this was probably part of the natural course of things. Sasha would definitely ignore the jealous feelings she had that her friend was probably pregnant, and she was ambivalent about going on a second date with the only relevant guy who'd shown interest in months.

She was not a bad friend, and this was about Hannah. Whom she found retching in the bathroom stall farthest from the door. Sasha knocked gently.

"Just leave me here to die."

Sasha ignored her and swung the stall door open. "That's not part of the deal."

"I did not sign up for this when I agreed to get sperminated." Well, if she had her sense of humor, she was probably further from death than Sasha thought.

"Didn't you?" When Hannah shot her a death glare over her shoulder, Sasha added, "Congratulations?"

"I was going to tell you today at brunch." Hannah clutched the sides of the toilet and puked again. They were definitely going to have to take a car home, and Sasha left the stall briefly to grab some of the plastic bags the gym provided for soiled workout gear for the ride. At least their misadventures in college had prepared Hannah to puke discreetly in the back of a cab.

"I would have guessed when you ordered an orange juice without champagne in it."

Hannah nodded pathetically. "That definitely would have given me away."

Sasha sighed. "How are we going to get you home?"

"I can't go home," Hannah whined. "I was supposed to meet with Father Patrick."

Sasha tried her best to ignore the frisson of awareness that just hearing his name spread through her. "What for?"

"The pre-K program is in some financial trouble, and Jack said that we'd help out." Hannah made a vague motion with her hands. "Set up a fundraiser."

"He did?" Sasha really liked Jack, but sometimes he was entirely too nice. And sometimes his too-niceness forced her and Hannah to commit to things that they did not need to commit to. But one fundraiser wasn't a huge deal. Her hesitation wasn't about the extra work.

It was about whom they were doing it for.

If it was any other priest who needed help saving a preschool program, Sasha wouldn't hesitate. She had to be careful not to hesitate now, or Hannah would know something was up. She might be incapacitated, but she was way too sharp, and they'd known each other for too long for Sasha to be able to obfuscate.

"I'll go to the meeting for you."

That got Hannah to raise her head. "You will?" She sounded so pathetic that Sasha had to fight off a smile. It was only since she'd met and fallen in love with Jack that she'd let herself be vulnerable around anyone.

"Of course I will."

"But you'll have to be alone with Father Patrick." Hannah had noted that Sasha avoided interacting with Father Patrick; that's how she'd figured out that Sasha had a crush. Best friend logic at work.

"It will be fine." Sasha tried to make herself sound nonchalant and failed.

It was Hannah's turn to sigh. "Okay, well, as long as your crush on him isn't going to be a problem."

"He's a priest," Sasha said. Again. Because they'd had this conversation before. "My crush on him is nothing compared to how he feels about *God*."

"God schmod." Hannah pushed herself up so that she leaned against the wall. Progress.

"Besides, he doesn't even like me. Even if he wasn't a priest, it's not like love would blossom." If he wasn't a priest, she might not have a crush on him. Or she would, but it would be because he didn't seem to like her very much. Better to imagine him pushing her against a wall and grunting. Saying some mean sexy stuff in her ear as he hiked up her dress and—

"Not true. Patrick likes everyone." Maybe Hannah just hadn't noticed the way that Patrick *looked* at her—through her. If she'd seen the way he turned away without greeting her the other night, Hannah would know like she did that Patrick barely tolerated her.

"Falling in love has addled your brain, my friend." As though since Hannah had fallen in love, everything and everyone around her was encased in a puffy pink cloud. Even those people who had made deliberate decisions in their life not to pair up. "And he *doesn't* like me. You should have seen the look that he gave me when I walked into Dooley's with a date the other night."

"Jack said that you had a date at Dooley's, but that Patrick seemed irked to see *your date*." Of course Jack would have mentioned that to Hannah. He'd sat with them for long enough that it had gotten awkward and Nathan had ended the date. "Jack said he seemed like a douche."

That was the conclusion that Sasha had come to, but it was disheartening to hear her friend's husband concurred. Still, she would probably go out with him again. Just because there hadn't been a spark over one date—maybe something would develop over time. She could see herself being friends with Nathan. Maybe that could grow to be more. And maybe she could stop thinking about Patrick and how he'd sound grunting and saying dirty things and doing under-her-skirt things.

Probably not. But that wasn't going to get Hannah home and taking care of herself. Even if Patrick didn't like her, and her crush on him was out of control, she needed to do this for her best friend and the only person who really seemed to understand her. Her ride or die.

"Anyhow, it doesn't matter." Sasha straightened up as much as she could. "I will go over to the church to meet with Patrick, and you will go home and go to bed."

"We have too much work to do." Of course they did; they owned a business.

"You are allowed to answer e-mails if you are feeling better this afternoon."

"Thanks, Mommy." Hannah must already be feeling better if she was calling her names.

"That's *your* new title."

They made it out of the bathroom, out of the gym, and onto the sidewalk to wait for a car before Hannah picked up the earlier thread from their conversation. "So, how was the date?"

Sasha shrugged. "It was just a beer at Dooley's—and your husband joined us for the second half." She didn't want to say too much, because he probably wouldn't call again. "No big." Wanting to change the subject, Sasha said, "Jack did mention wanting to talk to us about a favor, but he didn't say anything about it having to do with Patrick."

"Was he cute?" Hannah wasn't going to let this go, and Sasha wasn't going to put her in a car alone if she was still feeling terrible. "I need details. All Jack said was the douchebag thing."

Sasha understood the prodding. She used to get excited about a new prospect and spill all the details. But—for a while now—she hadn't felt like sharing a whole lot because it wasn't like anything permanent was going to come from her endless dates. It used to be fun to meet new guys and flirt and wait to see what kind of freaks they would reveal themselves to be.

Now . . . now it was just tedious. Hannah, more than anyone, should understand this.

"He works in the front office for the baseball team we don't like." She left out the part where Nathan had said that he'd seen Sasha at a couple of events before asking her out. She knew that would put up Hannah's creep antennae.

"Did you make out with him?"

Sasha made a face. For some reason, she couldn't imagine making out with Nathan because she'd been on a date with him in the same room as Father Patrick. The whole time, she'd felt his gaze on her back. The little hairs there had stood up. She had barely registered Nathan as a sexually viable entity because Patrick was there.

She was sort of mad at herself for ruining what could have been a perfectly good date for a cheap thrill. By all accounts, she should be into Nathan rather than Patrick. He'd been into her before her date, and it was her fault that it was awkward.

"If he calls again, will you go out with him?" Hannah's question made things clear.

"Of course. He was perfectly nice."

The car they'd called pulled up to the curb, and Hannah rolled her eyes before getting in. "Sounds like a ringing endorsement."

WHEN PATRICK WALKED INTO his office, he expected to see Hannah. He stutter-stepped when he saw Sasha sitting in the chair across from his desk—prim, as always, with her ankles crossed. How was it possible that she had sexy ankles? Jesus, her ankles? He really needed to say more Hail Marys.

She must have heard him padding across the ancient blue carpet because she stood and turned to him. He took a deep breath, which was a mistake because her smell got in his nostrils. If he still bet on those kinds of things, he would bet that her skin tasted like a ripe piece of fruit.

He cleared his throat and motioned for her to sit down. If she was sitting, maybe he wouldn't think about wrapping his hands around her nipped-in waist while she wrapped her mile-long legs around him.

"I'm sorry that it's me." She looked down, flushed. And the part of him that he tried to forget existed got a thrill from that. "Hannah is feeling under the weather."

"Oh, it's fine." It wasn't fine. He cleared his throat. "That is—I hope it's nothing serious."

Then, Sasha gave him a secret smile, a smile that made him regret being born. Because if he hadn't been born, he wouldn't have become a priest. He wouldn't have given up secret smiles from prim-looking women that he wanted to unravel. He was full of regrets when she smiled at him, because he knew her smiles weren't *for* him.

They were for guys like the one she'd come into the bar with the other night.

"How was your date?" Oddly, his question made her secret smile disappear.

Sasha made a rather inelegant noise. "It was fine."

"Just fine?" He was stupid for asking, but his curiosity about what kind of man a woman like Sasha would fall for ate at him. It goaded him into dancing on the edge of propriety.

"Yeah, you know how—" She stopped, seeming to remember whom she was talking to. "Well, dating is hard. It's hard to find someone you click with, and it's rare when it happens right off the bat. Sometimes I wonder . . ."

When she trailed off, he debated whether he should say anything. On the one hand, she seemed distressed about her date just being fine. On the other hand, he was relieved. But he shouldn't be relieved. It was not as though he could expect her to stay single. He was the one who'd made that vow. "You should give it another try. Sometimes it takes more than one date to get to know someone well enough to know if you're interested."

She looked up at him, her gaze sharper than he'd ever seen it. "How would you know?"

He liked it when she had her back up like this. Like, how dare he give her advice? And she was right; he had no business telling her how to live her life. She wasn't a part of his flock. They weren't even friends. But the way she looked at him made blood pump through his veins—it made him feel alive. And although he knew he shouldn't even get a thrill out of talking to her, he smiled. "I wasn't always a priest."

His voice was lower and more suggestive than it had needed to be, and she flushed again. This was going nowhere quickly, so he decided to get to the subject at hand.

"So, did Hannah give you the lowdown?"

Sasha looked at the sheaf of papers on her lap. "Yes, she said that you need to raise twenty-five thousand dollars by the end of the summer, or the pre-K program shuts down."

The furrow in her brow was supremely cute. If he were a different man, he wouldn't be able to resist smoothing it out with his thumb. He cleared his throat again. "Do you need a lozenge?" she asked, reaching for her bag.

"Uh, no." Patrick shook his head. "You're correct about the situation. We've never had such a large budget shortfall before, and Jack offered your help. If you're too busy with Hannah sick, I totally understand if you can't spare the time."

"Oh no." It was Sasha's turn to shake her head. "I did research on your program before I came over here. It's the only one in this part of the city that offers affordable pre-K education for kids with low incomes and special needs. It needs to stay open." She flexed her hand and hit her thigh a few times for emphasis, and any reservations he had about working with her would have to dwell in the back of his mind—exactly where he'd put the consistent ache she caused whenever they were in the same room.

She understood how important this program was to St. Bart's—and to him. There was no way he was going to let his inconvenient and unwanted feelings for her interfere with saving the preschool.

They could absolutely keep this chaste and professional. They had to. Sasha passed him a sheet of paper with a list of options. "I took the liberty of putting together a list of possible fundraising opportunities. Hannah and I can call on some of our other clients to pitch in, because it would be great PR for them."

"Helping out small children isn't satisfying enough?" he asked, knowing that Sasha would give him a look that partially unspooled his intention to maintain forbearance around her from just moments ago.

"I'll definitely remind them that God is—you know—involved," she said with a wave of her hand that should not have made him feel anything, but most definitely did. "But they will mostly care how good helping underprivileged children will look next time they have a scandal they need to paper over. It's a story as old as time."

Although he didn't like how cynical and world-weary that sounded, he knew she had a point.

"Tell me about this bake sale idea." If he couldn't take a bite out of Sasha, he was interested in getting something else sweet in his mouth—for the benefit of the program, of course.

"Well, it's just a start, and I don't think it will get us to twenty-five thousand dollars in one go." She brushed a strand of hair behind her ear with one finger. "But it will give us a good place to build from."

CHAPTER FOUR

PATRICK NEEDED TO WALK into the preschool class to see Sasha reading to a group of rapt three- and four-year-olds like he needed a hole in his head. Actually, walking into the classroom and clocking the dimples in her flushed cheeks as she giggled—*giggled*—at what one of the children said about Arthur the Aardvark made him wish he could step in for a quick lobotomy to drain the scramble his brains became whenever she was near.

He was ready to turn around and leave when she looked up at him. Although he couldn't avoid her, he wanted to spend as little time with her as possible. At the very least, he needed time to prepare before seeing her. He needed to steel himself against the awareness he felt when he was around her. Her popping in and out of nowhere was a nightmare.

Right then, he could smell the clean, fresh scent of her shampoo over the baseline musty-church smell that lingered all over the campus. He felt heat rise in his skin as she turned her smile on him. Her sable eyes and wide mouth stirred up wants that he'd controlled for more than a decade.

And it hadn't even been that much work to control feelings like this up until now. But something had switched when she came into his office with all her shiny, bright ideas for saving the pre-K program.

Before, he'd been able to relegate her to the slim part of his life he hadn't reserved for God. Sure, he thought she was attractive. And it bothered him to see her flirt with another guy. But those thoughts were passing, and he didn't ache from not reaching over to find out whether her hair was as silky as it looked.

He wanted to walk out. He should walk out. She'd seen him, but he could feign some pastoral emergency, and she wouldn't ever need to know how she tempted him.

But—unlike every time he'd had to make decisions over the past decade—he didn't do what he should. He leaned on the doorjamb and watched her as she got back to reading about Arthur and his teacher trouble. He drank in her smile and let it settle something in him that he hadn't realized was off-kilter.

When she was done reading to the children, Sasha stood up and smoothed the front of her electric-blue shift dress. He racked his brain for any time that she hadn't been totally put together around him. He couldn't think of one. It made him want to see her completely undone in a way that would totally destroy both of their lives.

As she walked toward him, he braced himself. For what, he wasn't sure. "What are you doing here?" That came out more harshly than he'd intended, and Sasha started. He liked startling her more than he should. It made him feel as though he weren't alone in being off-balance. It was selfish and wrong, but he couldn't help being those things around this woman.

"I came to talk about the logistics for the bake sale." Her words were wary, and her gaze was wide-eyed.

"And you decided to drop in on story time?" He softened his tone with this question.

He realized his mistake when Sasha smiled at him. That wouldn't help with Project Dick Go Back to Sleep—like, not at all. "They like you." He cleared his throat of the thing he wanted to say—*I want to put a baby in you*—and said, "You're good with kids."

"Small children are great. They're free." There was something wistful in her smile as she looked through the little window in the classroom door that he shouldn't probe, but with her he couldn't help himself. As long as he wasn't touching her, he would be totally fine. Totally fine.

"You're going to be great with Hannah's little one." When Jack had shared why Hannah was sick, Patrick had assumed that Hannah had told Sasha about the pregnancy. It wasn't public yet, but Hannah told Sasha everything. As soon as she looked at him, he knew that he'd not only made a mistake trying to strike up a non-business-related conversation with Sasha, but had said something *wrong*. Wrong in the way that made her eyes fill with tears. "I'm sorry if I—"

Sasha wrapped her slim arms around her waist in a way that made her seem like a wounded bird, and he almost reached out to pat her on the arm. The only sane part of him still steering the ship of his brain stopped him from touching her. She shook her head. "It's okay."

"It doesn't look okay." Totally should have dropped it, but he couldn't now. He tilted his head toward his office. "C'mon, we'll talk about cake. That always cheers me up."

He didn't miss her raised eyebrow and the look she gave his flat stomach. And he couldn't suppress the jolt of lust her gaze caused him.

"Well, I sort of came here to talk to Jemma." Sasha pointed at the teacher, who had taken over story time. "I wanted to chat with her to get a better idea of how we can really make folks reach deep into their pockets."

When Patrick looked over, it was clear that Jemma had more than enough on her hands. "I'm baptizing Jemma's baby later this week, and honestly, talking to her then would probably cause less chaos than carving out time now."

"I wouldn't want to intrude—"

Of course she wouldn't. "Hannah might be feeling better by then, and you can both talk to her."

"Okay, that makes sense." She crinkled her brow again, and Patrick thought he might perish on the spot. "If you're sure—"

"I'm sure." She followed him out of the classroom and her forehead un-crinkled, so it felt like success to him.

Once they were in his office and she was seated across the desk from him, he could relax a little bit. Her scent didn't fill his nostrils, and she had composed herself. He still wanted to know what had made her gaze shiny about what he'd said, but he could quell his curiosity enough to get through this meeting for the time being.

But Sasha didn't seem like she could let go of the way she'd lost even a little bit of her composure around him. "I should explain what happened back there."

"You don't have to—"

"No. I guess I consider you a friend, even though I don't even know if you can have women friends—"

"We're friends by association." He smiled at her, but it felt tight even to him. "That's allowed." Although it would be a lot easier if she was a friend the age of Mrs. O'Toole—his most faithful parishioner whom he pinned as somewhere between eighty and one hundred and twenty years old.

She took a deep breath as though she was deciding whether to say what she obviously wanted to say. Her full mouth flattened, and he held his breath. Everything in him wanted to hear what she had to say. "I'm really jealous that Hannah is married and pregnant."

Most of the time, confessions were pretty boring to him. Most of his parishioners were at an age that cheating at their weekly bridge game was a more likely sin than cheating on a husband. Sasha's words rocked him. He'd had an idea of what she was like from his very brief interactions with her—poised, competent, shy, *pure*. Like the Virgin Mary plucked out of Bethlehem and plopped down on the South Side. But her admission that she had negative feelings about her best friend, even though he knew how close they were, slightly shifted his view of her. It was like the vision of her messy and disheveled that he'd been trying to hold at bay rushed in.

He said none of this and tried to take on his pastoral persona despite the rioting thoughts that had her crawling across his desk and him pulling out her careful ponytail. "That's totally natural. We're at an age where most of our friends are getting married and having kids. And those are good things for them. And you want good things for yourself. Have you done anything about your jealousy?"

"Of course not. It's just a feeling. And I hate feeling that way. I want to be totally happy for her. And I am happy for her—both of them. I love Hannah like my own sister." She finally paused her explanation to breathe. "And I adore Jack. He's the only man that I could imagine loving my best friend the way she deserves."

That was all well and good, and it warmed Patrick's heart to hear that his best friend had found his match despite a rather rocky beginning. But Sasha wanted to be loved in the way that she deserved. "What about the guy you were on a date with the other night?"

Sasha looked down and blushed. "Nathan?"

Suddenly, Patrick hated everyone named Nathan that he'd ever met for no other reason than one douchebag named Nathan got to do what he could never do—take Sasha out for a drink with the intent of kissing her and doing a whole lot more.

"He's okay, I guess." Sasha didn't even sound like the guy was okay, and that prickled Patrick's guts.

"How did you meet?" He shouldn't be asking these questions. It wasn't any of his business. Sasha wasn't even a parishioner. But he couldn't help himself.

"At a wedding. Maybe you don't remember, but he was one of the groomsman, and he asked for my number as I was cleaning up. He was nice, and I couldn't think of a reason not to."

That didn't seem like a good reason to date anyone to Patrick, but his expertise about dating and relationships had always been limited and ended in college—right after his mother died and he decided that whole love thing was not for him. He'd been good at sex—he thought. None of his girlfriends had ever complained, and the vast majority of them had wanted more of that.

It was only when his heart had gotten involved that everything went sideways. He'd never have thought that losing his heart to a woman in the midst of the most awful period of his life would lead him to a lifetime full of administrivia and celibacy, but here he was. Celibate—but thinking about how much he would give up to touch a strand of Sasha's hair. To hold her and not have to pull away.

"Did you go out with him again?"

Sasha grimaced and nodded.

"How did the date go?"

"It was fine." Her tone sounded bright—overly so.

"Fine?"

"Yeah. I mean, if you've been on one second date, you've been on them all." She paused and scrunched up her nose in a way that was so cute he wanted to reach out and flatten that patch of skin with his thumb. Again. He just wanted his hands on her. "I guess you wouldn't know."

Instead of throwing his whole life away for a woman who thought of him as a friendly acquaintance, he laughed. "I went on a few dates." He winked, even though he shouldn't. The only thing he wouldn't do was end this conversation right here and right now, before he found any more things to like about Sasha Finerghty.

"Listen, you go out for drinks with one guy, and maybe he calls you, maybe he doesn't. As long as he doesn't do anything terribly offensive, you go on another date. And maybe things escalate until you decide you can't kiss him for the rest of your life, or he decides that he wants someone else. It's not interesting. It's not special."

That's not what Sasha deserved. It was decidedly less than what he would give her if he were a different man who had made better decisions a decade ago. But even though he was in so deep with her without even trying, he wasn't going to dig himself any deeper. "I think maybe you're a little cynical."

"It's just the way it is." Sasha sounded so defeated that he wanted to give her *something*.

"Maybe give this guy another shot, and he might not do what you think." He took a deep breath and decided to risk following up that statement that he knew was a lie with one thing that he knew was very, very true. "You're special, and you deserve someone who makes you feel that way."

He couldn't help but look away from her then. It was as honest as he could possibly be about how he felt about her without going too far. "Now, I understand that you brought me cake to try?"

YOU'RE SPECIAL, AND YOU *deserve someone who makes you feel that way.*

And then he just moved on to what Sasha had actually come over to the church for. He couldn't do things like that and expect her not to continue to crush on him—hard. It wasn't fair. Her mother's voice popped into her head. *Life isn't fair, Sasha. If it was, pantyhose would feel like sweatpants.*

She crossed her legs and sent a silent prayer of thanks that no one but her mother even wore pantyhose anymore.

"Yes, I do have cake for you to try." She'd tapped most of her favorite bakers in the city, and they had all agreed that they would donate products for the bake sale. "This isn't a full representation of the selection, but it's a good start."

Even though Patrick's words hung over the room, his focus seemed to be entirely on the task at hand as Sasha pulled out the brown butter vanilla birthday cake with French buttercream, the pistachio honey sponge cake with Italian buttercream, and the blueberry yogurt cake with American buttercream.

"I didn't even know that these were cakes that actually existed." Sasha laughed a little at his childlike wonder. "I'm a Costco cake guy, usually."

"Costco cake is delicious." Sasha pulled out the last one. "This one, however, is orange chocolate buttermilk cake."

Patrick's face scrunched up. "Chocolate and orange together is a no from me." When Sasha started to put the cake away, he added, "But Sister Cortona loves it. Maybe we can save that one for her?"

Sasha smiled at him, but he couldn't see her because he dove right into the other selections.

"This is delicious," he said about the Italian buttercream–topped cake with sliced strawberries in between the layers. "I hadn't realized there were regional differences between buttercreams."

He was usually so stoic and laid back. Seeing him excited about something was novel and made him more compelling. He was actually kind of adorable.

She tried to refocus and concentrate on getting approval for the list of chefs she'd lined up for the bake sale. It took a herculean effort not to preen under Patrick's utterances of approval. She knew better, and he'd just told her to go out with Nathan again. He clearly didn't think of her in a romantic way. He probably wouldn't even if he wasn't bound by his vows.

If Patrick wasn't a priest, he would have so many options. Sasha might be able to sustain his interest for a few dates, but according to Jack, he was sort of a genius—had a photographic memory for literature. He was also devastatingly handsome. With an expensive haircut and even one tailored suit, he would be a certified lady-killer.

Once they were done with their work, she stood to leave. He stood with her and surprised her by taking her elbow and leading her out of his office. The shock of his touch reverberated through her, and she felt it like a brand on her skin. She knew she would look down and touch her elbow later to memorialize the feel of his callused fingers on her exfoliated skin.

"I'll walk you to your car."

"Oh, you shouldn't."

He stopped and smiled down at her. He was close enough that if she rose on her tiptoes, she could put her lips against his. The fact that she couldn't do it only made her want it more. Everything he did made her want him more, and she'd never felt more right about the fact that her every impulse was bad—evil, even. He didn't know it, but her cynicism about relationships was the only thing that kept him safe from her. If she was even a little bit more romantic, she would throw all caution to the wind. Nothing would matter—not the Church, not what her family or friends would think. She would do her best to lead him into temptation.

Not that she would succeed, but she would try.

Something about that seemed to hang in the air between them. Like a promise and a warning.

"I might be a priest, but I can still be a gentleman and walk you to your car."

The last thing she wanted was for him to be a gentleman, but she didn't say that. Only the sliver of self-restraint left inside her made her stop. "That would be nice. Thank you."

She dipped her head, and they walked toward where she'd parked in silence. Her senses filled with the sound of Patrick's dress shoes slapping against the pavement in rhythm with the clack of her heels. She was so absorbed in the scant heat coming off him and the shame she felt from drinking in that heat as he walked beside her that she would not have noticed if the ground opened up underneath them.

That's probably why she didn't hear the screech of rubber against pavement from the car careening into the church's parking lot.

Drinking in Patrick was probably why she didn't freak out when she was walking toward her car one moment and on the grass underneath Patrick the next, the wind knocked out of her but otherwise unharmed.

Because she wasn't the good girl she portrayed while out in the world, she didn't immediately push against him to get up. She stared, dazed, into his eyes, which were so close and so green. And so concerned. "Are you okay?"

Sasha didn't usually have a problem getting words out. But right then she stammered, "I—I think so."

She did a mental inventory. Her head was cushioned by his hand. Her tailbone ached. Legs and ankles and back seemed fine.

But then she wasn't fine, because Patrick's gaze clouded over with something she'd never seen from him—anger. It was as close to passion as she'd ever get, so she still didn't push him away. It was as close as she would ever get to having his weight press her down into a flat surface, and she couldn't quite see her way to making it stop. Instead, she curled her hands around his upper arms and held him close.

She'd feel guilty about it later, but that was not a problem for now. The problem for now was that he smelled like Irish Spring soap, and she would never, ever be able to get that fact out of her head. Not ever.

"I'm okay." She had to make this stop, so she tried to sound sure.

"Fuck." She'd never heard him swear.

"You shouldn't say that."

With that, he levered off of her body, leaving her bereft. Him not touching her made her feel hollowed out and uneasy. She was afraid that she'd never feel easy again without him touching her. And him touching her again was not ever going to happen.

Patrick marched over to the car that had almost killed them both with rage in his stride. He looked like an avenging angel, and she half expected him to sprout wings and grow a sword from his palm.

Gah! She had to stop thinking of him as a hero in a romance novel. He would never be the hero in her romance novel, and this was unproductive. Having lascivious thoughts about Father Patrick would not help her find the someone special that he insisted she deserved.

She got to her feet and dusted herself off in time to see Patrick pull a youth out of the beat-up car that had almost mowed them down by the collar of their shirt. They were far enough away that Sasha couldn't hear what was said, but the kid looked like they had probably peed their pants.

Patrick let the kid down and walked away. The youth leaned against the car, looking just as happy to still be alive as Sasha was.

When Patrick marched back toward her, he didn't look any less angry than when he stormed away. He didn't stop his storming until he was in front of her. He grabbed her by the arms, probably too hard. But it was just hard enough for Sasha to feel like she was still tethered to the earth.

And he was touching her again.

"Are you sure you're okay?" He still sounded angry, so she paused before answering. She did not want to anger him by claiming to be okay when she really wasn't. "I can take you to the emergency room."

Then he looked her up and down for outward signs of injury, probably because she still hadn't responded to him. And she needed him to stop looking at her because she was pretty sure that her nipples were rock hard since he had touched her so much in the last two minutes.

"I'm really fine. A little bruised from the fall." That sounded like she was upset that he'd saved her life. "Thank you for saving my life."

He seemed to relax when she said that. And then he seemed to realize that he was still touching her. He dropped his hands and stepped back, clearing his throat. "Of course."

"You were kind of hard on the kid." Sasha motioned over to the car, which now didn't have a kid leaning against it.

Patrick's gaze hardened again, and Sasha tried not to shiver. "He almost *killed* you."

She could have fallen in love with him then. The idea of her being hurt or killed seemed to be so unacceptable to him that he stopped being the affable acquaintance she'd had for years now. His collar might have disappeared—just up and floated away. He was *so much man* in that moment.

It was impossible not to let her mind go wild with the possibilities that would open up if he was not a priest right now. If he was just a regular guy, the best friend of her best friend's husband, they might have already done it.

No, she knew they would have already done it. She would have made it happen. Just turned on the Finerghty-woman magic and made him hers.

Not that he would have had any idea of what was happening while it was happening. The Finerghty magic was much more subtle than all that. She didn't think her father knew that her mother had mapped out their courtship with a level of precision and strategy that would impress a four-star general. And her sister's husband had no idea that their meet-cute was nowhere near the coincidence he'd thought it was. Her mother and sister had scoped out all the first-year men in the Notre Dame freshman faces site and picked one out. Marlena had gotten a work-study job with her now-husband, Kevin, batted her naturally long eyelashes, and the rest was history.

Not-a-priest Patrick would have been almost as much of a gift. Granted, he hadn't gone to Notre Dame. But he was Irish Catholic, and he would have given Moira's grandchildren the prettiest green eyes. He would have been seen as acceptable as long as he'd gone to the right law school or medical school.

She must have had a dreamy look in her eye, because Patrick tilted his head. Thankfully, some of the anger leached out of his affect. "Are you sure you're okay?"

Needing a moment to collect her thoughts from the gutter, she cleared her throat. "Yes, I'm fine."

Patrick nodded, and the air re-thickened between them. He stepped back, and she felt his absence. She was tempted to throw herself in front of Mrs. O'Toole's Subaru so that he would save her again. Kind of.

The sensible part of her brain flipped back on now that she was no longer surrounded by the scent of Irish Spring and drowning in Patrick's clover-colored eyes. "I'll send you the final plans for the bake sale and get you the flyers to hand out at all the services this weekend. Hannah will send out a newsletter to our usual press contacts between bouts of extreme nausea to get some local, feel-good coverage. And we'll talk to Jemma at the baptism this weekend."

"Thank you." He grabbed the back of his neck, threatening her equilibrium again with the sheer amount of masculinity he was throwing off. "This is really too much."

"The work you're doing with those kids is really important." She kept herself from reaching out to touch his shoulder reassuringly. She wanted to give him comfort, and it was exceedingly difficult to remember that it wasn't her place to do that. He wasn't hers, and he never would be. "Their whole lives will be better because they had a nurturing place to go to learn kindergarten things before kindergarten."

Sasha had been given every advantage, and her family had always emphasized the importance of giving back. For them, it was all about image. For her, from the moment that she'd started going to the local South Bend preschool with Hannah to read to kids, it was about making a difference.

Maybe part of her wanted Patrick to think she was a good person. Reading to kids and planning this bake sale so that they had a place to go and learn also made her feel like a good person. And most days, especially days when she didn't feel like she was living the life that her family expected her to live, she really needed that. "It's not too much because St. Bart's needs it. The kids need it."

Patrick gave her a crooked smile, and all the parts at the middle of her body melted a little. She could pretend it was the adrenaline draining out, but that would be a lie. And she didn't even want to lie to herself in the presence of a man of the cloth.

"You really do deserve someone as special as you are."

God, he was trying to break her heart.

CHAPTER FIVE

SASHA MET HER SISTER Madison for lunch about once a month. She was the only member of her immediate family who didn't cause a knot to take up residence in her belly. Still, she had to keep some boundaries because Madison hadn't developed enough self-awareness to realize that their parents had really fucked all of them up.

Why would she? She'd followed all of Moira's rules and was married to a perfectly fine guy with a trust fund. When Madison swept into the restaurant late without so much as an apology, Sasha had to wonder how she spent all her time. It was the same question Sasha often asked herself of the stars of the *Real Housewives* franchise. There was only so much time that someone could spend on glam.

After they'd air-kissed and Madison sat down, she examined Sasha. It reminded Sasha of the thing her mother did whenever they came home. But Madison didn't usually say anything cutting right away. She kept her knives stowed for later.

"You look . . . great," Madison said. Sasha was not prepared for a compliment. "Clearly driving our mother up a wall agrees with you."

Sasha sighed. "I'm doing no such thing." She grabbed a piece of bread from the basket at the center of the table and ignored her sister's look of horror.

"I think the fact that you aren't doing anything is what's bothering her." Madison must have fielded a call from Moira after Sasha had hung up on her on the way to the gym the other day.

"You know, running a successful small business is doing something." Sasha slathered more butter than was strictly necessary on a second slice of bread. "Just because I'm not barefoot and pregnant like our parents' prehistoric standards dictate that I should be by my big age doesn't mean that I'm not doing anything." Madison's mouth dropped open. Sasha wasn't usually so direct with her criticism of their parents.

Still, Madison's brain didn't short out. She didn't skip a beat before asking, "So, are you dating anyone?"

Sasha weighed whether to mention Nathan. On the one hand, she liked to throw Moira a bone once in a while. But did she want to answer questions about Nathan at every lunch and brunch with her mother and/or sisters until she met the next guy that she tried to like?

There was never any question in her mind of mentioning the man who occupied her thoughts—Patrick. Madison would not understand why she had a crush on him. He didn't even have any money.

In the end, throwing the bone came out on top. "I've gone out with someone that our mother might like, but I don't think it will develop into anything serious."

"Because our mother would like him?" Sometimes Madison got her.

"Precisely."

"Well, she likes Tucker more than I do."

"Trouble in paradise?" Sasha didn't begin to try to understand her sister's relationship. She'd met her husband at one of their parents' parties. Sasha had always assumed that Tucker was a plant, and thus ignored him. But maybe Moira had just worn Madison down enough that she hadn't had the will to fight her any longer.

"Marriage isn't supposed to be paradise, Sasha." Madison popped an olive into her mouth.

"Yeah, I'm going to rush right into that institution." Sasha nodded at the menu. "Now, I'm going to order the pasta carbonara, and you're going to share it with me because you and I both know that you're not allergic to gluten. I've also swept the bar for our mother's spies, so it won't get back to her."

SASHA DIDN'T KNOW WHY she was seeking out a face-to-face with Patrick after-hours. Scratch that. She wasn't lying to herself anymore. She knew exactly why she wanted to see him. Against her better judgment and all the better judgment of anyone in the world—she liked him and wanted to spend more time with him.

She looked down at the thousand-piece puzzle that depicted the Sistine Chapel that she'd brought because she'd done all the other ones stowed away in a bookshelf, behind a corner table at Dooley's over the past couple of years. It wasn't as though she could seduce him with that. Plus, Dooley's would probably be busy tonight. She'd set herself up in the corner and work on it alone with a glass of whiskey.

But when she'd opened the door, only a few of the tables had patrons, and Patrick clocked her presence immediately.

"Hey." He raised his arm in a casual greeting that made her heart pick up speed. He was wearing a flannel shirt over a Henley, and she hadn't known that it was possible for him to look any better than he did in a clerical collar, but here they were. "What can I get you?"

Patrick didn't question her coming in, so she wouldn't either. It was totally normal for her to show up at the bar where she and her friends often hung out on a Thursday night. In her heart, she knew that she should be making more of an effort to see Nathan. He was really nice, and there was nothing wrong with him except for the fact that he was just so earnest. It was hard to get it up for a guy who didn't seem to have any flaws at all.

Flaws made people interesting. Maybe instead of giving it another shot with Nathan, she should be looking for guys with flaws that didn't come along with a vow of celibacy. Or maybe she should be looking a little more closely for Nathan's flaws.

"I'll have a whiskey." Another time, maybe. "And a spot to work on this." She shook the box and the puzzle pieces shuffled around in a way that was pleasant to her ears.

Patrick peered over the bar to see what she was holding. "You're into puzzles?" His question didn't sound judgmental, just curious and possibly a little bit excited.

"You too?" Sasha asked, hoping that he would answer in the affirmative.

Patrick poured her a drink, and she tried very hard not to notice how his forearms looked as he did that. He really shouldn't be allowed to lift weights. It wasn't fair, and it added too much to his mystique. She might have to take it up with the cardinal if this went any further.

"I mean, aside from moderate whiskey consumption, puzzles and books are really the only thrills left to me."

Before she could stop herself from saying it, "Well, you certainly get to partake in physical exercise, too" popped out of her mouth. She looked down at her hands and could feel her skin stain red.

For his part, Patrick totally glossed over the fact that she'd just admitted to checking him out. Like a damned gentleman. "I haven't done this one."

"So you're, like, really into puzzles?"

"People give me all the Catholic puzzles for birthdays and holidays."

"Makes sense." Sasha smiled at him, miraculously able to meet his gaze. He smiled back, and then it felt awkward again, but bearably awkward.

"Mind if I join you?"

Sasha had been hoping that he would ask that. In her fantasy version of the evening, it was just the two of them working on a puzzle. She forced herself to skip over the part where they were both overtaken by passion. Maybe she needed to add some thrillers into her reading rotation so her fantasy life could calm itself down just a little. Romance would always be her first love, but she could probably stand to add a little variety until her crush on Patrick waned.

But telling him that she didn't want his company would be rude. In addition to enjoying the way he looked and the way he smelled, she liked being around him. He made her feel good. It was sort of the same feeling she'd had when she'd started hanging out with Hannah. Someone who was curious about what she thought and felt, instead of what she could do and how well she was behaving, was so refreshing.

The atmosphere in her family was filled with so much pressure. She hadn't noticed it until she'd spent a good amount of time around someone who didn't pressure her to be or do something else.

From Patrick, it was probably just gratitude that she'd agreed to help him out, but her stupid heart didn't care about that. "Of course."

He came around the bar and led her to a well-lit table in the corner. That's when she noticed the boxes of puzzles stacked on a bookshelf in a little nook. "So, these are all your doing."

Patrick gave her a smile that she would classify as roguish from anyone else. "I don't think my brother could sit still long enough to do a puzzle, and my father's idea of leisure time is cleaning the house."

"You really do like puzzles."

"Would I lie to you?"

"Never." Sasha knew that. He had this honesty about him that didn't have anything to do with not sinning being his thing. He was easy to talk to, and he looked as though he would keep all of her secrets.

They sat down, and Sasha spread the puzzle pieces over the table. That was always so satisfying to her. Like her own personalized form of ASMR.

"Where did all these puzzles come from?" Patrick furrowed his brow as though he were in pain, and Sasha regretted the question. "Never mind."

"No, it's fine." He sifted his hands through the pieces and found a corner. "I used to do puzzles with my mom. Especially once she got sick."

"I'm so sorry." The last thing she'd wanted to do coming here was to make Patrick upset. She felt enough guilt at the idea of seeking him out, even though she had a sneaking suspicion that her crush on him was returned. That alone had the potential of being life-ruining. He didn't need her to remind him of his dead mom.

But he made eye contact with her then. "It's okay. It's a good memory. Thank you for reminding me."

Sasha wouldn't examine the way his genuine smile warmed her to her toes and made her willing to do anything to experience it again.

CHAPTER SIX

THE GOOD NEWS WAS that Sasha had stared long enough at Nathan during their third date that she didn't think he would ask her out again. The bad news is that she would probably be the subject of a Reddit post before the end of the night. The humiliation of going viral, even if it was anonymous, would probably make it so she couldn't leave her house again.

Now that Hannah was at about half capacity because of morning sickness, her only source of pleasure was "Am I the asshole?" posts. Hannah would definitely recognize her in one of those and put her on blast.

It's not like she had tried to seem like a total freak on her date. Going in, she'd only intended to try her hardest to grow an attraction to the man sitting in front of her instead of the man she couldn't stop thinking about. She knew how bad she wanted Patrick to forget about his vows wasn't healthy. It was probably pathological. She always wanted what she couldn't have. For her, wanting something was better than having it.

Patrick might believe that she was special. Then again, his

words might have been platitudes the other day. Maybe he could see that she was doe-eyed and smitten every time she laid eyes on him and wanted to pat her on the head and push her away.

That was probably it. If she truly deserved someone who saw her as special, she would have performed better on her date. Instead of squinting her eyes and trying to conjure a single, solitary dirty fantasy about the man across from her, she might have spent more time asking about his hobbies. According to Moira, this was much less gauche than asking about stock portfolios and investments directly—but no one with a serious skiing habit was lacking in funds.

At least that was the theory.

But no. She'd tried to imagine Nathan pushing her to the ground and pressing his body into hers. And then she tried to imagine him pinning her arms above her head against a wall and sticking his hand down her panties.

She couldn't.

Multiple times over the course of their very nice, expensive dinner, Nathan had asked her what she was thinking. And each time she'd turned red and said, "Nothing."

He probably thought she was completely daft or not into him.

The latter was definitely true, and she couldn't stop beating herself up over it.

Nathan hadn't had much to drink over dinner—just one beer. Sasha had three glasses of champagne in order to get herself in the mood. He'd probably thought she was drunk, which was probably why he didn't even kiss her at the door.

The good news was that he wasn't going to ask her out again. The bad news was that she wouldn't have anything to distract her from fantasizing about Patrick. But it wasn't fair to Nathan, and she knew that.

Still, the same part of her that had thrilled to Patrick's reaction to someone almost mowing them down in the parking lot wanted to witness how he would react to seeing her with a man who wasn't prevented from fucking her by sacrament.

If he'd just been placating her with the words that were quickly forming a tattoo on her soul, then he might not even react. He'd be friendly, avuncular even.

But if his reaction to the teen driver was an indication of more complicated feelings about her, then she could imagine his nostrils flaring like an angry bull's when she introduced Nathan at the bake sale.

She didn't want to use Nathan. But she also kind of did. That's why she'd felt so dirty after their date that she'd taken a shower before wrapping herself in a towel and rubbing in all of her lotions. Self-care was important, after all.

It was why she had traces of darkness under her eyes once she'd washed her makeup off. Her obsession with Patrick Dooley was messing with her sleep.

If only her brain would perform the same acrobatics with Nathan. After all, there was nothing wrong with him. And on their first date and second date and third date (before she ruined it), he'd really seemed like he wanted to get to know her.

If only that were an aphrodisiac in the same way that unavailability was.

She put on her silk jammies and flopped back on her pink-festooned bed—a birthday gift from her parents. She would have chosen differently, but she'd always had to choose her battles with

Moira. Exchanging the bedding would have been a whole lot of drama.

Ready to pass out after a date that was probably more emotionally taxing for Nathan than it was for her, she closed her eyes. Her phone buzzed on the nightstand, and she pried her eyes open and dragged her hand over to pick it up, expecting to see "Mom" flashing on the screen in the text notification.

Instead, it was Patrick. Even though they were on several group chats together, he'd never texted her directly before. She really should just leave it until the morning. Texting with a man late at night gave men late-at-night ideas. And, when it was Patrick, it gave her more late-at-night ideas than she'd previously had. A lot of late-night ideas.

She threw her arm over her face and took ten deep breaths and attempted to remind herself that she was going to keep acting the part of the good girl, even if that really wasn't what she wanted to do.

And even though Nathan would never ask her out again, she wasn't going to indulge in any flirtation with Father Patrick. He was committed to God and the Church.

She was never going to let her mind dwell on the way that his body had felt as he'd pressed her into the green grass. She couldn't allow herself to remember how massive he'd felt in comparison to her or how gentle his touch had been. She wouldn't catalogue the way his face had turned from relief at her safety to anger at the person who had put her in danger.

And, even as she told herself that she wouldn't allow it, her fingers drifted from her collarbone, where she'd felt his heavy breath against her skin, to her cheekbone, where his lips had brushed accidentally as he'd knocked her to the ground.

She tried to push thoughts of him away, but after about ten minutes of mooning, she realized that it wasn't going to stop until she picked up the phone. Her curiosity about what he could possibly have to say to her at this time of night won out over her vow to herself to behave.

Patrick: How are you feeling? Sore at all?

Sasha snorted a bit of laughter. She usually received a text message like that in a very different context. She doubted that Patrick even knew that there could be another meaning to his words. Even though he hadn't always been a priest—a statement that continued to plague her—he'd been one for long enough that he wouldn't have thought about how she could have taken that text.

Sasha: I'm just fine. No long-lasting damage.

She put the phone down, not expecting him to answer. They were friends. That was established, but it felt weird to be texting him. She could barely picture him working a cell phone, for some reason. Part of the point of being a priest was maintaining status as a luddite, and it muddied her mental picture of Patrick to see him using a phone.

Patrick: Thank God.

Patrick had looked like an avenging angel when he stared down at her on the ground. A dark avenging angel. It was hard to picture him differently now. She'd never viewed him as sexless, like the pastor of the church her parents attended at home. But after he'd pushed her to the ground to save her from a speeding car, she could only imagine him in the context of romantic hero.

Still, she should have left it alone. But her kink for authority figures wouldn't let her.

Sasha: No, thanks to you.

Patrick: What are you doing up so late?

Him asking after her well-being turned her on even more.

Sasha: Are you scolding me?

She'd like for him to scold her for more than her bedtime. If he only knew that she'd cast him as the hero of one of her favorite books, he would have a whole lot to punish her for. She'd like to kneel in front of him. The idea filled her with unruly, untamed lust.

However, she saw the ellipsis form in the text bubble on her phone, and she would not touch herself thinking about him while she was talking to him. It would be some sort of rude, nonconsensual thing, and it was a line that she would not cross.

Patrick: Scolding you?

Sasha: Yeah, shouldn't you be in bed, too? Don't you have an early day of preaching?

Patrick: I don't sleep much.

Was he up all night thinking about God and all the ways he'd failed? He probably had some sort of medical condition that made him an insomniac. She had to stop romanticizing him. There was nothing romantic about their relationship.

She was caught off guard by his next question.

Patrick: Do you believe in God?

Sasha wasn't quite sure what to say. If her parents asked, she definitely believed in God. But, when no one was looking, she didn't think there was anything beyond the present moment. She wasn't sure whether to give the honest answer or the answer that Patrick was probably looking for.

He definitely believed in God. Would he try to convert her if she told him that she doubted that God was anything beyond a fantastic human imagining to stave off the certainty and finality of death?

In the dark, it seemed like the right thing to do to tell the truth.

Sasha: Not really.

Patrick: I shouldn't be saying this, but that's comforting.

Sasha didn't dare say anything to him after that. And he didn't elaborate. If insomnia spread like a contagion, she would have been infected by that one ambiguous statement. What did he mean?

Her prurient interests were directly served by the idea that Patrick felt something beyond pastoral concern for her soul and friendly concern for her health and safety. It certainly put his anger at the kid who had almost mowed her down in context.

Sasha liked the idea that she was precious to him. She tossed and turned for at least an hour, knowing that if she could relieve the ache between her legs, she might get a few hours of sleep before she had to be up and out the door for the baby shower that she and Hannah had planned tomorrow.

But she couldn't get the idea of Patrick treating her like a precious doll out of her mind. That maybe the image of his benevolent gaze after he'd saved her from getting hit by the car wasn't about saving her from the fires of hell. That he was going to dive into them with her.

CHAPTER SEVEN

THE NEXT TIME SASHA came to see him—and he'd started thinking of it as coming to see him—he put product in his hair. He tried not to think about what that meant in terms of his vows, but it meant something and sat on his conscience.

He'd told himself that it was about the baptism that he needed to perform that morning. Jemma's wife, Marie, wasn't a member of the Church anymore because of the teachings on LGBTQ+ issues, but Patrick wanted to make them feel as welcome as he could, given his lowly position. It might get him in trouble, but it wasn't like the bishop would really do anything about it. He hadn't done anything but give Patrick a stern talking to before.

Besides, the Church couldn't afford to lose a priest over something as innocuous as baptizing a newborn—no matter who that newborn's parents were. He'd also performed their backyard wedding ceremony, but no one in the Church or at St. Bart's knew about that. Sister Cortona might suspect, but it was one instance in which she cut him some slack and didn't bust his chops.

Thank God.

Sasha and Hannah came in toward the end of the ceremony and sat in the back pew. Jemma held out her infant over the baptismal font for Patrick to perform the sacrament. Just some holy water and a few words and all the stain of sin wouldn't be able to touch this little guy anymore.

He'd performed the rite hundreds of times, but this time he was a bit self-conscious about it and he flubbed a few of the words. "I baptize you in the name of the—uh—Father, the Son, and the—uh—Holy Spirit."

It seemed fitting that his memory went wonky on the Holy Trinity when Sasha entered the room. But he had a job to do, and he would do it.

The fact that Jemma and her wife trusted him with their baby's spiritual life was the reason he stayed. Patrick knew that the bishop—his boss—and a lot of his fellow priests in the diocese weren't willing to baptize the children of LGBTQ+ couples, which was probably why Patrick had many members of the community as parishioners and the bigoted priests in the diocese didn't.

Patrick knew the catechism back and forth. He knew all of the rules, and he followed most of them. But he'd also been raised to always do what was right, even when it was against the rules. And—despite the pope's oblique references to a more inclusive Church that the other officials at the Vatican tended to walk back—the Catholic Church's official position on LGBTQ+ issues was flat-out silly. Looking down at baby Sullivan, he could no more deny him the sacrament and blessing of baptism than he could quit breathing.

It was one of the reasons that he'd stayed in the Church once he'd started to suspect that his vocation wasn't truly authentic. If he left, who would minister to the families in his parish in the way that they deserved? The bishop would probably replace him with some ultra-conservative prick who would preach homilies to increasingly empty pews.

And he might even fire Jemma because of the stupid "morality" clause in all the contracts that employees of the Church had to sign.

When he handed Sullivan to his teary-eyed and joyful godparents and they promised to protect him from hell—which Patrick knew existed here on Earth even as he had doubts about the meaningful threat of an afterlife—he felt more filled with purpose than he had in a long while.

Even when Sasha and Hannah filed into the last pew.

He was scheduled to meet with them after the baptism and discuss details for the fundraiser. Even though the timing was bad, he'd filled Jemma in on the financial situation with the pre-K program. She'd agreed to chat with Sasha and Hannah at the reception after the ceremony. They had an entire sheet cake, after all, and Jemma's wife wasn't keen on bringing most of it home.

After the mass, he found Sasha and Hannah chatting in the vestibule. His best friend's wife greeted him with a huge smile and warm hug. Even though they could not be more different, he and Hannah had gotten along immediately. Patrick thought it might have something to do with the fact that they were the only two people on Earth who had no problem telling Jack Nolan that he was completely full of shit.

Sasha smiled at him, but no hug. That was probably better for both of them. "Hi, Patrick."

He liked the sound of her saying his name far too much. A lump formed in his throat, and he nodded at both of them. "Jemma and Marie know you're coming."

"Are you sure it's okay?" Sasha asked, even though he'd assured her it was fine three or four times via text. "We really don't want to intrude on their celebration."

"Jemma is really invested in this program. She built it from the ground up." Marie was a high-powered lawyer at a law firm downtown, so they would be fine financially regardless. Still, the kids were important to Jemma, and Jemma was important to Marie. "And there's plenty of cake."

Sasha's eyes got a little wide. "The grocery-store kind with super-sweet buttercream?"

"No other kind."

They went into the atrium, where Jemma and Marie's family and friends had gathered. Jemma spotted them and handed off baby Sullivan to one of his grandparents, who accepted the infant eagerly.

She rushed over to them. "Have you had cake?" Jemma walked them over to the refreshments table, where Sister Cortona was cutting into the positively giant sheet cake.

"I have no idea why you got this much cake for a smattering of people," Sister Cortona grumbled. "And goodness knows your wife is going to stick me and Father Patrick with the leftovers. Neither of us will be able to fit through the rectory doors."

Jemma laughed. "That's because you've never seen my family eat cake before. And I'm sure we can find a good home for the leftovers that isn't yours or mine."

"You should freeze that corner piece." Sasha pointed to one of the flowers that hadn't been cut into. The frosting flowers had always been her favorite. "And keep it for when you want to celebrate something in Sullivan's life. Or a day when he's really driving you up a wall."

"That's a great idea." Patrick hoped that he didn't sound like a teenager with a hopeless crush. It was just rare that someone shared his cheesy sentimentality. If she shared his taste for corny jokes, he would really be in trouble.

Jemma didn't seem to notice that he couldn't seem to stop looking at Sasha, but he could feel Sister Cortona's pointed gaze on him. It made the hairs on the back of his neck stand up. If he wasn't careful, she'd rap the back of his hands with a ruler and make him stand in the corner.

"That *is* a great idea," Jemma said. "Patrick mentioned that you and Hannah wanted to do a bake sale to raise funds for the pre-K program?"

Hannah declined a slice of cake, citing a still-iffy stomach, but that didn't keep her from launching into a pitch. "It was all Sasha's idea. We've approached a group of our vendors and a few of the baking influencers we've been tracking on social media."

"There are baking influencers?" Patrick asked, incredulous about the idea.

Sasha rolled her eyes at him. "If you had any presence at all on Instagram, you would know that. By the way, I started an Instagram page for the church. I sent you the login details so you can put photos up."

Patrick could feel a flush crawling up his neck. He really should have thought of starting an Instagram page if he wanted to attract younger parishioners. But, according to his brother, Instagram was for "thirst traps." Considering his lifestyle, he had no use for those. Especially since the only person who'd made him feel anything resembling thirst was standing right in front of him.

Because he'd agreed to work with her. To save the church pre-K program. For the Catholic Church that he was the pastor of. Maybe if he could keep reminding himself of that, he would be able to stop looking at her like a moony-eyed bastard.

"Do you really think we can raise twenty-five thousand dollars with a church bake sale?" That question came from Sister Cortona, ever the skeptic.

Sasha turned to her. "I absolutely think we can. We'll have to make sure the invite list includes people from the surrounding community with deep pockets, but I don't see why not." Sister Cortona gave her a stern, narrow-eyed stare. "But if we don't meet the goal, we have other options."

Patrick found himself hoping that they wouldn't meet the goal on the first try because that would give him more time with Sasha. The sensible part of his brain told him that he ought to be rooting for their success. Just because her excitement was contagious and he liked to hear her laugh didn't mean that he deserved to spend more time with her.

What he deserved was time on his knees, praying to God that they met their goal with this bake sale and this stupid crush would go away.

"Listen, we're going to do the best we can," Hannah said before turning to Jemma. "We really think it would help if you spoke about the importance of the pre-K program. Maybe give some examples of the difference you've made."

Patrick could sense Jemma's panic at being asked to speak in front of a crowd. "I usually only talk in front of preschoolers. Influencers?" Her voice got high on the end.

"Well, if you don't do it . . ." Hannah's gaze lighted on Patrick. "We can always trot Patrick out. I know the gray-haired brigade will have their pocketbooks open if he turns on the charm."

Patrick looked at Jemma. "I think Jemma should do it. If we didn't have her on staff, the program wouldn't be nearly as successful as it now is. She's the one who's really responsible for the increase in test scores. She won't tell you all this, but she partnered with St. Bart's food pantry to make sure every kid who showed up hungry the first week goes home with a bag full of nutritious food every week. All on her own."

Jemma blushed. "I just—"

"I know you can do it, Jemma," Patrick said. "Just speak from the heart, and I'm sure we'll meet the goal."

Patrick hadn't meant to "turn on the charm," but he could feel Sasha's eyes on his face. As soon as he looked at her, she averted her gaze to something interesting on the atrium floor.

At least it wasn't just him, and they were both acting like teens with inconvenient crushes.

AFTER THEIR TALK WITH Jemma, they went outside for pictures. Sasha stopped to hug Patrick's friend Carlos on the way out, and he wondered whether she knew everyone. Then he remembered that Sasha had planned Carlos's wedding reception.

She took a beat to introduce herself to Maria and cooed over the baby. Patrick could picture her with a baby so easily, and he wondered what kinds of people she'd been dating who didn't want to give that to her. If things were different—if he was different—he would be jumping at the chance.

Once they were done with pictures and everyone—including Hannah—had left, Sasha was waiting for him, sitting on the steps leading to the sanctuary.

"Do you need more measurements for the bake sale?" He wondered why she'd lingered. More irritated with his reaction to her presence than her presence itself. "Or do you need something else?"

He didn't know if he could give her any more sage advice about her love life. Every time he thought about her dating someone, kissing them, or more, he got ideas about her doing those things with him. It was totally inappropriate, and no amount of prayer and contemplation stopped the thoughts from coming.

It reminded him of when he'd had his first inklings of joining the priesthood. It had always been his mother's hope for one of her sons. But he hadn't considered it seriously until he'd started seeing signs—his mother's favorite flowers in the patch in front of the seminary offices on campus, someone calling his attachment to routine monk-like—and then Ashley had dumped him. Apparently, his grief was boring, and she thought it was a "bummer" that he had to get up early every morning and go to Mass. His explanation that his mom had asked him to on her literal deathbed hadn't been enough for her. That had been the last straw.

When he'd gone to Mass after she left his apartment, he'd felt an inner lightness. A sense that he was where he belonged.

He'd been starting to doubt that he was called to the priesthood before he'd started spending more time with Sasha. Being around her intensified those doubts. He hadn't realized that he'd been missing that sense of lightness and belonging from his work until she'd brought it back.

He still derived satisfaction from baptizing babies, marrying couples, and helping people. But the routine that had saved him from his grief at his mother's death didn't make him feel settled to his bones anymore.

At times, the collar was too tight. It was ironic that it loosened when he was around Sasha and feeling his attraction to her. Maybe that was why he'd fought getting to know her for so long.

Sasha flushed. "I came back to look at the tables and see if I needed to rent some."

"One thing we have are plenty of tables." He motioned for her to walk around the building. It was a beautiful spring day, and it would be a shame to waste the time indoors.

Her soft steps in pristine white sneakers followed him. He didn't know if he'd ever seen her dressed casually before. He hadn't even noticed that she was more dressed down than anyone else at the ceremony. She looked younger, somehow, in a T-shirt and dark jeans, with her glossy dark hair pulled back in a ponytail tied with a scarf. But she didn't look any less put together.

He felt like he was falling apart a little bit and hoped that her overly observant eyes weren't seeing it. That was the thing about her that got to him. Even though she was scrupulously kind to everyone, he could tell when she didn't like someone. It wouldn't be obvious to someone who wasn't looking carefully. But then, he'd always looked at her closely. He just hadn't let himself think about it too much, because they'd never spent as much time alone before.

They got to the shed adjacent to the courtyard and he opened it up. "Behold the bounty of tables."

Sasha gave him a crooked grin. "Good. I'll just bring some tablecloths."

"Perfect. We usually have plastic." He stuck his hands in his pockets. "It'll class up the place."

He was about to ask her if she needed anything else so that he could leave, but then his phone buzzed. He pulled it out of his pocket and saw that it was his dad. He normally wouldn't answer the phone when he was with a parishioner, but Sasha wasn't a parishioner, and his dad never called without a good reason.

"Hold on, it's my dad."

"Of course."

He picked up the phone and without preliminaries, his father said, "Patrick."

His father hadn't exactly seen eye to eye with him on entering the seminary. He hadn't been inside a church since his wife's funeral, not even for Patrick's ordination. And he'd never gone to Mass with his wife. So, he never called him "Father Patrick"—*Not calling my own son "Father."*

"What's up, Dad?"

"Need you to come to the bar." That's when he noticed his father's voice sounded strained.

"What happened?" Concern for his father's safety replaced any thoughts about Sasha. His father's health had been more frail of late. And even though he was supposed to be at peace with all of God's whims—to trust that all was His will—he was afraid of losing his father. His father didn't call him "Father Patrick" partially because he didn't respect the institution of the Church. The other part of it was that Patrick wasn't a priest when it came to his father. He was a son.

"It's nothing. I had a little accident, but I need your help." His father was an old-school tough guy, and to admit that he needed help was a really big deal. A lump formed in Patrick's throat, and sweat slicked the small of his back.

"I'll be right over," he said as he hung up. He looked up to find Sasha still standing there, looking concerned.

"What's going on?"

"My dad." Patrick made a noncommittal hand gesture. "He said he had a little accident, and it sounded like he was hurt."

"Oh no. Should we call 911?"

Patrick could kick himself for not thinking of that. "I said—I said I'd be right there."

"Okay, I'll drive you. My car is right in front."

He could have argued with her or just walked off to his car. Inviting her further into his life was a bad idea. She knew his father in passing, but she wasn't an emergency contact. Having her come with him when his dad could be seriously hurt felt really intimate to him. But her car was closer, and he was afraid. She would probably get them there faster and more safely.

So he followed her as she ran-walked to her parking space.

He tried to call his dad six times in the ten-minute drive to Dooley's. He didn't answer, and Patrick's anxiety amped up another level every time the phone clicked over to voice mail. Every time he heard the recording, *You got Danny. Send a text next time*, he wanted to throw the phone.

"It's going to be okay," Sasha said, even though she couldn't know that.

"That's my line." He didn't know how to accept the comfort she was offering. He was usually the one doling it out. And, for once, it felt like a relief to let someone else bear the burden of keeping things together. He was so good at staying composed that he'd become a professional. But the prospect of being an orphan was really straining that ability.

After shifting, she reached over and gently touched his forearm. Though he'd thrown her out of the way of a moving car, he'd only been touching her for a few seconds. This lingering caress wasn't meant to do anything but offer comfort, but it felt like more. He was so touch starved, it was as though his body didn't know what to do with the oxytocin.

He didn't want to push her hand away. She didn't mean anything by it. He was the one with the problem having her around. Even if she'd noticed his attraction to her with her too-astute gaze, she hadn't changed her behavior toward him.

SASHA DIDN'T LIKE THAT Patrick was worried. She'd seen him concerned, but she'd never been able to feel his anxiety spike like this. He and Chris—despite the latter being a total douchebag— loved their father. And Danny Dooley was a gruff but good man. If Sasha and her parents were as tight as Patrick was with his father, she would be apoplectic at getting that kind of call.

She didn't flinch when Patrick pulled his arm away to grab at his hair. She'd hesitated to reach out because something seemed to have shifted between them when he'd saved her from getting run over. It was as though there was something unspoken between the two of them that had created a delicate tightrope they had to walk. Any touching could lead the tightrope to fray. If they fell—well, who knew what would happen?

Once they got to Dooley's, Sasha parked the car while Patrick went inside. In her rearview mirror, she saw him tugging at the locked front doors. It was before noon, after all.

He ran around the side of the building to the alley, and Sasha followed him after she'd locked her car. Once inside, she ran through the back hall to the storage room, where she could hear the two Dooley men yelling at each other.

"I'm fine. How many speed limits did you break on the way

over? Last fuckin' thing I need is to put my son in the ground alongside my wife." Mr. Dooley seemed fine.

"You call me sounding like you're dying and then you fail to answer the phone, I'm going to break some speed limits." Patrick sounded exasperated but relieved.

Sasha stepped into the room. "I'm afraid any law breaking is my fault."

Patrick's dad didn't appear to be in serious distress, but he was sitting on the floor with his back supported by one of the shelves of booze. There was a pile of boxes and a broken bottle of whiskey next to him. When Mr. Dooley saw her, he smiled and then winced in apparent pain. "Why would you bring a pretty girl to see me looking like this?"

"Mr. Dooley, I was just at the church."

"If I'd get a woman who looked like you visiting me, I might have to consider the priesthood." Sasha and Patrick both laughed, but there was tension there. Mr. Dooley didn't seem to notice because he followed that up. "Of course it's wasted on this one. Such potential he had."

"I'll leave you on the ground, old man." Outside of yelling at the kid who'd almost run them over, Sasha had never heard Patrick be anything less than beneficent, so hearing him tell his father off was sure something. She wouldn't admit to herself how much she liked to see this side of him. The human side.

"No, you won't. You're worried about going to hell." He reached up to where Patrick was crouched. Patrick gave him his arm and helped his—not small—father to his feet almost effortlessly.

Why did he have to be so strong? If he were weak, he wouldn't be nearly as attractive to her lizard brain. But apparently, her avaricious, lustful nature was being tested with this one.

"What happened?" Patrick asked. His father looked like he was going to wave him off, but he pressed. "Did the employee that Chris and I hired for you not show up today?"

"He's not coming in until nine." Mr. Dooley stuck his chin out stubbornly, and Sasha saw the son in the father right then. "My back isn't what it used to be."

She could see it pained the man to admit it.

"Well, he'll be on his own since you have to go home now."

Sasha felt like she shouldn't be there. This was a private conversation. "I'm just going to grab some stuff to clean this up so no one cuts themselves."

By the time she got back with a broom and dustpan, a mop, and a bucket full of soapy water, Danny Dooley was on his feet and Patrick had taken off his priestly collar to move the rest of the pile of boxes onto shelves.

Sasha's gaze stuck on the back of his head where drops of sweat raced their way down to his neck. She could picture the muscles moving underneath the black fabric, and it made her a bit weak in the knees.

She would have stared forever, but Mr. Dooley hobbled past her saying, "Like I said, an absolute waste."

Patrick looked at her then, and she said, "I have a broom and mop." When he reached for the broom, Sasha snatched it back. "I've got it."

"Be careful of sharps. I avoided one trip to the hospital today. I'd like to avoid it altogether," he said, but he let her get to work.

And she was careful not to get cut. She wasn't careful enough to let her curiosity about what she'd seen between father and son go, though. "So, what's the deal with your dad and you being a priest?"

"My dad's not really a God guy."

Sasha had to laugh at that. "So, how did you become one?"

Patrick was silent for so long that she figured he wasn't going to answer.

"My mom was really devout, and she always wanted one of us to become a priest like her brother."

Sasha tried to imagine Chris as a priest and failed instantly. Anything that didn't involve being a jackass wasn't going to be Chris Dooley's calling. He was like a relative that you couldn't get rid of because by containing him you could keep his damage levels under control.

"After she died, I just felt called. It was so obvious to me that I should be pursuing it that I couldn't avoid it."

"Did you want to avoid it?" Sasha couldn't imagine trying to parse out a religious calling from her parents' wishes. She'd been pursuing marriage to the "right kind" of man and having children so that she'd get their approval for as long as she could remember. Her parents would probably be thrilled if she decided to enter a convent—both because it would be something that they could brag about in the lobby of their church and they wouldn't have to worry about her shaming them anymore. But they weren't fervent believers, and neither was Sasha. If she believed and then felt called, it would be difficult to resist.

"Not at the time, no."

Sasha knew one thing with certainty as she finished helping Patrick clean up and then went home—assured he could get back to the Church without her staying. Her crush on him had to go away, because he was where he belonged.

CHAPTER EIGHT

"I WANT TO HAVE sex with a priest." Sasha just said it. She wasn't going to spend thirty minutes of their forty-five-minute session forcing her therapist to tease this dirty little secret out. Not like the time she'd admitted to lusting after her college English professor. Besides, whenever Sasha made Pam pull her deepest, darkest stuff out, Pam laughed like a drunken hyena when she got to the big reveal. Pam was an unconventional therapist, but her methods worked.

"Is this the beginning of a joke?" Pam inquired gently, after she stopped laughing. Sasha sometimes came in with jokes. Pam never laughed at those, but it helped Sasha acclimate to telling someone the truth about how she was feeling. Other than with Hannah—and not even with Hannah all the time—Sasha kept a very tight lid on her emotions.

That was what Finerghty women did. Needless to say, therapy was very difficult for her.

"No, I am infatuated with an actual priest." Sasha wrung her sweaty hands in her lap and tapped her foot. The lust was like its own person in her body, with its own kinetic energy. The lust wanted to *move*.

"A *Catholic* priest?" Pam sounded incredulous.

The only sound Sasha could get herself to make was a squeak. Luckily, she'd been seeing Pam for a few years. She'd started seeing the septuagenarian Jungian when she'd realized that she had a habit of lying to herself and those close to her without even thinking about it. They weren't harmful lies; they were the kinds of things she would say to make sure everyone around her was comfortable.

For example, she never told anyone that anything they were doing was a bad idea. She would tell them that she supported them and hope the concerned look on her face shone through enough for them to know that they were about to make a huge, catastrophic, gigantic, life-altering mistake.

It had a fifty percent chance of working—higher with her sister because facial expressions were their common language. Some families had love languages like acts of service or quality time; the Finerghtys had telling each other off with nary a raised voice. For that matter, after the age of thirty, there was nary a raised eyebrow due to the compulsory, preventative Botox.

Even after five years of sitting in Pam's eclectic office once a week, learning to tell the truth, she couldn't say the whole truth all the time. She had to dole it out in pieces. It often made things much more complicated.

"Well, does he want to have sex with you?" Pam's question caught Sasha completely off guard.

"What does that have to do with anything?" It wasn't as though they could sleep together, so what did him wanting to sleep with her have to do with her massive, unruly desire to rip off his collar and ride him like a pony?

"You're both consenting adults." Pam shrugged, even though Sasha knew for a fact that her therapist had grown up a devout Catholic. "It could be a whole lot worse."

"The problem is that I've gone on three dates with a perfectly nice groomsman."

"Do you want to have sex with the groomsman?"

"Not yet." Sasha was at the point where she liked Nathan enough to hope that someday she would want to have sex with him. But the overpowering need to feel all of his skin against hers hadn't shown up yet. Maybe it was a fake-it-until-you-make-it sort of thing. Not orgasms—she'd finally stopped faking those when Hannah and Bridget had staged an intervention/sex toy party. She'd been so traumatized by her forced feminist awakening that she heard the sales rep's voice telling her that her fake orgasm would propagate fake orgasms with any woman that her lover slept with every time she was tempted to fake it.

Sasha was a terrible person, but she really didn't need that kind of karma. Better for guys to think she was cold and withholding if she was only having sex with them to be polite.

"Not yet?" Pam parroted her words.

"We've only been on three dates—like, four hours total!" Patrick was right. She should give it a chance. Unfortunately, Patrick being right about everything was another attractive thing about him. If only he didn't have those twinkly eyes and godforsaken dimples, maybe she *could* give Nathan a fair shake.

"So you want to want to have sex with the groomsman, and you seem frustrated that you actually want to have sex with a Catholic priest?" Pam summarized her problem perfectly.

"Yes!" Sasha threw up her hands and stood, pacing to the window that she couldn't see out of because there were too many plants vying for the scant sunlight. "I know. I know. I know. I always do this. I always want what I can't have and just totally discount what I have in front of me. I'm ungrateful, and I can't seem to do what's good for me."

"You're not ungrateful," Pam said, interrupting Sasha's self-directed diatribe.

She turned around and folded her arms across her chest, knowing that Pam would read that, rightly, as defensive. "What!? Of course I'm ungrateful. I should be kissing the ground in front of Nathan that he's interested in me, considering I've almost reached my expiration date."

Sasha tried not to talk about her expiration date with Pam. The first time hadn't gone so well. Her therapist had turned red in the face and given Sasha an entire stack of literary fiction about women in middle age who learned something and then usually died to read as homework. After that, Sasha had kept her worries about aging out of desirability to herself.

"You know, I don't know your mother, but you sound a whole lot like your mother right now," Pam said.

Sasha gasped. "Take that back."

"That's not how therapy works." Pam looked pointedly at the seat that Sasha had just vacated.

"You're not supposed to traumatize me in here. I know that's not how therapy works either." But she sat down.

"Let's talk about this whole 'expiration date' thing."

God, it sounded so unbearably stupid when Pam said it. She was totally holding Patrick responsible for having to talk about this. If he didn't scramble her brains, if he had just let her get hit by that car, she wouldn't be here trying to explain to a woman of indeterminate age why she had to get married and have two babies within the next four years or literally perish from the weight of her mother's disappointment.

"I am—I feel like—I'm running out of time."

"For what?"

"To get married and have babies." Sasha made a rolling motion with her hand. "And all that stuff."

"You want all that—stuff?" Pam looked over her glasses at her. "Or does your mother want it for you?"

Sasha was so tempted to say that she really wanted to get married and have babies, but then she remembered when Pam had almost kicked her out of therapy during her second session. *If you're as happy as you say you are, why are you here?*

"I don't know. I feel like I should. I've been training my whole life to be a wife and mother."

Pam squinted in the way she usually did right before she was about to drop some knowledge. "Have you, though?"

"What do you mean?" Sasha tried to be perfect. Really hard. And when she wasn't perfect, she buffed it over. She did what was expected of her. Always. Even if it was the opposite of what she wanted.

Oh.

"Yeah, if you wanted to be married, you'd be married." Pam doodled on her pad. After one of her sessions, Sasha had peeked at Pam's yellow legal pad. A diligent researcher, she'd wanted to know if Pam had written anything down that would help her be better at therapy. She'd been disappointed to just find doodles. "More precisely, if you believed that you deserved to be married, you'd be married."

"So if I didn't want to sleep with a priest, then I'd be attracted to Nathan?"

"None of these men have anything to do with you, other than how you feel about them is a reflection of what's going on inside of you."

This was only making things muddier, when she'd come to therapy in order to get clear. If her feelings for Patrick were a reflection of her feelings about herself, did that mean that she didn't deserve to get what she wanted? And to prove that to herself, she had the hots for a priest?

"I want Patrick because I don't think I can have what I really want?"

Pam nodded. "And you don't want Nathan because you won't let yourself want what you can have."

It all made sense, and it made her mad—at herself, the world, the Church, Patrick for being so enticing. It even made her angry at Nathan for being too perfect. Maybe if he had a hint of bad boy, she would want to touch his bathing suit parts.

"What do I do?"

Pam shrugged like she always did when Sasha asked her that question. After the tenth time she'd asked, the confounding woman had stopped saying, *That's not what therapy is for.*

Sasha wished it was more like a rule book. Even if her unruly desires were running rampant, Sasha could follow rules. She understood rules. Dark lines between good and bad and right and wrong. She wished there was a list of steps she could take to root out the things her body wanted and put her brain back in charge. Or a list of ten easy ways to forget how it felt to have Patrick's body pressing hers to the ground. Maybe a handy guide to aphrodisiacs to get her motor running for a guy who wore pleated-front pants.

She giggled, forgetting where she was a for a second because dealing with her therapist looking at her and waiting for her to have a breakthrough was a little bit too much for her.

"What's funny?"

"I wish I could just be fixed, you know? Like, I wish I could wake up one day soon and just love the right people."

"You love some of the right people."

That was true. She loved Hannah and Kelly and Bridget and their other friends. She loved her family as long as they kept their distance. "I wish I could fall in love with the right man."

"There's no right or wrong with who you love, just what you do with it."

"I can't do anything with the feelings I have for Patrick." She wouldn't call those feelings love; that would make them too urgent. "And I can gin up feelings for Nathan."

"Are you going to see him again?"

It was pointless, and yet . . .

"Of course I am."

"Are you going to talk to the actual object of your affections about how you feel about him?"

Also pointless, and yet . . .

"Of course I'm not."

CHAPTER NINE

ST. BARTHOLOMEW'S WAS AN old church in an old building. It was the kind of place people imagined when they thought about a Catholic Church if they hadn't been inside a sanctuary for several decades.

Although the sacraments that took place inside the church had modernized, all of the original architecture—that had survived the fire—was intact. The confessionals were only there in the name of architectural preservation. But if someone wanted to confess one-on-one, Patrick usually sat next to them in a pew.

The confessionals, akin to wooden, stand-up coffins, were a great place to hide, though. Today, Patrick was hiding in the confessional, reading a book of poetry by Seamus Heaney, which he hoped would inform his homily this Sunday, because Mrs. O'Toole, the president of the parish council, was on the hunt for him.

She'd been the sole dissenter at this month's meeting, where they discussed the plan to save the pre-K program. She represented the contingent of the congregation that didn't like change and wasn't particularly welcoming to outsiders. She grew up in a period during which the Church didn't have to try to get butts into pews on Sunday.

Mrs. O'Toole had decided that the parishioners should provide the baked goods for the bake sale. To prove her point, she'd been bringing over baked goods every day. Patrick had as much of a sweet tooth as the next guy, but there was a limit. And his limit was a loaf of lemon bread and a dozen rhubarb muffins the day after she'd brought over mini blueberry loaves.

If he ate any more sugar, he'd go into a flat-out food coma.

He wasn't expecting Sasha to be the person who found him.

"What are you doing in here?" She looked so pretty and fresh in jeans and a sweater. Her eyes were shiny and her pink lipstick made her teeth look impossibly white. Although the gloomy dregs of winter were holding spring off for the moment, she was like fresh air.

"Did anyone see you come in?"

She glanced around behind her, smirking when she looked back at him. "No. Why do you ask?"

He inclined his head toward the other side of the confessional. "Get in." He wouldn't be able to see her, but they could talk, and she wouldn't blow his cover.

Sasha followed his instructions, which he liked even though he shouldn't. He didn't have a whole lot to say for a long beat. Maybe a joke? "Anything you want to confess?"

She laughed. "I thought we established the fact that I don't believe in God the other night."

That had been such a dumb thing to ask. "Sorry about that."

"Oh, it's totally fine." He heard her clothes rustling as she shifted her body. The shadow at the other side of the screen seemed like it was closer to him, and he could smell her shampoo. Being this close to her was more intimate than he would otherwise be allowed to be, and it was a terrible idea. "Why did you ask?"

He wasn't going to tell her the real reason—that he felt guilty about his prurient interest in her, and he would feel better about it if she wasn't one of the faithful. "I was . . . curious. We've known each other for a while, but we don't really know each other that well."

"Hmmm."

"What are you doing here today?" That sounded less welcoming than he wanted it to sound. Not that he welcomed her surprise visit more than any other surprise visit. He didn't like her or anything. "I mean, is there something you need from me?"

"You sound like you're afraid that I need something."

Patrick scrubbed a hand over his face. He was tired. It wasn't just the work; it was the work that went into making the work look easy. "A lot of people need a lot of things, but I can always make time for a friend."

"Even if I'm a heathen nonbeliever?" Somehow, her teasing him made him feel better. It filled him with energy.

"You were still baptized, right? So, you're still Catholic." He might sound like he was trying to be helpful, but he was so selfish. He wanted to see inside her head and know what made her tick. And he couldn't let himself think about the reasons why.

"But I'm not a good Catholic." Was she trying to kill him? Saying that she wasn't a good Catholic to him was like waving a red flag in front of a bull. Because, thing was, Patrick adored sinners. He loved how interesting they were, and how they tested his faith.

"What do you mean by that?" She paused and he caught the glimmer of movement through the screen, as though she was brushing her hair behind her ear. He didn't like that he made her nervous. "You went to Catholic schools long enough to know that you're not a bad person. You're a child of God."

If only Patrick could remember that when he was around her. She wasn't for him to lust after. She just wasn't for him. And yet, he was dying for her to give him anything of herself. He had a conflict of interest here, but that didn't mean he was going to do anything about it.

"Are you trying to tell me that you're not like regular priests? That you're a cool priest?"

"Are you quoting *Mean Girls* at me?"

"You've seen *Mean Girls*?"

"Come on! I didn't come out of the womb a priest. And I can still watch movies."

Sasha laughed. "I guess I just think of you as outside ordinary life."

"If I couldn't understand ordinary life, I wouldn't be a very good priest." He was in close contact with how ordinary life felt right now. Spending time with Sasha was reminding him of what his life might be like if he wasn't a priest.

Sasha surprised him by laughing again. "No one in the Church understands ordinary life."

"Listen, I'm not like the other priests."

"We've established that you're a cool priest." Her derision got to him in a way he wasn't going to dwell on. She'd come here for a reason, and this was about her, not his growing dissatisfaction with his vocation. "But you're part of an institution, and bound by the canon laws of that institution."

That was true. He really didn't have anything to say in response to that.

"I get it that you try not to come down too heavy on people, but you have to admit that a lot of the rules are pure bullshit designed to control the sexuality of marginalized people all the while the institution at large is basically a child sex abuse ring. How is someone with common sense supposed to get their head around that?"

"I've never come up with a good answer to that. The only thing I know—" He hated how she'd turned the tables on him and made him feel vulnerable. But he also wanted to be honest with her because he felt as though a lot of people blew smoke up his ass and didn't tell them how they felt about his faith or his vocation. "I can only try to be a good priest. For me . . . I've always been a man of faith."

His mother had brought him to daily Mass with her every morning before he'd started school. He'd learned to pray rosaries and novenas from her. Chris had rejected all of it, but Patrick had stuck with it because his mother's religiosity had been their only point of connection.

From the time he was five or six, she'd encouraged him to consider becoming a priest. He'd resisted it for a long time, feeling like Catholicism was just something he did with his mother—that it wasn't really the sum total of who he was.

He was interested in girls and video games and hanging out with his friends. If it hadn't been for two things that happened during his senior year in college, he probably wouldn't be here. He might even be a piece of shit like his baby brother.

First, his mother had gotten sick. She hadn't told anyone she hadn't been feeling well for a long time. By the time his father had insisted that she get checked out by a doctor, it was too late. She was gone so fast that it felt like she'd slipped through his fingers—almost as though she could slip back up through time at any moment.

And then, the woman he'd been in love with, the one he thought he would marry, decided that he wasn't good enough. Or maybe she'd gotten tired of dealing with him when he was deep in his grief.

His father and brother were silent types. On the outside they looked strong, but they were just masters at dissociating. Patrick never felt like he could talk to them. So, he'd thrown himself into his mother's religion. It had felt like his only remaining tie to her. He'd just inquired about seminary school, and they had sort of pounced on him.

Although there was a lot of lip service about discernment, everything picked up momentum and—even though he had doubts pop up about committing his life to serving the Church—it had become harder and harder to think about leaving.

Because, honestly, what would he have if he did leave?

He didn't have a useful major in college, a plan for his life, or even any desire to come up with one.

And so he was here. Talking to a woman who aroused the same doubts—only they seemed intensified. "I just want to help people the way that the Church and my faith helped me."

It was the answer he always gave when people questioned why he'd made the rash leap into taking holy orders.

But Sasha wasn't going to let him get away with that. "You know that there are better ways to help people, right?"

"What turned you sour on the Church?" He knew, through casual conversations over the years and stories that Hannah had told, that Sasha's family were Irish American and Catholic and total nightmare human beings. But he didn't know any specifics.

"I don't think anyone in my family ever believed or had faith.

We went to Church every Sunday because it would look bad if we didn't. Sacraments were less about the ritual and the changing relationship with God than they were about who spent the most on the luncheon after everyone had their first communion."

That made Patrick sad, but he also sensed something deeper behind it. Was that why she was here? Was she not a believer, but God-curious?

He was probably reading too much into this. She was probably dropping by for some totally unrelated reason, but he'd pulled her into this meandering conversation about the meaning of faith.

"How did you turn out to be such a sweet person, then?" He'd never seen her be anything but exceedingly kind to all of their friends—excepting his idiot brother. She gave him dirty looks because he'd hurt her friend, Bridget, when they'd broken up and after. And he couldn't get the image of her reading to that preschool class out of his head. She'd been so fresh and lovely and excited and engaged. She'd made all those kids feel like they were the only ones in the room.

She made him feel that way every time she talked to him. And he didn't deserve to feel that light on him because his brain was turning it into something prurient, when she probably didn't mean it that way.

"I'm not a nice girl, Patrick." She didn't sound wistful about that. She sounded suggestive. "My sisters are nice. Marlena and Madison are very nice."

"How did you escape an 'M' name?"

"My mother took one look at me, decided that I was the most dramatic child that she could ever contemplate, and gave me a name to match." Sasha's voice dripped with good humor, despite the fact that what she was saying was heartbreaking. "She decided that I didn't belong in her cabal of M's. My father's name is Steve, though."

He ignored that but probed on. He couldn't help himself. "I still don't believe that you're not a nice girl."

"I always want to do bad things." She sighed. "My first instinct is always the wrong one."

"That's just being human," he said. "The important thing is that you do the right thing." He'd never seen her do the wrong thing. Although her mildly suggestive tone might be skirting the border. But she wasn't religious. It wasn't wrong for her. It was wrong for him to be having thoughts about it. He was a fucking mess.

"But how do I know if I'm doing the right thing if I don't believe in anything?"

Patrick had to laugh at that. "Beats me. You know I need to have the rules."

"I don't want to live by the rules that my parents set out for me, and I don't want to live by the rules of a church. How do I know that I'm a decent person?"

"You look inside and you look around. You think that you would have friendships that have lasted for fifteen years if you were a shitty person?"

"I mean, Jack is still friends with your brother."

She made him laugh—again. This was starting to be a problem. He was pretty sure this confessional had never seen this level of mirth.

"You've got me there. I think that Jack is just too attached to the idea that Chris might grow and change. I hold out hope, too. But it's very faint."

"That's really saying something—specifically, that your brother is a real jerk—if even a priest thinks he's past saving."

"I deal in hope and faith, but I can't turn off my reason."

"Is that why you were so cool with Bridget when she told you about her abortion?"

That was a complicated issue for him. There was what the Church believed—what he was required to preach—and what he believed in the privacy of his own heart. He liked to think that life-and-death decisions were between the person making the decision and God. He tended to think that forcing people to stay pregnant was petty, misogynist cruelty.

He avoided preaching about it in general and tried to take individual cases as they came. "Bridget did what she needed to do to save her own life, and I respect that."

"Hmm." Sasha was silent after that for long moments, until she said, "This is a cool confessional."

Thank goodness, something that didn't involve faith and redemption. "We don't really use it anymore, but it's a good place to hide."

She gave one of those unexpected barks of laughter that made her sound both amused and world-weary. He could drink that sound and feel like his soul was new again. "What were you hiding from?"

"Baked goods. You've caused a bit of controversy bringing outsiders and professionals into the domain of the parish council."

"I haven't caused too much trouble for you, have I?"

A loaded question. Every time he thought about her, he was in trouble. It was the vague sense that his life wasn't good enough. He knew what he should do about it—prayer, contemplation, reconciliation. But he couldn't bring himself to cut off the source of his sinful thinking. It just didn't seem like an option to lull himself back into a sense that he was here in this life and therefore that meant that his vocation was right with God.

"No, you haven't."

"Good. I actually came here to invite you to the Art Institute. They're doing an exhibition of some of the items that were at the Met Ball the year that they did Catholicism as a theme, and I couldn't think of anyone who would enjoy it more."

SASHA HELD HER BREATH waiting for Patrick to answer. Once they'd started talking about God, she'd immediately regretted coming here. They had been flirting about God, and now she'd basically asked him out on a date.

He was definitely going to say no. He had to say no. He probably had plenty of generous, virtuous shit to do. And she'd asked him on a date.

Well, if the mortification killed her, she would at least know that she was headed straight to hell for asking a priest on a date.

"I'm sure you have other things to do—"

"I'd love to," he said. "It'll get me out of here and away from the clutches of Mrs. O'Toole's rhubarb muffins."

"That actually sounds really good." She stepped out of the confessional, stretching her arms over her head. Those things had been built when people weren't as well nourished in their youth—and thus they were too small for twenty-first-century Americans.

She caught Patrick's gaze on the exposed skin between her sweater and jeans. At the same time that she delighted in the fact that he noticed her, she felt a stab of guilt.

She shouldn't have come here. They were friends. He'd saved

her life. She was helping him out by raising money for the pre-school. But he was still a priest, and she was still a woman who had a crush on him despite the fact that he was a priest.

All of this was a very bad idea. "Are you sure you have time to play hooky?"

His gaze snapped up and met hers, and he smiled the smile of a man who hadn't taken a vow of celibacy. Did he even know the effect he had on her and other people who liked black hair and green eyes and a cut-glass jaw?

"You can't take the invitation back now. I am all excited about seeing the pieces on loan from the Met."

Sasha decided to just go with it. He knew his limits, and he was the one bound to follow the rules. If he could keep this friendly and platonic, then she could as well.

CHAPTER TEN

SASHA MIGHT NOT BE a fan of Catholicism as an institution, but she was impressively knowledgeable about Catholic art.

"I was an art history major at Notre Dame, so half of the required courses dealt in iconography," she said.

"I was an art history major, too."

She stopped in her tracks and looked away from the tryptic taken from ruins in an old Eastern-sect church and stared at him with a narrowed gaze. "I thought priests weren't supposed to lie."

"I'm not lying. I took the first class to meet girls freshman year." Sasha's cheeks pinkened, and he wondered if she was thinking of him trying to meet girls. He would have been trying to meet a girl like her. If he was a betting man, he'd put money that they would have gotten together, given the right time and the right place.

Sasha looked back at the piece, which depicted the Madonna and Child, surrounded by rudimentarily rendered farm animals.

He touched her elbow and she started, so he pulled his hand back immediately. "Sorry."

"It's okay. I just wasn't expecting—"

"I just wanted to thank you for bringing me here. It was incredibly thoughtful." It was a weekday, and there was a newer exhibition in the Modern Wing, so they were virtually alone in the gallery. There were no children to run between them and cut the tension. If he was allowed to, he would brush her hair back over her ear right now.

As it was, all he could do was stand there and look at her, but not for too long. He was here to see the art.

It was Sasha who ended his moment of weakness. "The dresses are in the next gallery."

He followed her over, and she explained why several dresses that looked like they would be incredibly uncomfortable were rare and important and cost more to make than Patrick made in a year.

She was at home in a world where a dress could cost twice as much as the car he had use of as pastor. He used the opportunity to attempt to convince himself that they did not belong together—they wouldn't even if he wasn't bound by ordination to serve as a priest until he died.

If he weren't a priest, he probably would have taken over Dooley's from his father. He would work himself to the bone to keep the place open, occasionally arguing with his old man that they ought to update things, but losing most of the time.

Sasha wouldn't look at him twice if he wasn't a priest.

He usually didn't dwell on his own shortcomings, but Sasha had him thinking in stark terms about what he'd chosen for himself. He never should have allowed himself to touch her. It had been untoward, and it was dangerous to his composure.

She seemed unbothered by it all as she wandered the room. She stopped at a photograph of Jared Leto carrying a duplicate of his own head. He stopped next to her.

The image reminded him of the Spanish Inquisition. Since they seemed to have a mind meld about everything else, he wondered if she was thinking the same thing. "In the past, there would have been much more barbaric ways to get you to accept Christ's love."

"That's very macabre, Father." He liked it way too much when she said that.

As he looked at the photo and listened to her talk about couture while he lit up from the inside just being with her, he knew he was screwed.

CHAPTER ELEVEN

PATRICK WASN'T READY TO see her again. He hadn't been able to stop thinking about her for days. Not after she'd dropped him off after their museum visit and he'd gone to his office to wait out his hard-on.

Not a short wait.

It was made shorter by Sister Cortona walking in and telling him about the backed-up toilet outside the sanctuary. Nothing like a graphic description of a fetid stench to take his mind off the way that Sasha had felt underneath him in the grass.

He was surprised that Jimmi Rafferty's parents hadn't called to yell at him about how he'd manhandled their kid. He'd been totally out of line. But something had come over him that he couldn't explain and hadn't been able to control. He hadn't gotten in a fistfight since he'd entered the seminary almost a decade ago—bar brawls weren't exactly becoming for a man of the cloth. And he hadn't been much of a fighter before that. Most of his altercations had been in defense of his brother, who was a dipshit on the best of days. And his brother's scrapes had never aroused the metallic taste of rage he'd felt when he'd seen that car coming toward Sasha.

An image of a world without Sasha Finerghty in it had flashed in his mind, and it made him angry. She might not be for him, but he needed her to be alive. It was imperative.

Still, his rough treatment of a careless kid wasn't excusable. He could control his attraction to Sasha—he had to. But he also had to control the feelings that were fallout from those feelings—rage, confusion, and the idea that there was something outside the Church to hope for.

He knew all too well that hope for anything other than his faith would yield nothing but heartbreak. He would not—could not—indulge the idea that whatever he felt for Sasha and her kindness would be enough to sustain him.

Love was an illusion. People he loved either died or left him. The only thing that hadn't left him was his faith, even though God seemed to be talking to him less and less now that he was the pastor at St. Bart's. Or maybe he just wasn't listening over the sound of his own ego and desires.

He knew that he could put Sasha out of his mind and keep her in a very platonic place in his heart. He had to.

Resolved, he walked out into the courtyard to make sure that all of the donations were in place. He fixed a smile on his face that he wouldn't let falter, even if Sasha showed up with the guy that he'd been dumb enough to encourage her to continue dating.

Sister Cortona had a clipboard and was directing volunteers to put fabulous, layered confections on tables covered with linens a whole lot nicer than anything the parish could afford. They must have come from Sasha, and he said a silent prayer of thanks that he hadn't made the massive mistake of tasting her mouth the other day when they were almost run over. He'd been so tempted to lean over and kiss her that his lips tingled for hours after. She would have run screaming, and the pre-K program would be doomed. Besides, the flush on her cheeks and fast-beating heart had been all about the adrenaline.

None of it had been about him.

"About time you arrived." Sister Cortona smiled when she said it. "We're just about done setting up."

Patrick nodded his head. "Thank you."

"Who are you looking for?"

Patrick hadn't even noticed that he was looking for anyone, but sure enough, his head was on the swivel. Luckily for him, Jack arrived. Patrick looked at the sister and winked, even though his charm never did any good with her. "I have to make sure my heathen friend spends plenty of money as penance."

The sister rolled her eyes and walked away, sharply telling one of the volunteers to "keep her filthy mitts off the petit fours."

Patrick approached Jack, who embraced him in a backslapping hug. "Hannah couldn't make it. Apparently, the thought of baked goods is enough to make her 'ralph' these days."

"I thought we left the term 'ralph' in the 1980s?" At least, Patrick hadn't heard it in a while. Not that being a priest kept him up on the current slang. Latin phrases for a whole lot of shit, yes. But dead languages yielded no slang.

"So did I, but it seems pregnancy has caused all sorts of regression." Patrick would have been concerned if Jack hadn't been smiling while he said that. "She hasn't been able to keep down anything but blue-box mac and cheese in weeks."

Patrick was confused by his friend. Jack had always been sentimental when it came to love. Even before he'd met his wife, he'd been a relationship guy. He'd never gone more than a few months between serious girlfriends and had always seemed to be happy to arrange his whole life around a ladylove.

The one time Patrick had tried his best friend's tack, everything had gone disastrously and he'd ended up swearing off relationships for good, with emphasis. Patrick couldn't even pretend to understand the depth of love that Jack had for his wife. It was really quite something to see how they revolved around each other—as if each were a planet and the other was the sun.

He didn't think about it very often because it made him feel weird. He liked Hannah, but she also scared him—partially because of how twisted up his best friend was over her after years together and partially because Hannah was very formidable. "She's okay, though?"

Jack shrugged, a little bit of concern clouding his sunny disposition. "I hate that she feels miserable, but it's supposed to pass in a couple of months."

"And then you're going to be a dad." Patrick had baptized babies for people that he and Jack had gone to school with for years. But this was the first time that one of their core group was going to become a parent.

Patrick had never thought much past making sure that he was never in the position to become a dad. He'd never thought past the practice portion of the program. And thinking about that now made him think of Sasha—again—and blood rushed to his pelvis—again.

She was five-foot-six and weighed about sixty pounds less than him, but she was breaking him in pieces all the same.

"Good thing I have such an awesome one to live up to," Jack said. And it was true. Sean Nolan was a lion among men. Patrick's dad was cool and laid-back but had always left the mushy stuff to his wife. Mr. Nolan had always been dialed in—especially after his rocky divorce.

Patrick put his hand on Jack's shoulder and squeezed. "You're going to be just fine, man."

"Put in a good word with the big guy, won't you?" Jack cast his eyes to the sky. His best friend had never been particularly religious. His church attendance was sparse, but Patrick wasn't going to point out that he could stand to chat up "the big guy" one-on-one. It just wasn't his place.

But then Sasha walked in, trailed by five people in white chef's jackets, and Patrick forgot all about ministering to his friend through sarcasm. He had been about to say that he wasn't sure if the big guy was listening, but that statement was no longer accurate at all.

Looking at Sasha, he *knew* that God had forsaken him for sure. She was just wearing another of her prim, pastel dresses, and yet he couldn't seem to catch his breath. Were the dresses getting tighter? Or was he just more in tune with the way her curves filled them out? Was the architecture of the way she moved that much more ingrained in his spirit?

He had to turn away. Just his luck, he looked right at his best friend smirking at him.

"Wow," Jack said.

"Shut up." Patrick meant it as a warning. He could not, would not, go there with Jack. Even though they'd been friends since they'd both been wearing diapers, he had an image to uphold. Even if the image didn't seem to have the vocation attached to it that it used to, he would not let it slip. At least not more than it already had.

He fixed what he hoped was a neutral look on his face. Just a hint of a smile that hopefully would bely the turmoil inside. "Sasha."

Her face lit from within, and he started saying prayers in Latin in his brain—the intellectual equivalent of a cold shower in his world. She introduced all the pastry chefs. He smiled and shook their hands, thanking them. He wouldn't remember any of their names. Sasha was too close.

His gratitude when she led the chefs to where their goods were displayed knew no bounds. He didn't want her away from him for even one second, but she had to get away from him. He was never going to last through the afternoon with her this close. He felt as though he'd either combust or lose control or do something unforgivable like take her hand and lead her around the corner, press her against a wall, and tug that pretty yellow dress up around her waist.

"Dude." One word from Jack and he felt a flush creeping up his neck. He'd been busted. "Are you okay?"

Patrick grabbed the back of his neck, and his palm came away damp with sweat. "I'm fine. I just really want the bake sale to work, you know?"

What he wasn't saying was that he really hoped that Sasha and Hannah's suggestion that they *start* with a bake sale was actually a promise. He didn't like the idea of only seeing Sasha from across a crowded room when they were hanging out with their friends.

"Sure." Jack gave him a jerk of his chin, telling him that his friend was going to leave his obvious thing with Sasha alone for now, but would revisit the increasingly problematic problem later.

They'd developed a shorthand through the years of their friendship, and the whole thing sort of operated like the suspension of a car. They'd never actually gotten into a fight because whenever either one of them tiptoed to a boundary, the other compensated for it. It had always worked perfectly, but Patrick hadn't felt this kind of turmoil in a decade. And, even then, he hadn't allowed his friend to see how he was feeling. So used to being the solid center of their crew of friends, he was not about to throw anyone else off-balance with his agitation. That wasn't part of the bargain of their friendship.

As he'd accustomed himself to doing over the past few years, he pivoted in his mind and put his attention on the parishioners who'd come to support the bake sale as well as the new faces he assumed came as a result of Sasha's publicity campaign.

He managed a middling amount of success; his gaze only caught with hers three times. For the rest of the two-hour ordeal, he was able to focus and place his attention on the people he spoke with, sharing the success stories about the pre-K program with the surprisingly eclectic crowd in hopes that the Catholics would feel guilty enough to be generous, and the non-Catholics would catch some of that emotion in the air and open their wallets as well.

He hadn't prepared himself for when it was all over and he was alone with Sasha again. He could never prepare himself for that.

Even though she'd been running around for hours, he still caught a whiff of her fresh scent. Not a hair out of place or a wrinkle in her dress. She smiled at him, and it didn't have the same strain that her smile of greeting had had earlier in the day.

It was like having sunlight hit him for the first time in the spring, but just as quickly it was gone. She went back to counting what looked like a large pile of cash.

He wanted to flee, but he couldn't just leave her here. Without anyone else there, he had no reasonable excuse to avoid Sasha. Sister

Cortona had gone out with Mrs. O'Toole and few other parishioners for supper after the event. Usually they would have invited him, but they hadn't bothered for some reason.

She was managing to ignore him much more successfully than he was her. She drew him in just by sitting there and breathing. She mesmerized him with the way her hands moved over the cash. The small smile curving her lips was like a siren song.

"Good haul?"

She looked up at him as though she was surprised to see him standing that close to her. "Very good haul." Her eyes lit up.

Fuck.

Dammit, she shouldn't talk to him with that breathy voice. It was lethal for his resolve. "Eh?" She was making him inarticulate.

"Along with everything that was deposited directly into the church's bank account, almost twelve thousand dollars."

That shocked him out of lusting after her. His surprise must have shown in his expression, because she gave him a you-poor-sweet-summer-child look and said, "Did you doubt me?"

Her tone was flirtatious, and he desperately needed to not think about that. "Well, no."

"Almost halfway there."

On the one hand, he was glad that her idea had been so successful. On the other hand, he knew that would mean that he would be stuck with her for longer. She was so effective that he would be foolish not to accept more of her help if she was still willing to offer it. The war between his gratitude to her for helping and his fear that she would lead him into temptation was bloody.

"That's amazing. You're amazing." She deserved to hear that.

Then she stood up and was way too close to him. He should

have stepped back, but he didn't. He felt her breath on his chin, the heat of her body against his.

She didn't step back either. Instead, she looked up at him, with her lips parted as though she was waiting for something. He'd barely have to bend down to kiss her, to taste the sugar on her breath and the inherent sweetness of her mouth. The heat inside him was painful. It made his skin feel too tight as well as his pants.

The black pants that he wore every day, along with the black shirt and collar, that reminded him that *he was a fucking priest*.

And a priest kissing the pretty girl who had just gotten him halfway to saving the pre-K program would not only be breaking his vows, but would be making a very stupid professional decision even if he weren't a priest.

He stepped back, still aching from being so close to her and only wanting to be closer. "Thank you."

For her part, Sasha stuffed the cash into one of the vinyl bank envelopes that Sister Cortona used for deposits. Patrick reached out his hand to take it from her. He could do that without making contact.

But she surprised him by wrapping her arms around his shoulders and hugging him. His body went rigid—all of it. He didn't dare move because then she would feel the evidence that his vocation hadn't deadened him below the waist. He fought not to sigh at the way her feminine curves pressed into his body, how he would never forget how this felt, how on his deathbed he wouldn't be thinking about the face of God or if there was really any everlasting reward. He would be thinking about Sasha Finerghty's embrace.

Somehow he kept himself from wrapping his arms around her waist and feeling her elegant back under his palms. If he did that, he would be lost. She made a sound that he didn't dare to categorize as a breathy moan before stepping back, leaving him shaken and changed. She put the envelope in his still-outstretched hand.

He was speechless. He was *never* speechless. Luckily, despite the possibly breathy almost moan, Sasha could speak. She smoothed one perfectly manicured hand through her dark bangs and said, "I will call you next week?"

Patrick somehow made himself nod. "Yes." His voice sounded as though he hadn't used it in days—broken. "I'm free. I mean. Most days."

Why did he sound like such a blathering fool? He was never like this. He dealt with people for a living.

Sasha gave him a break, though. Thank God. If she did something like hugging him again—even squeezing his arm—he wouldn't be able to resist the urge to touch her more. And if they became touching friends, they would become kissing friends. And then he would really be in the shit, because they would become fucking friends. It would be secret and temporary and messy. And he would ruin both their lives.

In that moment, he knew he would throw it all away for her. But he had nothing, and there was no reason that she would want him. She flirted with everyone; he was no different. She'd hugged him for completely platonic reasons. They'd become friends in planning this thing, after all. That was all there was to it, and it had to be.

They couldn't be anything else.

Knowing that didn't stop him from saying, "Do you want a drink?"

CHAPTER TWELVE

SASHA LOOKED AROUND TO make sure they were alone. Had she heard him right? In another context, it would seem that he'd just asked her on a date. Of course that wasn't what was happening. He was a priest. They were just friends. This was just a friendly drink. He didn't—couldn't—know how attracted to him she was. It would look weird if she turned him down.

Totally weird. She had to say yes.

"Of course." The smile he gave her almost set her panties on fire, but he obviously had no idea of that. Luckily, he probably missed her full-body flush, because he turned around and led her out of the empty courtyard to the small building at the back of the church—the rectory—where she presumed that he lived.

He opened the door for her, and she didn't brush up against him. In fact, she was as far away from him as she could get. And she didn't look up to see how he was looking at her.

Even though they'd been alone before, they'd never been alone at night. The part of her that wanted to do bad things thrilled at the intimacy of the situation. They were going to be totally alone. And drinking.

"You'll have to be quiet," Patrick said, and his whispered tone thrilled her to her bones. "Sister Cortona gets all het up when I disturb her beauty sleep."

Sasha very much doubted that the nun spent a lot of worry on anything quite as frivolous as beauty; she'd never met a more practical person in her entire life. She couldn't stop the giggle that came out of her mouth, but she made it quiet.

Patrick led her into a utilitarian kitchen that smelled of the same industrial cleaner they used in the church, without the incense over it. He pulled out a chair for her and she sat down, which gave her the opportunity—which she took—to ogle his very fine rear end as he moved to a cabinet next to the refrigerator.

"Do you like scotch?" He looked at her with one eyebrow raised. It was almost shockingly rakish, and she felt as though she might disintegrate into a puddle beneath her chair if he didn't stop it immediately. She managed to nod and smile and make some sort of affirmative noise that got him to turn around and pour them both drinks.

She'd always wanted things she couldn't have and had fought against her baser impulses for literal decades, but that didn't completely explain her reaction to Patrick. Never in her life had she felt like she was on fire around another person. No one elicited the reactions that Patrick did. Nor did she understand why someone as vital and—well, virile—as Patrick would sign his life away when he was barely twenty-five.

Maybe if she understood more about him, she could demystify him in her own head and they could move on as just friends.

When he sat down, she'd resolved to ask more questions and find out more about him. "Why did you become a priest?"

He sat back in his chair, as though her question had blown him away. "Getting right down to the heart of things, are we?"

It didn't help her lady parts situation that he winked at her. That wouldn't do at all. "I just want to know more about you. I mean, we know each other, but like—I don't know anything about you."

"I guess I like that."

"What do you mean?"

"I like people telling me things." He looked down into his glass, and she felt like she might have made a mistake. If anything, having him on the precipice of revealing himself to her made him even sexier. "And it's hard for me to tell people about myself."

She really shouldn't have asked. "You don't have to—"

But he cut her off. "It was about a girl."

"Want me to kill her?" Any woman that could prompt this man to give up sex and romance with the degree of emphasis that he had deserved to die. For sure.

"Not necessary." He smiled at her again. He had to stop that. "It probably wouldn't have lasted anyway."

"You're going to have to elaborate if you don't want me to track her down."

"It was just a pedestrian romantic disappointment. Nothing for a priest to condone murder over. But it came at the right time. My mom was sick and dying, and she was more fervently religious than anyone I knew at the time." Sasha held her breath, not daring to stop him now that he was spilling all the beans. She could hear the pain in his voice when he talked about his mother and wanted to comfort him. But that wasn't something she could do.

It hit her then how wrong it felt that a class of people in an organization—any organization—were expected to dole out comfort and advice and spiritual succor without ever getting any in return. It was like priests were expected not to be human. But Patrick was very human. He was flesh and bone but denied himself the comforts of being human deliberately.

It was bewildering and intoxicating at the same time. Instead of saying this, she took another sip of scotch, burning the words that threatened to come up.

"And, like, I'd only directly experienced the good that the Church did. I knew about all of the bad stuff, but still believed that the faith could do some good. Hell, it felt like the only thing I could hold on to after my mom died and this girl dumped me."

"Felt?" The way he talked about his vocation, it seemed like he didn't feel the same way anymore. Or maybe she was just fishing around for reasons that she could try to entice him into breaking his vow of chastity and not feel as bad as she should about it.

"Yeah, some days I feel like it's just like any other bureaucratic job. There's a strict hierarchy, and the whole thing is more concerned about perpetuating itself and consolidating money and power at the top than it is about—helping people."

"And helping people is the point for you?" Sasha hadn't known a lot of people growing up who put helping anyone over money, sex, social standing, or power. It wasn't until she'd left home and been exposed to others who came from different walks of life that she'd realized there was another way to live.

Hearing Patrick talk about wanting to help people made her feel small—in the emotional and spiritual sense. They were totally different animals, and that had to be what attracted her to him. He had all of these things inside him—depth, spirituality, altruism—

that she hadn't known until she'd made her own friends into family.

There was always this sinking feeling inside her that she wasn't good enough to really love with the depth that Hannah and Jack loved. She felt doomed to perpetuate the bullshit façade that her parents and sisters did with their cookie-cutter perfect lives and perfect dinner parties and perfect everything with a rotted core.

She didn't realize how long she'd been quiet, thinking her head-up-her-ass thoughts, until Patrick asked, "What are you thinking about?"

"How different we are." That was as honest as she could get without spilling all of the ugliness inside her out on the table. Patrick took that on from everyone in his life. He didn't need it from her.

He laughed. "We're not that different. I think you and I have a lot in common." Simple words, but so incredibly provocative.

"You don't know me that well." She prided herself on very little but keeping all the ugliness that coated her insides from everyone who saw her. When people looked at her, they saw what she wanted them to see—someone put together, competent, a consummate rule follower. They saw the daughter and sister who was almost perfect—who hadn't gotten married yet. They saw someone who didn't shake up the status quo, who saw how the patriarchy operated but didn't have the juice to do anything about it. They saw someone bloodless, almost robotic—but well-meaning.

"I know more than you think."

"Oh really?" Most people didn't spend a long enough time thinking about her beyond how fucking basic she was. Patrick knowing more than that—thinking about her more than that—made her brain fuzzier than the scotch in her hand. It compromised her veneer so much that she asked, "What do you know about me?"

"I know that you don't like yourself very much."

Direct hit. "What makes you think that?"

"You're always minimizing yourself." Patrick paused as though he weren't sure he should say the next thing. "You don't trust yourself to be imperfect."

Jesus. Maybe he really did know her. "Are you usually this confrontational in confession?"

"This isn't a confession." He raised his glass and took a drink. She mirrored his gesture. There was palpable electricity in the air between them. "Besides, I think you can take it."

"I'm just a delicate flower." She shouldn't be teasing him. It was too close to flirting.

"Delicate flowers don't get Michelin-starred pastry chefs to donate thousands of dollars' worth of product for a church bake sale."

Sasha flushed, and Patrick pointed at her. "See? You're blushing because I brought up that you did something wonderful, and you can't take it in."

She didn't deny it because it was the truth. Somehow, he'd said in fifteen minutes what it had taken years of therapy for her to admit out loud.

"You have me pegged, I guess." Sasha felt vulnerable and exposed, and it made her want to strike back at Patrick. "But I still don't understand why you'd become a priest."

"You're thinking about the sex thing, aren't you?"

"Another way in which you have me pegged."

"I'm going to need you to stop saying 'pegged.'" Her eyes got wide when she got the double entendre. And her eyes got even bigger when he said, "It's not usually hard."

116

"I'm going to need you to stop saying 'hard.'"

Patrick laughed and held up his empty glass. "Another?"

That was a terrible idea. "Only if you tell me the whole story."

"Not tonight."

Fair enough. Someone who didn't get the option of unburdening himself very often probably wouldn't want to rip off the bandage all at once. And they'd devolved into middle school teasing. Probably not condoned for priests.

"Thanks for the drink." She stood up and smoothed her skirt.

He got up from his chair and rounded the table so that he was far too close to her. "I'm glad to know you, Sasha Finerghty."

CHAPTER THIRTEEN

SASHA HAD NO IDEA how she got home, but somehow she got out of a Lyft in front of her condo building with her purse and not looking like she'd almost jumped a priest in his own rectory with the likely salacious addition of a nun being able to hear.

Although she'd always been more of a cultural Catholic, there had to be some higher power that had allowed her not to fall on Patrick's baloney rocket like her mother after coming back from juice fasting in the desert on anything with simple carbs.

She was so off-balance after the intimacy of her—encounter— with Patrick that she didn't notice the light coming through where her door was open or the fact that her doorknob was hanging out of place on one side until she was on the top step.

She didn't often miss the actual presence of a husband or significant man in her life, other than when she had to snake a pipe— and now when her apartment was potentially mid–break in was the only other time.

She should have gone outside and called the police. But she was exhausted and horny and confused. Instead of doing the smart thing, she opened the door as quietly as she could and grabbed a long umbrella from the container next to the door. She choked up on it like a bat.

The light and noise were coming from the kitchen, so Sasha walked that way after she slipped out of her shoes. Only when she saw who was rifling through her cupboards did she relax and put the umbrella down.

"What are you doing here?"

Her sister Madison turned around and shrieked, dropping a bag of quinoa that spilled all over the floor. "You scared me."

"So I see." Sasha looked at the thousands of pieces of pseudo-grain that her mother had purchased the last time that she was in town. "What are you doing here?"

Her sister composed herself and put the greatly diminished bag on the counter. "Why don't you have any snacks without gluten?"

"I don't have a gluten allergy." Seeing that—as per usual—her sister wasn't going to offer to clean up after herself, Sasha went to the closet where she kept the vacuum.

"Everyone has a gluten allerg—" It was a lot more satisfying than it should have been to turn on the vacuum and drown her sister out. It also gave her a few seconds to come to grips with the fact that she wasn't going to be able to retire to the bathtub to rub thoughts of Patrick Dooley right out of her clitoris and to prepare for the onslaught of drama.

If Sasha's great sin was that she always wanted what she couldn't have, her sister's was that she always got what she wanted and was never happy when she got it.

By the time that Sasha had triaged the floor/quinoa situation, she was ready to listen and nod and fix whatever was fucked up in her sister's perfect life without rolling her eyes or complaining— within view or earshot of her sister.

"What are you doing here?"

"I'm leaving Tucker."

They hadn't been married that long—two years—and this was the third or fourth time that her sister had made the declaration. It was, however, the first time that she had made it all the way to Chicago, so Sasha couldn't discount the fact that this time might be for real.

She'd never liked her brother-in-law that much, but she hadn't disliked him. It seemed almost unfair to dislike someone that dull. Their mother had been delighted when Madison had "snagged such a catch" (eye roll), and Madison had seemed as happy as she ever was—about two steps above miserable—at the time. So Sasha had kept her mouth shut until their mother had started hinting at the eligibility of Tucker's younger brother. Then she'd sort of noped out in the most gracious way possible.

"What happened?" Sasha had some ideas. The first time she'd left him, he'd suggested that they go birdwatching on their six-month anniversary. The second time she'd walked out, he hadn't told her that he was bringing his boss home for dinner. Sasha had never seen such fifties-housewife bullshit, but it was none of her business. Honestly, Sasha would have slipped the boss a hundred if she was married to Tucker—less time listening to him prattle on about painting miniatures.

Then again, Sasha would have burned all of Tucker's pleated-front pants before the wedding and then denied all knowledge or culpability. But her sister had more fortitude than that. She'd married for security, and she was at peace with that. Or so Sasha had thought.

"Did Tucker give all of your money to a fin domme?"

"What's a fin domme?"

Sasha shouldn't have brought it up. This was going to be worse than the time she'd had to explain pegging to her sister to talk her out of leaving Tucker after Madison had found a strap-on in his drawer. And she definitely wasn't going to think about pegging when she could still hear Patrick saying the word with a wry smile in his voice.

"That doesn't matter. Did he lose all his money?"

"Of course not." Her sister turned and started rifling through the liquor cabinet. Much more likely to find something gluten-free in there. When she found a bottle of red and two glasses, she turned back to Sasha.

Sasha took the glass Madison offered her and sat on the couch. "So what happened?"

Her sister's brow furrowed, which hadn't happened in over a decade to Sasha's knowledge. Things were really dire if a Finerghty woman started laying off on injectables. "I'm not in love with him anymore, and I was just looking at him wearing his awful pants while talking about some bird that I'd never heard about and I just couldn't do it anymore."

"So you just walked out?" Sasha finally examined her sister's outfit and noticed how off it was for her. Like Sasha, her sister had had proper decorum drummed into her practically from birth. Slacking was never allowed short of arterial blood loss. And even then, it was frowned upon.

"Yeah, I grabbed my purse and my passport. And I left." Madison sounded bewildered by her decision.

"And you came here?"

Her sister took a big gulp of her wine and asked, "Should I not have? Were you going to have a boy over?"

Thinking about the boy she'd like to have over if it were possible to have him over wasn't going to lead anyplace good. She had to put Patrick out of her mind entirely, but it was especially important while her sister was here. Even if Madison had committed the cardinal sin of leaving a marriage and possibly bringing scandal down on the family, she probably wouldn't be able to stomach her thing for Patrick.

"Nope."

"Why not?"

"We're not talking about me." Sasha took another sip of wine. "Did Tucker cheat on you?"

"God, no!" Madison reared back and made a sour face. "Can you imagine Tucker cheating?"

Unfortunately, Sasha kind of could. Her sister wasn't nice to her husband, and it wasn't his fault that he was deeply uninteresting. It wouldn't surprise her if Tucker met a woman who shared his interests and left Madison for someone who appreciated something beyond the fact that he'd checked a box for her.

"Are you going to get a divorce?" That would cause the greatest scandal in Finerghty family history. It would be a cataclysm that might very well kill their mother and pickle their father in very expensive scotch. For one moment, Sasha allowed herself to revel in the possibilities of relinquishing her title as the disappointing sister, but concern for Madison ultimately won out.

"I hadn't even thought that far ahead." Madison squinted. "Do you think that's even possible?"

"I mean, it is legal to get divorced in every state, still. Although Mississippi is teetering, I think."

"Stop being facetious. How would I even live on my own?"

Sasha allowed herself one eye roll. Madison had never held down a job before, but she had skills. She'd mostly done volunteer gigs and sucked off the family teat before getting married. Sasha was fairly certain that Madison could figure out how to be an adult. "Get a job and some alimony."

That brought a pall over the room. "Mommy always says that you're way too independent."

"And you and *Mommy* are living in a whole other century. Join me in the 2020s instead of the 1920s where virtually no one gets stoned for being a witch if they wear makeup."

"Stop being sarcastic." The judgmental version of her sister was back, and Sasha was much more comfortable with this dynamic. Pam had warned her that this was likely to happen the first time she'd had a breakthrough in therapy—that when she was around her family, she would regress.

Sure enough, it was happening now. But Madison had never let Sasha off the hook, and Sasha's job was to reciprocate when her sister was about to come into the light of freedom and join the twenty-first century.

"Do you know how privileged we are?"

Her sister squinted and drank more. "Are you going to attempt to talk to me about race again? You know that I don't see color, and donate every year to the NAACP—"

"No, Karen. I'm not going to make that mistake again." Sasha gave her sister a warning look when she sensed her about to retort. "I'm talking about how we've been given everything our whole lives, and never had to work for anything. It kind of makes me mad at our parents. They didn't prepare us for being disappointed—only being disappointments to them. Like, it's not a promise that everything will work out if you get married to an 'advantageous match.'"

"They just want us to be happy."

"But they never wanted to let us decide for ourselves what would make us happy."

"You've got a point there."

Sasha thought this was going to be a bigger fight than it was turning out to be. But she really didn't want to fight with her sister. She wanted to help her through what seemed like some very real turmoil.

"Did you ever love Tucker?"

Madison sighed. "Maybe?"

"You don't sound so sure about that."

"I think you're right about our parents. They don't know what happiness is because they were miserable."

She'd never thought she'd hear her sister say anything like that. Their family religion might officially be Catholicism, but the true liturgy of the family had always been the gospels according to Moira and Steve. Their family sacraments were looking perfect, acting perfect, getting into the right school, and marrying the right person—preferably one that your parents handpicked.

Sasha had tried to hang on to some of it—the parts where she did what she wanted and didn't lose her parents' approval. But that plan wasn't terribly realistic, so she'd moved far enough away that they couldn't keep tabs on her through spies in the community.

And sometimes, in her head, she still couldn't get free of the specter of ancestral disappointment at her choices. Her family religion was fucked.

"What can I do?" That was not a rite in the family religion. The question "What can I get?" was more a part of the ritual. Maybe that was why Patrick was so compelling. She doubted that he'd ever asked himself that question.

PATRICK HAD NEVER BEEN an avaricious man. Not even before he'd taken his vows. His ambitions before the priesthood had been humble and realistic. His family did well enough because they owned the building that housed the bar and a few other businesses, but he'd never seen himself leaving Chicago for warmer climates. He'd never regretted the fact that he didn't eat at fancy restaurants like Jack and didn't feel comfortable rubbing elbows with high society like his brother.

He'd never wanted something that he couldn't have or that anyone else would say he shouldn't strive for. Granted, he was a white dude, so there weren't many things in that category. He knew that.

And he'd never thought that wanting something he couldn't have would ever actually be delicious. But the way Sasha smiled, the sweet scent of her, the way she was so effortlessly competent and organized. It was intoxicating.

After she left him in the rectory—aching and alone—he went through his bedroom and straight into the shower. If he'd had a large store of extra clothing, he would have burned what he was wearing. He could still smell her on every bit of it, which was wild. They had barely even touched.

He wanted to do a lot more than hug her, and he let himself go there in his mind as he turned the water all the way to hot. He should turn the water to its iciest setting, but he couldn't do that.

He didn't want to let go of how being around Sasha made him feel alive in a way that he'd maybe never felt.

It was as though his skin was on fire. Perhaps it was a good thing that they could never truly be together. He wasn't sure he would actually survive being able to dig his fingers in that thick fall of hair, messing it up as he pulled her face to his.

Her lips would be so soft. They would turn a deep red after he kissed her for hours. Even though he knew that—in reality—he wouldn't last very long if having sex with Sasha was an actual thing that was going to happen, he liked to imagine spending a lot of time exploring every centimeter of her body. He'd want to learn every freckle and scar.

As the hot blast of water hit him, he gave in and took himself in hand. According to the rules, he wasn't supposed to even allow himself to do this. But this was an emergency. If he didn't do this, he might actually maul Sasha the next time she gave him a sassy smile as she licked whiskey off her bottom lip.

Of course he could just avoid her, but he wasn't about to lie to himself. He knew himself well enough to know that he wouldn't do that. He could try, but he would fail. And the way he felt when he looked at her was sinning—what was one more sin to add to the pile? There was a line—actually acting out what he wanted to do with her—that he would not cross. He promised himself that and hoped that God heard if He was indeed listening to him anymore.

And then he shut thoughts of God out as he imagined sucking on Sasha's probably cherry-colored nipples, hearing her cry out and moan with a throaty yell as he touched her clit with his fingers and found the spot that made her lose control.

That's what he wanted—for her to lose control because of him. Maybe it was some sort of lascivious justice in his own mind; she made him feel like he was going off the rails, and he wanted to do the same thing to her. That's why he'd said those things to fluster her when she was sitting in his kitchen, drinking his scotch, daring to look edible after a full day of grueling work.

He was a mess, and he had a feeling that she knew what she was doing. The part of him that didn't identify with being a priest, the part that had been sleeping for a long, long time, felt entitled to seeing her fall apart. The brake pedal on that impulse, the vows he'd taken, kept that drive in the realm of his imagination but still allowed him to run free there.

He wondered if she'd like him to wrap his hand around her collarbone, mimicking choking her. He didn't want to do that, but he sort of did. And he wasn't going to allow himself to think about how much that turned him on—the thought of her pupils dilating at being totally at his mercy.

His forearm muscles strained as he worked his dick over faster and faster under the blast of the water. He could lube himself up with soap, but he didn't deserve it. He wanted to know that he was sinning as he worked himself over for the first time in a long time to the thought of fucking Sasha from behind, admiring her plump ass as it bounced against his hips—fuck.

That was the last image in his mind before he came against the wall in the shower attached to the room where he slept alone because he was a priest and he'd made vows. Two things tempered the cataclysmic orgasm that made his knees unstable and his pounding heart practically echo off the walls: Sasha wasn't here having a screaming climax along with him, and she never would be.

As the orgasm faded, so did Patrick's resolve that indulging in thoughts of Sasha was superior to acting out his desires. Thinking about it only made him want her more. He was pretty sure Jesus had to think about turning water into wine or walking on water before he actually did it. Thinking about the impossible things he wanted to do to Sasha could only turn him down the road of making the impossible—having her—possible.

He felt stupid and ashamed. Still, he didn't ask God to help him figure out what to do. He knew that he should make a confession, do his penance, and never, ever see Sasha again. He also knew that he wasn't ready to do that. Maybe ever.

CHAPTER FOURTEEN

"I HUGGED HIM," SASHA said, not quite believing she'd done that.

Hannah shrugged the best she could while getting fluids for her very severe morning sickness. Sasha had hesitated to visit because watching Hannah vom was a situation she never wanted to repeat.

But she wasn't currently vomiting. She was sitting on her couch in a caftan. The only thing that was different about this than their regular hangs was that she had an IV in her arm instead of a mimosa in her hand.

"You whatted him!?"

"I hugged him." Sasha struggled to find the words for how the hug had evolved into an almost kiss.

"And?"

"I felt something."

"Did he have a hard-on?"

Sasha felt her skin pinken. For a second there the night before, she'd thought that maybe Patrick had a hard-on for her in the small sense even though he could never have one for her in the sense that would lead to anything other than her doomed crush.

"So, he did have a hard-on." Hannah nodded and looked at her arm, cringing when she saw the fluids instead of a drink. "Pregnancy is not for the weak of spirit."

"I'm sorry you're weak of spirits right now." Sasha took a sip of her own drink, thankful that her friend did not require teetotaling on the premises during the pendency of her confinement. "But at least your terrible sister hasn't moved in with you."

"That's because I'm an only child, and I have no terrible sister." Sasha had often been jealous of that over the years. "Is it Marlena or Madison?"

"Madison."

"Oh good. At least it's not the pregnant one."

"I'll drink to that." Sasha raised her glass and took a sip.

"What happened?"

"She left her husband." Sasha still couldn't quite believe the words coming out of her mouth. "She wasn't happy anymore."

"That seems like a good reason to leave your husband," Hannah said. "Not that I would know."

Yes, her best friend was blissfully happy, and Sasha was only a little bit jealous. "Jack's treating you like a queen, isn't he?"

Hannah smiled when she said, "It's almost annoying."

"It's what you deserve."

Hannah leveled her a look that told her that her best friend knew that she'd been trying to change the subject. "What are you going to do about Madison?"

"I have no idea." They'd never spent that much time together as adults, and they were almost like strangers. "She's been just lying around and drinking my wine. She eats nothing. It's starting to worry me."

"Well, maybe if you put her to work?"

"Doing what?" Her sister had never held an actual job in her whole life, but her experience volunteering might be put to good use. Still, Sasha had serious reservations. "She might be able to plan a decent tea for the Junior League, but she's not a professional event planner. If I set her loose on a bride, she would just end up getting us fired by telling her that her taste is unrefined."

"Then don't let her plan weddings." Hannah was either delusional about the extent of Madison's awfulness or trying to tank their business. "Or let her menace the vendors when I have my head in the toilet."

That wasn't a half-bad idea. "I'll think about it."

"Good." Hannah nodded in that way she did when she knew that she'd won.

FOR A FEW DAYS after the bake sale, Patrick felt as though he'd gotten away with something. Like when he was a kid and he and Chris had pulled a prank. There'd always been a few days— before Chris had opened his big fucking mouth—that they'd gotten away with it. It was a heady and exhilarating feeling, and that made him feel guilty, along with the fact that he'd technically broken his vow of celibacy for a semi-satisfying wank in the shower.

But he'd always had to pay for the giddiness, like when he was a kid and put toads in the assistant principal's desk after she'd called his brother stupid. And it was no different this time.

Sister Cortona was meaner than that principal, though. They

were going over the music director's plans for a fall concert series when she lowered the boom.

"What do you think you're doing with that girl?" she asked.

Patrick felt the red flush work its way up his neck, but he still decided to deny it. "What girl?"

Sister Cortona just rolled her eyes and leaned back in her chair on the other side of his desk.

"She planned a bake sale." Patrick shrugged, knowing that it wasn't going to end there, but needing to buy himself time. "We made quite a bit of money."

"And then you invited her back to your place for a drink, like someone who can actually date. Someone who hasn't taken a vow of celibacy."

She had him there. Drinking alone with Sasha wasn't technically a violation of the rules. He could have a social life. But it had tempted him to do things that were outside the rules. Oh Christ, had Sister Cortona heard him masturbating? The level of mortification in that was greater than when his mother had simply started replacing all of his and Chris's socks on a monthly basis instead of cleaning them. He wished she was around for him to apologize for that, but he also wanted to ask her why she'd thought a little pervert like him should have become a priest.

Regrets, he had a few. But he wasn't about to let Sister Cortona in on that. They didn't have that kind of relationship. She wasn't his confessor—she couldn't be because the Catholic Church was a patriarchal institution. That was why he didn't really say anything about the frank and bracing way in which she liked to insult him. And this time he really deserved it.

"It won't happen again."

"So you admit that it shouldn't have happened in the first place?" Jesus, why couldn't she just let him off the hook?

"Nothing happened. She did the parish a solid, and we had a drink and a chat afterward."

"Did you touch her?"

"We hugged." He should not have admitted that.

"And you don't think about her like you think about Mrs. O'Toole." Sister Cortona sighed. "You think about her like one of the chippies that probably tried to get you to quit the seminary."

Nope. None of the women he'd dated after Ashley dumped him and his mother died had seriously tested his vocation in the way that Sasha was. But he wasn't ready to confess and do penance to his actual confessor, and he wasn't ready to fess up to Sister Cortona either.

"We're just friends. I'm allowed to have friends."

"I see the way you look at her, and it's a dangerous game." Sister Cortona stood up, and Patrick thought better of reminding her that they still had actual church business to discuss. She was gearing up to have the last word. "I know you, and I know you don't want to cause a scandal for the church."

"I'm not going to cause a scandal—"

"I'm not going to be part of covering things up for you." She pointed a finger at him, and he was chastened. He wouldn't expect her to cover up for him. He had his feelings for Sasha under control. He did. "Be sure she's worth you destroying your whole life and turning away from your vocation if you take things further."

It wasn't worth it. First of all, his feelings were one-sided. Sasha politely flirted with everyone, and he had no indication that her interactions with him were different or special. And even if she was attracted to him, she was dating someone else—something he'd encouraged her to continue doing. Finally, there was no reason to think that their attraction—if it even existed—was anything beyond just that. If he broke his vows to be with her, there was no indication that it would be anything beyond sex. It wasn't like she would want him to give up being a priest for her. She came from money and had a lifestyle to maintain. It was clear from whom she was dating that she didn't want a defrocked priest/househusband hanging around her apartment with nothing to do but service her sexually. She needed—deserved—more than that.

"Nothing's going to happen." He hoped he sounded more sure about that than he actually was.

"If you want, I will deal with her going forward." That idea stabbed Patrick in the heart. He was at peace—sort of—with the idea that he'd never be able to touch Sasha. He'd never kiss her, never know for sure that her skin was like velvet, or know the sounds she made when she came. But he wasn't okay with never seeing her again.

"It's okay. Nothing's going to happen."

"See that it doesn't," Sister Cortona said before sweeping out of his office with what he could have sworn was a flick of her habit. She looked at him imperiously over her shoulder as she reached the door. "Oh. The bishop called, and he wants to have a chat with you in the next few weeks. I can guarantee that it won't be as pleasant as the one you had with Sasha last night."

CHAPTER FIFTEEN

IT WAS NEVER A great thing to get called to the bishop's office. Like being called in to see the principal, there was an outside chance that he would win an award, but it was more likely that he was in trouble for something.

Sort of inevitable, really, given that Patrick put a priority on welcoming people that the Church had done its level best to alienate over the millennia. Until now, he'd maybe been in a honeymoon period with the diocese. They were just happy to have him at first. But he knew that the leash would eventually tighten.

Patrick did not like the bishop. He was an ambitious man who'd become a priest with the express purpose of elevating himself to the College of Cardinals and eventually becoming the Pope.

Bishop Rafferty didn't say this out loud, but it was widely known all the same. And his ambition ruled everything that was in his domain. Politically, if he thought that something that Patrick was doing at St. Bart's would ultimately help him climb higher, he would support it. Any whiff of scandal, and Rafferty would stomp it out with his expensive Italian ankle boots.

As soon as the bishop's secretary ushered Patrick into Rafferty's lavishly furnished office and Patrick saw the smile on the other man's face, he knew he was in trouble.

Rafferty got up from his desk and patted Patrick on his back so hard that it jangled his insides. "Patrick, my boy."

Patrick stepped back and shook the bishop's hand when it was offered. "You asked to see me?"

Since this was his boss, something inside Patrick wanted to keep things as professional as possible. It was hard, given that their relationship was spiritual as well as professional, but Patrick would do his best. Bishop Rafferty cared more about his political aspirations than the spiritual well-being of his flock, and Patrick would never make the grave mistake of forgetting that.

Patrick's tone knocked the bishop off his game a little, but it only flashed across his face for a moment when he realized that Patrick was not going to play this game. He motioned toward a chair, and his tone when he said, "Yes, sit," was clipped.

"We have a problem," the bishop said, going right in, "with the pre-K program."

Relief washed through Patrick. This was a budgetary issue. The pre-K program had provided nothing but positive publicity for the diocese, so maybe the bishop was going to lend his support to saving it. "Well, we're doing a fundraising bake sale next week. I know it doesn't sound like much—"

"That's not what I called you for." Rafferty sighed, leaned back, and laced his fingers together over his stomach. "You didn't tell me that the teacher was married to another woman."

Patrick said nothing. He'd known that eventually someone conservative in the diocese might find out that Jemma was technically in violation of the completely archaic "morals clause" in her contract, but a lot of parishes declined to enforce that stupid rule.

When Rafferty realized that Patrick wasn't going to give him the satisfaction of squirming, he continued. "I just think that we need to be very careful and considerate here. I know the Holy Father occasionally strays from the Church's teachings in public statements, but the Church's position on gay and lesbian members hasn't changed."

He didn't know what he'd do if Rafferty demanded that Patrick terminate Jemma's contract. He didn't have the political juice to just defy him. Rafferty could have him sent on a mission to Siberia if he wanted to.

A kernel of the rage formed in his belly. It was an old, familiar friend. Every time he'd visited his mother to see her more wasted away, the same ravenous beacon had formed in his gut. The fact that he was not in control right now made him so angry. He tried to remind himself that he had chosen this. In his experience, so little of his life was in his control. He'd become a priest partially because it required controlling himself and regimenting his life. And it allowed him to give comfort, the deep, spiritual kind that he hadn't been able to offer his mother. She'd been his parent up until the end of her life, and he regretted that to this day.

And right now, he was on the verge of losing control of something good that he'd been able to cultivate in his community. But he wasn't going to give up without a fight. "No one at St. Bart's is upset by Jemma's marriage."

Rafferty raised his brow. "They don't have a marriage in the eyes of God."

Patrick wasn't going to touch that one. "She's a great teacher. We couldn't have the program without her."

"Which is why the diocese didn't fund it next year."

Patrick was going to flip the desk like a Real Housewife after too much pinot grigio if he didn't get his emotions under more control. He knew that his face was probably red and his jaw was starting to ache from biting back all the choice words for Rafferty. He might be a man of the cloth, but he was a hot-headed Dooley first and foremost. Always.

Rafferty had known about Jemma and Marie the whole time, and he'd kept that information in his back pocket for when he could use it against Patrick. He took a deep breath, ready to defend himself. But Rafferty cut him off.

"We could fund the pre-K program fully if you found a more appropriate teacher. I was willing to look the other way, but then you performed the baptism."

"You're really reading our Church bulletin pretty closely, aren't you?" Didn't this man have bigger fish to fry? Like a cardinal's ass to kiss or something? "I'm not going to fire her. You and I both know that the negative publicity that would garner for the Church would be worse than leaving things as the status quo."

Rafferty sighed. He must know that Patrick spoke the truth. "You can be replaced as pastor, you know."

"I'm sure it will look great for you to fire me because I wouldn't fire a pre-K teacher you don't approve of." Patrick knew that he was playing his last card and calling the bishop's bluff might backfire horribly. But he didn't feel like he had a choice.

He hadn't realized how much it would sting to curtail his choices by joining the priesthood. He hadn't realized how much it would chafe when he became fully an adult. And he'd never re-gretted becoming a priest quite as much as he did now. He'd thought it was an honorable thing to put the needs of the Church—something enduring—ahead of his own earthly desires. He'd been so naïve to believe that the Church wasn't filled with men who used the Church's rules to wield their own desires and need for power.

And God wasn't there to take away the anger he felt in that moment. He didn't have the wherewithal to jockey for power in the same way that Bishop Rafferty did, but he was smart enough to use the few tools at his disposal.

"I'm still not funding the pre-K program if she's there." Rafferty sounded resolute in that.

"That's fine. We'll find a way." Patrick only hoped that he was speaking the truth.

SASHA DIDN'T SEE PATRICK for several weeks after the bake sale, and she convinced herself that it was a good thing. She didn't have much time to think about it, because her sister was auditioning to be the most depressed soon-to-be-divorcée in a nonexistent cosmic contest.

By week three of her sister drinking a bottle of wine a day, starting at around eleven on her couch, Sasha decided that Hannah's plan of putting her to work was indeed the less disastrous option. Especially after Madison had drunkenly reorganized her closet while she'd been at an event sponsored by the Art Institute auxiliary board.

Sasha still couldn't find her favorite pair of shoes.

Keeping her sister close enough to keep an eye on her seemed like the most prudent course of action.

It actually worked out pretty well. Madison was seventy-five percent as effective as Hannah at menacing vendors to deliver on time and on budget, and that freed Sasha up to smooth the feathers of nervous brides and mothers of brides who reminded her of her own mother. The terrifying ones.

And although she hadn't seen Patrick, she'd gone out with Nathan two more times. He was starting to feel like a friend, and she was counting that as a good thing. She wasn't in lust with him, but that was fine. The man she was currently in lust with was the furthest thing from good for her. And if she couldn't rid herself of impure thoughts about Patrick Dooley, it just meant that she had to work harder to replace them or learn to live without lust. People did that, right?

Regardless, Nathan hadn't tried to get physical with her. Sasha must be giving out a very strong "don't touch me" vibe. She felt like she should just be grateful that he kept asking her out, which gave her the chance to clench down really hard and try to form feelings for him.

He was smart, funny, and passionate about his job and hobbies. She should be falling for him and forgetting all about Patrick any day now.

She also should have known that the peaceful accord she'd reached with Madison would not be allowed to last. Moira had a sixth sense for when her daughters were not pushing each other to be their best—or at least not at each other's throats. She had to stamp out their impulse to be friendly, or at least humane, toward one another so that her daughters would not rise up against her and stop taking her bullshit.

So, of course, Moira showed up in the condo that she had a key to because Moira and her husband owned it. She was lying in wait when Sasha and Madison came home from a wedding that had gone well. They were laughing when they came in the door, so

Moira's face was markedly constipated when she stood up and said, "So this is where you've run off to."

Moira Finerghty looked perfect, even though she'd likely been traveling all day. Her dark brown bob was as severe as it always was, swooped down almost over one eye. She was dressed in a black cape, a crisp white blouse with a pussy bow, and wide-legged wool pants that emphasized her ruthlessly maintained lean figure.

Even though Sasha was about the same height, somehow her mother always seemed to manage to look down at her. It was really quite the feat.

Sasha put herself between her mother and Madison. She was used to the slings and arrows of her mother being a total bitch, but Madison had always done the right thing. She'd always been one of the two golden children. Her mother's judgment would hurt her more because she hadn't had the time or the reason to develop a thick skin.

"You look tired, Sasha." Her mother looked her up and down and the room filled with oozing, black derision.

"Thanks, Mom." Moira hated being called "Mom." She thought it sounded too pedestrian. She much preferred being called "Mother."

Moira sniffed. "Would you excuse yourself from the room? I'm here to see Madison and talk some sense into her."

"I think she's making plenty of sense for a change." Sasha couldn't believe that she'd said that. She almost expected to get slapped across the face. Or have her mother drag her into the bathroom by her ear and wash her mouth out with Dr. Bronner's soap.

She was shocked when her mother merely shook her head as though she'd been slapped by the words and said, "I see you've been trying to influence her." Moira pushed past Sasha and put a gentle hand on Madison's arm. She was smart enough to know that she couldn't just savage her youngest daughter right out of the box. She would try to urge and cajole Madison back into her version of marital bliss—which was being married at all. "You can't get a divorce, Madison."

Madison surprised both her mother and Sasha by saying, "Why can't I?"

"Because we don't do that in our family." Moira looked at Sasha over her shoulder and said, "Just because your errant sister seems to think that she has forever and a day to find a husband doesn't mean that you can let a perfectly good one slip away."

Sasha rolled her eyes in her sister's direction, hoping to give her strength. It seemed to work. "Of course I can. Just because he's perfectly good doesn't mean he's perfectly good for me."

Wow, wisdom from her basic-as-fuck sister in the crucible of their mother's twisted sense of traditionalism.

"People get divorced every day." Sasha was trying to be helpful, but she had to back up when her mother rounded on her.

"Not in this family."

Madison pushed past her mother into the room. "It's not really your business, Mom."

"Of course it's my business." The vein in Moira's forehead was throbbing, and Sasha was afraid that she would have a stroke.

"Can I get you a martini, Mother?" That might calm her down a smidge. Or at least keep her occupied deriding Sasha's choice of gin.

"That would be the least you can do."

Sasha busied herself doing that while her mother sat Madison on the couch and harangued her. At this rate, her sister would be back on a plane to New York within the hour. Sasha gave thanks for the fact that she'd fled the family roost after high school, never to return. That move had disappointed her parents, but it had set the tone for the rest of her adult life. They didn't *expect* her to bend to their will, and that meant she was off the hook when she wasn't on the phone with them or at their home. Out of sight, out of mind.

She brought her mother a martini, which she downed in three gulps. "Terrible. You need to get your gin from someplace more upscale than Total Wine."

Yes, everything was terrible at the moment. Madison gave her a look that could only be interpreted as an SOS in the version of visual Morse code that only sisters knew. "How about we find you something better, then?"

SASHA WAS ALWAYS WALKING into Dooley's when Patrick was least expecting it. It was as though she knew when his resolve not to think about her was weak. Actually, that was a lie—he'd added lies to his list of sins. His resolve not to think about Sasha was always weak.

Sister Cortona's words ran through his head and mingled and rioted with thoughts of Sasha and the way she'd looked reading to the preschool kids. He looked at her and saw forever, and it was wrong, wrong, wrong.

She'd left a couple of phone messages with ideas for another event to raise money. He'd saved them and listened to them over and over, lying and telling himself that he needed to hear her voice to properly mull over her ideas.

After his conversation with Bishop Rafferty, he'd been feeling like the whole enterprise was for naught. All the community outreach he'd done over the past few years, trying to get people to give the Catholic Church another chance, was based on the premise that he could do something to make the Church more welcoming. Not that he could change canon law, but that he could make a difference around the edges.

Intellectually, he'd known he was wrong about his individual efforts to make change for a while, but the conversation with Rafferty had really driven it home. And his ambivalent feelings about the Church were now all wrapped up with his growing feelings for Sasha.

He didn't really doubt his calling anymore. He had the growing suspicion that it was bullshit. His mind was scrambled. And he would probably think more clearly if he didn't have a cockstand from the gentle timbre of her voice.

The only voice message that he didn't listen to over and over was the one that referenced that the guy she was dating—he refused to say the man's name, even in his mind—could help out with a church carnival in a month.

He loved the idea, but the prospect of watching that guy with his hands on a woman that he shouldn't think of as his, but that he did, was enough to muddle his thoughts even more. He wished that he hadn't agreed to work with her to save the pre-K program, even though he couldn't have done it on his own. He'd known it was dangerous to spend too much time around a woman who aroused him that much, but now that he knew her a bit more, he craved her presence.

It was both heaven and hell when she walked into Dooley's followed by an older woman with a sour expression on her face—had to be her mother—and a woman about Sasha's age who, he would place money on, was her sister.

Sasha looked tense, like one more thing would make her snap in two. He ached to fix things for her. He knew her family was difficult and she remained entangled with them financially. Even though what he truly wanted from Sasha in his heart of hearts would mess up her life, he would never allow himself to actually do that. She came here tonight for a reason, and he would help her with whatever that was.

"What can I get you?" he asked. Sasha's relief was palpable, and that was like a balm to him.

"Mother, Madison, this is Father Patrick Dooley."

The woman that she'd indicated was her mother looked around the bar like she'd sucked on a moldy lemon. He took an instant, decidedly unchristian dislike to the woman. And his insides turned cold when she turned her gaze on him. "Why would a priest be working in a bar?"

"My father owns it, ma'am." The woman winced when he called her that. "And what can I get you?"

"Do you have any decent gin?"

In part to counter his dislike of Sasha's mother, he reached for the top shelf of dusty bottles that his father charged through the nose for in the event that a rich asshole wandered into his bar. In case they got lost or something.

It came in handy for moments like this.

He didn't miss Sasha's gaze on him as he shook the very dry martini and poured it into a glass in front of her mother. Nor did he miss the hungry look in her eyes as she asked him for a Guinness.

"Well, I don't even know what to do with you if you aren't even watching your figure anymore." He didn't think many people actually went to hell, but Sasha's mother might be a great candidate.

"I'll have a vodka soda, then."

Patrick raised his eyebrows as he leaned down into her space. "Are you sure that's what you want?"

He hoped that he was conveying a silent offer to find a way to extract her from the situation.

"It'll do for now." He thought she sounded breathy—definitely. He might have mostly tuned out people flirting with him over the past decade, but he wasn't completely daft. Sasha was flirting with him. In front of her mother. She must be running on the fumes of her last few fucks if she was doing that.

He couldn't dwell on it, though. Because he wasn't going to do anything about it. Sasha was merely flirting for sport. So he turned to her sister. "What'll it be?"

"Can you go back in time and get me adopted by a nice family?"

Her sister was funny. Sasha might not have much in common with the rest of her family, but there was that.

"You know, the Church frowns on me using my powers of time travel, but how about a mixed drink?"

"I'll take a pinot grigio."

"You don't want the pinot grigio here. How about a whiskey sour?" Madison giggled and brushed a hand over her hair, and he moved down the bar to make their drinks.

He wasn't out of earshot, so he heard their mother say, "I can't believe you two, shamelessly flirting with a frocked Catholic priest."

"I was just being friendly," Madison said.

Sasha was silent, and he noticed that her glances at him were much more sidelong after that.

SASHA KNEW THAT HER mother wouldn't miss her thing for Patrick. And still she'd brought her and her sister here so that she wouldn't have to go through a whole meal at her mother's hotel. Her choosing to go to Dooley's and doing very little to conceal her flirtation with Patrick was dangerous. It hadn't been intentional at first, but it had taken some of the heat off Madison for abandoning "poor Tucker."

The only redeeming quality about poor Tucker "T-Dogg" McGovern was his ability to empathize with others. That was what had made him such an attractive marital prospect for Madison in Sasha's opinion. But if Madison no longer wanted to be married to the man, Sasha would support her sister. And changing locations to a place that would put Moira's focus on Sasha's failings and off Madison's was effective. Her mother drank three whole martinis, and Sasha found a puzzle from the corner bookshelf to focus on so she wouldn't choke Moira before she started in on Madison.

But eventually that tactic failed.

"I can't believe that you would throw your whole life away," Moira said in a near-wail of grief. She did that when she'd had too much to drink. And yet she always held her daughters to strict standards of decorum and didn't see the irony in her dramatics.

"She's not throwing her life away." Sasha tried to use a soothing voice, but you couldn't soothe her mother when she was in this state. "She's trying to live it herself."

"Thank you, Sasha." Her sister had been much more subdued in her alcohol consumption tonight, but she still wasn't standing up for herself the way that Sasha wished she would. Sasha could admit that Madison was actually playing things smart. She would eventually have to go back to New York and somehow figure out how to survive. If she remained sympathetic and marginally compliant, chances were that their father's checkbook would remain open.

But that wasn't on the table tonight. Not even a little bit. This was more an airing of grievances. It would last until they could get their mother into a car and send her back to the hotel where she would fall asleep after calling her husband and screaming about how her children didn't love her.

Sasha hated the sympathetic looks that came from Patrick standing behind the bar. Although she'd confided in him about her terrible family, it was many times more embarrassing for him to actually see it.

After her mother had admonished her, she'd been careful not to flirt with him again. The last thing Patrick needed was her mother calling his manager—the bishop—about a wayward pastor trying to corrupt her daughters, especially since her thoughts drifted to how she'd like to corrupt him plenty of times.

Especially the way he looked tonight. He didn't look like a priest at all. He was tall and brawny, and the skin at the base of his neck—the skin that was normally covered by his collar—was visible and completely tantalizing. She wanted to put her mouth there. Somehow, without the collar—which he didn't have to wear when he was off duty—he was earthier and more alive. It was as though the collar was a shield. When he wore a flannel shirt with the sleeves rolled up, there was nothing hiding his appeal. She'd seen him before. She'd always seen him. But after hearing him make suggestive jokes, she could actually feel his sexuality in his bones.

He startled her when he approached to see if he could get them anything else. Of course her mother noticed and gave her a look. And she really wasn't prepared for it when he reached over her and put one of the puzzle pieces in place.

"Anybody need another drink?"

Before her mother could answer, Sasha said, "We're good for now."

"I wouldn't say we're good," her mother said, pointing at Madison. "This one is getting a divorce."

Her mother seemed to be waiting for Patrick to register shock or disdain, which didn't happen.

For her part, Madison shrugged at Patrick. "Sometimes things just don't work out."

Patrick nodded sagely and Sasha liked him all the more for it. Her mother and sisters were all lit matches. Someone considering what they said before it came out of their mouth was truly refreshing. He pointed to where one piece of Sasha's puzzle was missing. "See this piece?"

Madison nodded, and Patrick continued, "It didn't come inside the box. I looked for it for days, even thought about cutting out a piece of cardboard and painting it to match. But it wouldn't have looked right no matter what I did. It was never going to be whole. Eventually, I had to accept that it would never be complete and move on."

"I don't see what this has to do with my daughters," Moira said, looking like she was winding up for another wailing session.

"The point is, a marriage, a business, a—" Sasha thought for a moment that he was going to say *calling*, but instead he said, "—a career is made up of a lot of pieces. If there are too many missing pieces, or if even one really important piece is missing, nothing you can do is going to make it whole. Sometimes you just have to move on."

It knocked Sasha on her ass to hear him say that, and Madison looked a little shell-shocked as well. Moira was the only one who wasn't speechless. "You're certainly an unconventional priest."

Patrick smiled at her and shrugged, nonplussed. His dimple crinkled, and he walked back to the bar.

That whole exchange made her wonder what it would be like for her to be able to introduce him to her family as a boyfriend. She'd never been excited about doing that before. It had always been a complicated operation that filled her with dread. But Patrick was so different from anyone she'd ever dated. He was magnetic, and left her mother—a woman who was rarely without words—without anything that could make a direct hit.

"I think I want to go to bed," Madison said. Sasha begged her sister with her eyes not to leave her alone with their mother. "I'm grabbing a car back to Sasha's."

"You're just going to abandon me?" Moira was back to the wailing again, but Madison was out the door faster than Sasha had ever seen her move.

Sasha tried to think of a way to get them all back to where they were supposed to sleep in one piece without saying anything they would regret. She was coming up blank.

Patrick came to her rescue. "I'll call you a car, Mrs. Finerghty." His beneficence shone down upon her like divine light.

Her mother's whole being bristled, but she said, "I suppose that would be acceptable."

Thankfully, she was only drunk enough to be mean, not enough to need to be carried out of the bar. It wasn't a chore to get her out.

But then Sasha was alone with Patrick. The rest of the patrons had cleared out when her mother was at about a martini and a half.

This was very bad.

She should have left that very moment—actually, she should have dragged Moira out when her sister had announced that she was going to leave.

But she hadn't. Part of her had wanted this from the moment that she'd suggested that they come here. She hadn't seen Patrick, but she'd felt him with her every day. He was in her mind, her fantasies, and he was starting to burrow his way into her heart. It didn't matter that it was hopeless. That they had no future. That her feelings for him were sinful.

She wanted it, and that was all that mattered. She was everything her parents told her she was. She was selfish, lustful, craven, and had all the wrong desires.

But Patrick stood there looking at her—not like a priest looked at a penitent or a friend. He looked at her like a man looking at a woman he wanted.

It was so much more real in that moment. She was filled with power and lust and regret all at the same time.

"Want to stay for a drink while I clean up?"

She should obviously say no, but how could she turn him down?

CHAPTER SIXTEEN

SASHA DIDN'T SAY NO, and part of her wanted to celebrate her good luck at Patrick playing into her fantasy. "Sure. I'd love to keep you company."

Patrick started turning over chairs and putting them on top of the empty tables. Without words, Sasha joined him. They worked in silence until they were done, and Patrick returned behind the bar and started making her a whiskey sour.

Burning, sweet, and tart. Just like she felt around Patrick Dooley.

"Your family is a trip."

Sasha didn't stifle her laugh. It was a relief to not suppress her emotions after spending hours with her mother. It was so automatic that she didn't even realize she was doing it half the time. "That's an understatement."

"How'd you—"

"Not end up being a total bitch?"

"That's not what I was going to say."

"But that's what you *meant*." She leaned toward him and the danger of being too close to him.

Patrick shrugged, respectful enough not to deny it.

"I guess it's because I try to do the right thing even though I want to do the wrong thing. I pretend to be the good girl they want me to be." He put down her drink in front of her and she took a sip, meeting his gaze. "Even though I want to be my own person and live by my own rules."

"Is that what this . . ." he said, motioning between them, ". . . is?"

The fact that he'd noticed there was something between them was a cataclysm. His words made her want to throw everything she'd just said to the wayside and jump over the bar to kiss him. She wanted to forget all about trying to be good and just allow herself to be fully bad.

But she stopped herself. If only to dig in to what he'd said before humiliating herself. "What do you mean?"

Patrick rolled his eyes, and she got a picture of what he must have been like as a wayward adolescent. It was another un-priestlike thing that she needed to file away for when they both came to their senses. They would both come to their senses, right?

"I might be a priest, but I haven't forgotten what *this* is like." He made the same motion.

Still, Sasha shook her head. "You're going to have to elucidate. I'm still not clear."

"Chemistry. Heat. The whole thing."

Each word hit her right in the abdomen, turning it liquid and hot. "Are you trying to seduce me?"

"No." The word was like a bucket of cold water, leaving her whole system confused. "I can't seduce you."

"If you could?"

Patrick raised his brow and poured himself two fingers of

scotch. He leaned down against the bar so that his right forearm was close to her left forearm. "If I could, I would have ages ago."

It was as though the bucket of cold water had never happened. "How?"

He canted his head toward her and said, "I don't think it would be all that difficult."

"So you think I'm easy?" God, she loved teasing him. When had she ever had this much fun around a man? Definitely not with Nathan. Maybe not since college, when the stakes were a month-long fling rather than a lifelong commitment.

"No, I don't think you're easy. I think this would be easy."

This. She loved how he said it and wanted him to lay out what *this* was.

"How are things going with Chet?"

Sasha was confused for a moment, and then she realized that he meant Nathan. "Nathan and I have seen each other a few more times. I like him," she said, more to convince herself than Patrick. "He's a good guy."

"You talk about him like he's a long stint downstate," Patrick scoffed. "Or lima beans."

That made Sasha's spine stiffen. He didn't have the right to flirt with her. They couldn't touch. They could certainly never kiss or fuck or make babies. Why did he think he could judge her trying to ease herself into a lovely relationship with someone who could give her all of those things?

She leaned her head so that she met his gaze. So close that he could kiss her with the most minor tilt of his head. "What's it to you?"

"I hate it that you don't have this," was all he said before he kissed her cheek. It was the most intense kiss she'd ever had, and it wasn't even on her mouth. The feel of his soft lips against her skin was incredibly sensual. She was already warm all over from being near him, but this was far too much.

And when it was over, in what could have been a month or a minute, she turned her head so that she could meet his gaze. It was molten and intense. She was drawn to it like a flame.

"What was that?"

"I'm sorry." He might be, but she wasn't. "I didn't mean— I couldn't help—"

"I couldn't help it either."

"So you and that other guy don't have this."

Sasha shook her head and Patrick closed his eyes as though the disturbance in the airflow caused by her movements was a caress. "No."

"What do you want from me, Sasha?"

How could she answer that when the answer was absolutely everything? She wanted him to lay her out on top of the bar and strip off all of her clothes. She wanted him to lick and suck and bite at her skin until it was bruised and aching for any other reason than needing him to touch her. She wanted him to completely lose control and empty himself inside her body.

But she couldn't have those things because there was guilt marring his perfect features from just a kiss on the cheek. It seemed that he didn't expect her to give him an answer either because he said, "I thought about you the other night in the shower."

"Did you touch yourself?" She might not be able to tell him all of her thoughts on what they should do with this, but that certainly wasn't going to stop her from a follow-up now.

He nodded. "I hadn't done that in—a long time."

That admission filled her with a level of pleasure she hadn't previously known. It filled her with electricity and sensual power, and she wanted more of it. "How did it feel?"

"Amazing." More sparks across her skin. "And terrible." Even more.

"I haven't let myself do the same." She didn't know why she admitted that. It had the potential to give him the wrong idea—that she didn't want him at least three times as much as he wanted her. "I don't think I could stop."

She bit her bottom lip, and his gaze dropped there. The moment stretched and morphed and the stuffy air in the bar turned even thicker. The faint smell of his fresh sweat wafted off his skin. They breathed each other in for what felt like a millennium. She could see his brain working behind his green eyes. They almost glowed at her. She was sure that they were having the same thoughts. They both wanted to take this further than thoughts and furtive masturbation sessions, but they couldn't. And how much she wanted him felt like physical pain. He reached out one finger and smoothed the crinkle in her brow. His touch was electric.

"I should leave." Sasha had let this go way too far.

He shook his head and didn't lose her gaze. "Stay."

"I want to." She couldn't breathe, but she wanted to drown in him.

"Show me."

At first she didn't understand his words. Her brain was too scrambled up in what was happening right at the moment and the things she wanted to happen that maybe, probably, never could. But his words sank in eventually, and somehow her brain got the message to her hand that it should move up to cup her own breast.

She gasped when her thumb grazed her nipple through her bra and the flippy sundress she'd put on just for the man in front of her.

He looked down and just watched. He made no effort to touch her, and she didn't think he would. This was just fair play. He'd thought about her while touching himself, and she hadn't allowed herself that. So she got him watching her touch herself, and that would punish him for what he'd done.

It was penance.

"More." It was a grunt, not a word. She didn't question what his words meant, even in her own mind. She slipped her hand under the hem of her skirt and touched her pussy through her panties. She was wet, and she moaned at the contact.

Patrick reached around her shoulders then, and she stilled. He wasn't supposed to do this. This wasn't supposed to make things worse. But he didn't touch her, just the back of her stool to push it back. "Lean back and spread."

She did it without thinking. Slipping her fingers inside her panties, she touched herself the way she did when she was alone. She touched herself like she did when she wasn't pretending to like the way the man whose ego she was responsible for not sinking touched her.

For his part, Patrick was fascinated and transfixed on the way her fingers moved under her skirt. Almost like he was cataloguing and learning for the future the way she wanted to be touched. She was beyond reminding herself that there was no future.

Between the two of them, alone in a mostly dark bar, there was no time. This was happening before he was a priest and after they were both dead in graves, the bodies that they inhabited at the moment being subsumed by the earth itself.

Energy filled her body, and all her muscles went taut. The only sounds were his heavy breaths, him chuffing with his apparent effort not to touch her, and the sounds her body made—moans and her wet fingers rubbing.

"Let me see."

She growled at him in frustration, and he chuckle-grunted, so she did what he asked. She flipped up her skirt and moved her panties aside to show him. For a moment, he dropped his forehead to the bar and made an anguished sound that filled Sasha with power and brought her back to where she'd been before he'd interrupted her flow.

He lifted his head when she started moving again, and he wasn't looking at where she was touching herself. Their gazes met and held, and she kept going until she thought her orgasm would break her into pieces.

It had never felt like this before. *This* was like nothing else she'd ever felt. It was bigger, and it would devastate her when she was done. That was the only thing that held it off for long moments before it hit her like a tidal wave. She couldn't help but close her eyes. Her body bent and her forehead hit the bar.

When she stopped moving, that was when he touched her. Just his palm on the back of her sweaty neck. She could feel that he was trying to tell her it was okay, but it wasn't.

It was fairly clear in her mind that it would never be okay again. She would never be able to get the awed look on his face out of her mind. She'd never felt sexier, more powerful, less tethered to the expectations of her family. All her life, she'd been a handmaiden to those expectations. But now, she wasn't sure that she could do that anymore.

His grip tightened, and so she didn't move for long moments. The cool mahogany against her skin a reminder that she wasn't in some celestial cocoon out of space and time, that she'd just jilled off in front of a frocked priest in a bar that wasn't even locked.

And she didn't feel guilty at all.

However, she could feel the remorse coming off Patrick in waves. She was sure that he regretted it. How could he not? In his mind, he'd already sinned. In hers, she'd twisted this so that this would somehow even the score.

But the way he'd looked at her—he'd loved this just as much as she had. This would stain his psyche as much as it would hers.

This was a problem.

That was the thought that made her lift her head. This time, he didn't meet her gaze. He looked down at her wrinkled skirt and sighed.

"Are you okay?" That he asked that, even when it was clear that he was not, made her heart ache for him. And somehow that was worse than the fact that she still wanted him to fuck her. What they'd just done had done nothing to dim her lust. No, she wanted him inside her even more. The way he'd pulled on all the right strings and pushed all the right buttons without even touching her told her that anything else they did would maybe create a tear in the universe.

The idea made her feel more than a little destructive. And the only thing that kept her from pushing things farther, from asking him to touch her more and condemn himself, was the sweat on his upper lip.

The fact that he was trying so hard not to want her, that there was something about this life he had that made him stop, made her stop.

She straightened out her clothes and nodded, finally answering his question. "I'm okay. Are you?"

He nodded but didn't speak.

"I'm going to go." She wanted him to stop her.

But he didn't. "That's probably—" He didn't finish his thought. Whatever he was going to say would definitely hurt her and it might hurt him. But she wasn't going to stick around to ask, because every time they talked, the talking led to them both doing something that they knew they shouldn't.

The problem was that doing it made her feel less like a bad person—instead she felt free.

But her freedom came at a price—and it was the fact that he thought that some higher power was actually keeping tabs on what people did with their genitals and meting out punishment based on how much fun they were having.

This thing with Patrick was making her realize how deep that patriarchal bullshit had seeped into her veins. Breaking all the rules—fooling around with a priest instead of the man who wanted to date her and was free to do so—was setting her free. It was making her brave.

But it was not doing the same thing for the man in front of her. She was ruining him, and this had to stop.

"Let's not be alone anymore." That was the only way this was going to stop. If they weren't alone, they couldn't give in to this.

He nodded.

"I'm going to go."

He nodded again, and she stopped waiting for him to say something. Still, she walked to the door slowly, in fading hope that he would stop her.

She opened the door and looked back at him. There was nothing left to say. Her body was filled with light, and she'd never felt closer to who she imagined herself to be when no one was watching. But he was devastated, and she wasn't sure that he would go seeking absolution from his God. She wanted to give it to him, hoped he accepted it, and knew that he probably wouldn't. Still, she said the words.

"Go forth and sin no more, Father."

CHAPTER SEVENTEEN

AFTER THE SCENE IN the bar, Sasha called him a few times. To Patrick's relief, she'd returned to her normal businesslike self. But something had changed inside him the other night. Whenever he heard her voice over the phone, an even stronger hit of possessiveness filled him. He couldn't control it, and he couldn't help it when his jaw tightened at her mention of her new boyfriend Nathan's employer helping out at the carnival by having some of the players—a few of them were Catholics—volunteer to run a bunch of the booths.

Like the bake sale, it would expand their audience beyond the parish and make them a lot more money. He could save the program and then move on with the work of trying to save his job and maybe his soul.

But, even though he shouldn't, every time he heard her voice, images of her touching herself sitting at his bar assaulted him. And he didn't have the strength to stop them. She was talking about ring tosses and dunk tanks, and all he could think about was how he'd missed the chance to sink down on his knees and drown himself in the nectar between her legs.

He couldn't get the scent of her out of his nostrils anyway. What was one more degree of sin? She'd looked like a queen sitting there, coming for him. It had been sacred and profane all at the same time.

And he was changed from it.

Although, after Sister Cortona's scolding, he'd promised himself that he wouldn't go any further, he'd let himself get too close. Just talking to Sasha was an aphrodisiac. She was intoxicating to him.

And now, after she'd fallen apart doing his bidding, making him feel all-powerful and so small at the same time, not seeing her again was actually killing him.

He'd tried to wring her out of his bones through exercise, but he couldn't run far enough or fast enough. He'd tried—running along the lakefront until his heart felt as though it was going to beat out of his chest. He'd hit the weight room at the YMCA until he was afraid that he was going to blow up his quads. After their weekly three-on-three game, Jack had joked about Patrick playing like a demon.

Patrick didn't mention that ever since that night at the bar with Sasha, he felt as though he were possessed by one. In fact, he said nothing about the night with Sasha. It was a precious, secret sin that he couldn't get himself to confess. He couldn't get himself to confess it because it didn't feel wrong.

That it didn't feel wrong filled him with the sort of existential angst that he'd become a priest to leave behind.

But directing Sasha as she gave herself pleasure—along with

the risk that someone would walk in the bar and catch them—had brought him back to when he was still a layperson. That was exactly what he'd liked to do. He'd liked to be in control.

What he hadn't liked was the out-of-control feeling he'd always had after sex was over. He'd never liked the idea of watching someone he'd shared that with walk out the door. He'd hated that feeling so much that somehow becoming a priest, thus foreclosing the possibility of losing that kind of control, had been appealing to him.

And he'd succeeded. By giving up choices and shutting out romantic connections, he didn't have to feel that intensity. Until Sasha.

When he knocked his brother Chris to the ground after they'd both gone up for a basket and had missed, his emphatic push and flagrant foul had been about that anger.

He needed someplace to put that intensity that wasn't pounding into Sasha's gorgeous frame. Now that he knew what the core of her looked like, he couldn't stop thinking about putting his dick there. The fact that it was a sin and violation of his vows—the fact that it put everything he'd built at St. Bartholomew's at risk—didn't sink in past the surface of his thoughts.

"What's with you, dude?" Chris got up and brushed some loose pieces of asphalt off his shorts.

"Yeah, man." Jack just *had* to pipe up. "Usually we don't see this kind of aggression from you."

Patrick was the easygoing guy that his little brother and his best friend had always been able to count on for a friendly ear or a ride home after a rough night. There was no way that he could turn that all around and sit this on their laps.

"How's Dad?" He knew it was dirty pool, but Chris was always worried about their dad. Patrick tended not to worry as much because their father had always needed someone there to keep him organized and on track. First, it had been his mother. After she'd passed away, the responsibility had fallen to Patrick and Chris. As the baby of the family, Chris's help was more in the form of worrying than helping. He just blasted that worry onto everyone else and let them worry about the consequences.

He totally understood why Jack's sister, Bridget, had dumped his ass, and he hadn't found anyone else to take him on.

It was a real bitch to be able to see everyone else's problems clearly, and not be able to solve his own. That must have been why he turned to Jack and said, "I have a lot on my mind."

"The pre-K program?" Jack picked up the ball, dribbled it, and took a shot that missed. "I thought Sasha had you almost sorted with that."

"Yeah, she does." And that was the problem. "It's bigger than that." It was hard to say that his own petty problems were bigger than his vocation and his parish. Wasn't God supposed to be bigger than everything?

Jack certainly looked shocked that he'd revealed something about his inner life. "Whoa," was his only response.

Patrick felt guilty for laying this on him. Chris had wandered off to practice layups. Patrick's father was a man of few words, and his brother didn't have enough range to listen to problems beyond client development that would help him move up the ladder at his law firm, so Patrick wasn't used to revealing himself. What was the point?

But when Jack inclined his head toward the bleachers, Patrick knew his best friend (since they were in diapers) saw him. And Patrick thought it was maybe time to let him in.

They sat down and Patrick took a few seconds while toweling off the back of his neck to figure out what he should say.

In the end, he figured it was best to just spit it out. "I have a thing for Sasha."

"Well, obviously." Jack said that like it was clear as day, and Patrick had to go back and comb his mind for times he would have slipped up with Sasha in front of Jack and/or Hannah. "The only real question is what you're going to do about it."

"Obviously," he said, mocking his friend's derisive tone, "I'm going to do absolutely nothing."

"See, that's not what I think you should do at all."

"Dude, you know I'm a priest, right?" Patrick was almost ready to take his friend's temperature. "You were at the ordination and everything."

"Yeah, but dude. I supported you and all, but I never really thought that this was the right thing for you."

"I can't believe that you're telling me this now."

"I couldn't really tell you anything after your mother died and Ashley left you practically at the altar." That was true. Before his mother had died, telling him in one of her last lucid moments that she could only rest easy if one of her sons took orders, he'd never really thought about becoming a priest. His behavior certainly hadn't been anything close to celibate.

But he couldn't understand why it had seemed to fit him so well for the last decade until—BOOM—everything changed. And Jack was right, he wasn't really hearing reason after his mother's death. The only person in the world who he felt really understood him was gone, and he hadn't trusted his friends enough to open up.

In addition to giving him a way to let his mother rest easy and feel closer to her, becoming a priest had been an extremely convenient way to shut off his own needs—to shut out the world.

But the world had a way of crashing back in. This thing with Sasha felt like a tidal wave. He didn't understand how he could feel so in tune with her while spending so little one-on-one time with her. Not that he'd have any more of that now that he'd screwed it all up.

"Has anything happened between the two of you?" Jack, his friend the journalist, was always going to dig a little bit deeper. He should have told Chris, who would have shrugged and told him to "nail Sasha and worry about it later," or his father, who would have grimaced and gone back to worrying about money.

"I don't want to talk about it." And he didn't. He also shouldn't. What had happened between the two of them was wrong in the eyes of the Church—no question—but it was also between the two of them.

"Dude, she's Hannah's best friend."

"And what of it?"

"Hannah will gut you like a pig if you hurt her best friend, and I don't think being pregnant has slowed her down at all." His friend said that with a smile meaning he was very happy to be married to a woman who threatened to gut priests like pigs.

Patrick allowed himself to wonder if he and Sasha could be that happy if he wasn't a priest. If he could just wave this one huge obstacle away, what kind of couple would they be?

He'd had an idea of who Sasha was—polite, contained, upper-crust girl from the East Coast. Part of him must have known that she had the potential to blow up his life because he'd never allowed himself to dig deeper. Even though he knew that everyone he met had a secret story in addition to the one they told the world.

"I need what I'm about to tell you to stay in the vault."

"I don't know if I can do that."

Patrick needed to talk about this, and Jack was really his only option right now. It wasn't like he could call up any of his friends from seminary with girl problems. "It would hurt her if she knew I told you and Hannah rode in trying to fix things. And you know Hannah would try to fix things."

Jack leaned back on the bleacher behind them and said, "All right. Shoot."

"Her family is way fucked up. More than like most families."

"That's not a secret, my good dude." Jack shook his head. "I could have told you that from the way she usually looks at the phone when one of them calls her. And they call her on the phone instead of texting. It's weird."

"Yeah, but she's got this idea that she's a bad person because she wants—"

Patrick was at a loss for what Sasha wanted that was bad enough to make her think that she was a bad person. It wasn't like she'd taken vows. And she wasn't a true believer. There was a whole other fucked-up system in her head—aside from the Church's misogynist teachings on women and sex that had trapped him. Since when had he started feeling trapped?

"Anything. She feels guilty for wanting anything."

Jack blew out some air. "She sounds like someone else I know."

"Who, me?" Patrick certainly didn't think that he'd been describing himself. He'd always thought that his needs and wants were simple enough that he could make do with what he had. He'd always had enough—maybe not all that he wanted, but enough.

"Yeah, you." Jack laughed again, and Patrick sort of wanted to punch him. He wanted to punch a lot of people these days. "You're both dummies."

"Says the dummy who lied to his now-wife for almost a month about why he was acting like a bozo."

"She was lying, too. And we cleared that up." Jack put up a hand. "This isn't worth arguing about, and you're changing the subject."

Caught. "It was a bad idea to mention anything."

"Why?" Jack looked hurt. "I'm your friend. If you're worried about something, I want to hear it."

"There's nothing to worry about, because I can't change anything about the situation." He could only try to forget how Sasha made him feel—made him want—and go back to his life by plowing forward. Besides, how he'd acted at the bar after Sasha had come made sure that she wouldn't want to change anything even if they could.

"You can change anything. People change all the time. You changed after your mom died. Who says you can't change again?"

"The Catholic Church." It wasn't a guarantee that the Church would allow him to be laicized. It was a big fucking deal. But that wasn't the only thing stopping him. If he left, he was pretty sure his mom's spirit would become a ghost and haunt him. That wasn't a part of the catechism, and it was likely blasphemy. But he still believed it. And who was to say that he couldn't walk out of the Church a free man and end up alone anyway? Thinking about it made him dizzy. "And what if it doesn't work?"

"You know better than almost anyone that there are no guarantees. Honestly, if I let myself dwell on everything that could go wrong—especially now that Hannah's pregnant—I wouldn't be able to get out of bed. I wouldn't be okay if I lost her. I know that. But I know that someday I'll lose her, or she'll lose me. Our kid will lose both of us. But we're here now, and that's what matters."

"I just don't know. I don't even know if Sasha wants me, or if she thinks she wants me because she can't have me."

"You were never this afraid before."

"It never mattered this much before."

Patrick dropped his head in his hands. When did his best friend become the smart one? It was like falling in love had made him silly and then wise. But he didn't know and couldn't be sure about how Sasha felt about him. He knew that his life had value as a priest. He helped people every day, whether it was listening to some of the elderly ladies who came in for confession but really just needed someone to talk to or delivering food and supplies to people who needed them.

And he couldn't get the hurt look on Sasha's face as she'd walked out of Dooley's out of his head. In the past decade, to his knowledge, he hadn't hurt anyone—not like that. It was selfish of him to want more of Sasha when wanting her as much as he did left her feeling like that. It was wrong, and he should leave it alone.

"The real question is, do you love her?"

Shit. He hadn't been thinking in terms of love. He'd only been thinking about what she did to him in making him remember that he was just flesh that would turn to dirt in the end. And she filled that flesh with something other than the Holy Spirit. Something he hadn't let himself want for a long time. He didn't—couldn't— know if it was right to let that thing win.

And part of him thought his faith was being tested. The question of whether he loved her was minor. And whether he loved her was separate from the question of the right thing to do about it. If he loved her as a man of God, he would protect her from what his flesh wanted. Her lack of belief wasn't important in that equation. If he loved her just as a man, then he would have to change his whole life and his faith wouldn't be in God and His love anymore—it would be in one person.

And that was too scary to contemplate. All of that made him say, "No," and return to the game.

CHAPTER EIGHTEEN

THE NEXT TIME SASHA went to St. Bart's to meet with Father Patrick, the forbidding nun was in his office with him. When she entered, her spine straightened, and she fought the urge to curtsy.

Nuns had always terrified Sasha, since before she attended her Catholic elementary school—the one that still allowed teachers to beat the children. Before that, Sasha had always found nuns in full habits who floated around like penguins on unseen dark clouds to be very scary. This was before she'd known any cool nuns who rode around on buses to protest the death penalty.

She had the feeling that Sister Cortona was not a cool nun who protested poverty. She seemed more like one of her elementary school teachers that slapped small children across the face for taking the Lord's name in vain.

When Patrick motioned for her to sit, her training kicked in. She glided into the chair, crossed her ankles, and folded her hands in her lap over the tablet she'd brought that held the contracts that she needed Patrick to sign.

Maybe it was spending five whole days with her mother before she and Madison had convinced Moira that her charities would simply not be able to go one more day without her adept guidance that made her so jumpy. Or, at least, that was a convenient lie she told herself to cover up that she was still shaken by what had happened in that bar with Patrick. She was using all her pretty, polite manners to cover it up.

Thankfully, Patrick seemed to be buying it. She was grateful to the mean mugging nun for that.

It was all going to be fine. Patrick would sign the contracts for the donated equipment—mostly assuring the vendors that the parishioners wouldn't wreck their stuff—and she would leave.

She wouldn't have to see him again until the carnival, and there would be a crowd. Hannah would henceforth handle all of the weddings at St. Bart's.

"Are you going to sit there all day staring at each other, or are we going to get down to fucking business?" Sasha started when Sister Cortona spoke. She'd never heard a nun use the f-word before.

"Um, if you can sign these contracts," Sasha said, opening the cover of her tablet.

Before she could hand it over, Sister Cortona grabbed it. "Let me look at that."

"I went over all the pertinent points with Father Dooley over the phone." Sasha was a little miffed that the nun was acting as more than just a chaperone. She was miffed—at herself—that they needed a chaperone at all.

"I don't know what you went over with him on the phone, and he doesn't understand numbers." If looks could kill, Sasha would be lying there dead.

"Oh—okay." Sasha wasn't sure what was going on, so she

looked at Patrick. He looked as though he were trying really hard not to laugh. And that made Sasha feel like she was going to laugh. It was like church giggles on steroids—the energy bouncing between the two of them no less potent than the energy between them the other night.

Patrick broke first. His laughter ended the silence in the office and not even a glare from Sister Cortona stopped him. And then Sasha broke, and she laughed so hard that she was doubled over and gasping for air.

When they wound down eventually, the nun was glaring at both of them. She didn't say anything, but she didn't have to.

The only thing that saved them was a ringing sound from inside her voluminous robes. She looked down to check her phone, muttering, "Oh, for Christ's sake," and stalked out of the room, leaving the tablet teetering on the edge of Patrick's desk.

After she left, the mirth between them turned to tension. And not the delicious kind that led to a fabulous orgasm and days of tortured guilt. It was the kind between people who were trying to be good and succeeding.

"She's not normally like that," Patrick said. "She's just concerned about me."

"You told her?" Sasha's face turned hot. What level of detail did he give? Why would he tell anyone?

For his part, Patrick also looked horrified. "Of course not. She guessed."

"That we—"

"No. She guessed that I have a thing for you."

"Are we that obvious?" Sasha rarely let her carefully cultivated façade slip. She'd gotten ghosted more than once by men who—when she ran into them later—told her that they'd stopped calling because they couldn't tell if she liked them or not. It was usually because she was only pretending to like them until she could figure out if she could actually see herself with them. The fact that she couldn't hide her feelings for Patrick was an entirely new thing. "Not that there's a 'we.'"

Patrick grunted. He had to stop doing that, especially when they were alone. It turned her on too much. Dear Lord, she had to get out of here. He must have had the same idea because they reached for her tablet at the same time, causing it to stop teetering and fall.

They both went for the falling tablet, but Sasha caught it. And when she tried to lift her head, her hair was caught in between the metal links of Patrick's watch. She tried to yank away, but that caused a snap of pain. She stopped struggling when he said, "Stop moving."

Whenever he told her to do something, her body just did it before her mind could get defiant. It should bother her, but it was for her own good in this case.

"If you move slowly around the desk, we'll get your hair untangled."

She got up into an awkward half-crouch, hoping that none of her bits were on display. She skirted the desk in that position until she could stand up with Patrick's forearm resting on top of her head. It would be laughable if it wasn't quite so dangerous. It didn't even matter that they'd started out this meeting chaperoned and six feet apart. And now they were touching—a mere breath away from kissing. If she still believed in God, she would think he was trying to fuck with them. Setting them up to fail.

"Hold on." Patrick lifted his other hand and tried to disentangle her hair from his watch. It gave her the chance to study him from up close. She didn't know when she'd have the chance again, so she drank him in. She tried to memorize the way he smelled, the way he quietly talked to himself as he worked.

She loved the shape of his jaw. Some might call it severe, but it read to her as strong. Steady. If she raised up on her tiptoes, she could run her lips over it. What would it be like to be able to do that? She knew she wanted that despite it being impossible, not because it was impossible.

In her mind, she could close her eyes and imagine waking up to that jawline every morning. She wanted to hear him muttering and cursing over fixing things in a small house that they shared. He made her think of white picket fences and family meals. It wasn't what her parents wanted for her—charity galas and auxiliary boards—but she didn't care. She'd never felt like she really fit anyway, which made her good at her job. She could always see everything that could go wrong, so she fixed it. The picture in her head of what kind of life she could have with Patrick—if he wasn't a priest and he wanted to make a life with her—felt like it fit. Thinking about it felt like sinking into a warm bath.

And she could see this beyond the undeniable sexual charge between them now. She could see growing old with Patrick, taking care of him the way he took care of everyone else.

"Just give me another minute." He glanced down at her. God, it was unbearable to be this close to him without being able to touch him. It made her want to crawl out of her skin.

"Just yank it." Sasha was getting too excited being this close to him. She wasn't sure what she might do if she didn't get away from him and out of this office right fucking now.

"No."

His being so calm about it made it even worse. "Why not?" It wasn't even that much hair.

"I like your hair attached to your head." He looked down and met her gaze. She froze and stopped struggling.

Even though he'd referred to their mutual attraction, he'd never mentioned anything in particular that he liked about her appearance before. The idea that she affected him in a primal and visceral way and not just in his head was appealing. She didn't understand it when she usually felt the opposite—she'd always worried that the men of her acquaintance cared more about what she looked like than what she felt or thought.

Sasha maneuvered the few millimeters between them and planted her lips against his. And then she didn't do anything else because this was a huge mistake. But that didn't make her pull away.

PATRICK HADN'T BEEN KISSED in well over a decade. Until Sasha planted her pillow-soft lips against his, he hadn't realized how much he'd missed it. This was a terrible idea. Sister Cortona could walk back in at any moment, and then she'd for sure report him.

The other night had been too far, but this—her mouth against his, open and breathing her fresh minty breath into his mouth. It was ruin. She was ruin. And he wasn't going to let it go.

They stood there for so long, lip to lip, that she started to pull away. The part of him that was touch-starved and lonely and needed relief more desperately than he did salvation grabbed at her waist and stopped her. Instead of pulling away, she bent her head toward where his watch was still tangled up in the silk of her hair and licked his lower lip with her tongue.

He shuddered at her touch and flexed his palm against her. She let out a throaty laugh/moan hybrid, and he broke.

He could have gotten her hair untangled faster, but he'd been greedy for a reason to keep her near. And—God help him—he wasn't sorry at all now that her body was pressed against his, and their tongues danced.

He'd thought about the taste of her so much, and the reality was so much better than he'd ever imagined. He was a starving man, and she'd put a banquet in front of him. If he could have managed it without hurting her, he would have her bent over his desk and begging for him to give her the release she'd given herself in front of him the other night.

It was depraved, but he was past caring.

Their bodies moved against each other awkwardly until he dropped the hand that was stuck to her and cupped the back of her head. That only brought her closer, and he groaned and cursed.

She turned him into a man that he'd forgotten he'd ever been—selfish, greedy, a man who wanted things that he couldn't have. She'd ruined his hard-fought contentment, but somehow it didn't take the legs out from under him. He felt more alive than he had since before he could remember.

She turned and sat on the edge of his desk. He backed her up until his thighs wedged hers open. He wished he could see the skin on her thighs as her dress rolled up, but he settled for squeezing one. He was so beyond the idea that he wasn't going to cross his own line and think about this while he relieved himself in the shower for decades to come that it wasn't even funny.

He wasn't sure how long the kiss lasted, but he knew when it ended that Sasha was holding scissors and a huge lock of her hair was floating down to his desk.

Then, she was a few feet away from him—looking stricken. He wanted to take that away. This wasn't her fault, and he was starting to think it wasn't his. Their connection was rare and precious and felt like nothing else he'd ever experienced. He wanted to go to her, to put his arms around her and reassure her somehow.

But she'd cut off a hunk of her hair to get away from him, which must have meant that she was thinking a whole lot more clearly than he was in that moment.

"I have to go." She was right, but it didn't cut him any less. Sister Cortona could still walk in at any minute. If she saw them now, there would be no question that they had been up to no good.

Instead of saying what he wanted to, instead of asking her to stay, he nodded and she was gone.

CHAPTER NINETEEN

SASHA HADN'T CALLED FOR an emergency girls' brunch in years, and not since before Bridget joined their group. But times were desperate. And, even though she was a relatively new friend, Bridget came through in the clutch in a huge way.

Bridget was divorced from and also engaged to the scion of an extremely wealthy and politically connected family that made the Finerghtys seem hopelessly bourgeois. And now that she'd fully embraced the idea of marriage, she enjoyed little more than giving away her ex- and future husband's money. She said it was a "recovering Catholic thing," but Sasha wasn't willing to dwell on the concept of recovering and Catholic in the same sentence.

Hannah and Sasha had gone to Bridget and Matt's house because she'd not only ordered brunch in, she'd arranged to have a hairstylist fix Sasha's truly atrocious situation while they triaged the damage that Sasha had done in her—and Patrick's—life.

She told them everything. Even the bar masturbation part. Both of her friends were truly shocked. A piece of *pain au chocolat* fell out of Hannah's mouth, and she'd never before wasted pastry on something so inconsequential as one of Sasha's stories about a man. Bridget, for her part, had finished three mimosas by the time Sasha arrived at the part where she'd cut her hair off so she wouldn't fuck a frocked priest on his desk.

"I'm going to hell." Of that, Sasha had no doubt. Still, telling two people who might understand was such a relief. She felt like at least half of the elephant crushing her internal organs was off her chest.

"We're all going to hell," Bridget said, motioning with her empty champagne flute. "I mean, I'm obscenely wealthy."

"And I'm a total bitch," Hannah added.

Sasha looked at her friend. She didn't know how many times they were going to have to go over the fact that there was a difference between a bitch and the c-word. Hannah was a bitch, but she largely used her powers for good. Since she was in a delicate condition, Sasha pointed at her. "No."

"Honestly, I don't see what you did that was so bad," Bridget, the lifelong Catholic, said.

Sasha put a piece of fruit in her mouth. She had been so sick about her inability to stop seducing Patrick, even though she'd really, really meant to, that she hadn't been eating. "I cannot control myself around him."

"Which I am totally grossed out by, by the way," Bridget said. "He's like my brother."

"You were engaged to Patrick's brother, which meant you were sort of engaged to your own brother." Hannah had a smirk on her face that said she'd thrown that out just to get a rise out of her sister-in-law. While Sasha appreciated her friend's effort at levity, this was a truly serious situation.

"Yeah, he was like my brother, which was one of the many

problems with our relationship." Bridget poured Hannah more orange juice and pulled another bottle of Veuve Clicquot out of the refrigerator. "Speaking of. The last time we talked, you were dating some guy who it sounded like you mildly preferred to major surgery."

"Nathan is nice." Sasha didn't know why she was defending him. She didn't want to have dirty sex with him. Which was fine. Because the only man she wanted to have sex with was definitely off-limits. Why weren't her friends more scandalized by this? Patrick was their friend, too. Sasha was ruining his life. "Why aren't you guys more upset about this?"

"Because the vow of celibacy is total bullshit. And Patrick is nothing like my brother, so I can see what a huge waste of— potential—that is." Hannah grabbed another croissant. It was good that she hadn't turned a little bit green even once this morning. "I think you should suck the celibacy right out of him."

"Hannah!" Both Bridget and Sasha yelled at the same time.

"What? You both know I'm right."

"I just wouldn't have said it that way," Bridget said. "Listen, the way I see it, there's the letter of the law and the spirit."

Of course Bridget would come at it like the prosecutor she once was. "Well, we've broken both."

"And there has to be a reason for it. Did Patrick seem as into it as you were?"

Patrick had instigated the kiss beyond what she'd intended. She'd just been reacting, and then he'd acted. His touch had been possessive; thinking about it now gave her a chill. That night at the bar, there had been no question of who was in control: him. She could have said no, but she would have done anything he asked, short of a crime.

"Yeah."

"So you're both breaking the letter and the spirit of the law. This is a conspiracy and there's no victim here." Bridget shrugged.

"It's not that simple." There was a victim—multiple victims. Sasha hadn't missed how the people in the parish regarded Patrick. They looked at him as though he were the Savior himself, and not just because his crooked smile was enough to turn water to wine and panties to dust. Even when he was stern, his compassion and generosity were a beacon. Even if she didn't believe in God, he was a good man, and he brought something good to people's lives. She refused to believe that she wasn't one hundred percent responsible for his downfall, and she refused to participate anymore.

"Hannah, I need you to handle the carnival."

Her best friend grimaced. "I'm in a delicate state."

Bridget called her out. "You've been back in spinning for weeks now."

"Fine," Hannah said. "But I think you're running away, and I think it's a terrible idea."

"My wedding's going to be a mess. Again," Bridget said with a laugh. She was getting married to Matt again two weeks before the carnival. Patrick would be a guest. "I fucking love it."

"What the hell am I supposed to do?" Sasha asked, not really expecting an answer. She was already a disappointment to her family, and even though her friends wouldn't judge her, she was worried that Patrick would grow to hate her. She'd seen his commitment to the parish, to the pre-K program, and whatever he thought God was. If she asked him to walk away from all that, and they didn't work out as a couple, there was no way he wouldn't grow to hate her.

She couldn't survive that. She'd rather have to see Patrick from afar and wonder if they could have been something great than fail at a real relationship with him.

Sasha was saved from having to confess all that when the hairstylist arrived. When she saw the thick strand of hair that was sticking up on top of Sasha's head, she blanched. But she recovered quickly, and said, "So, what are we doing today?"

"Cut it all off."

PATRICK ENJOYED SPEAKING AT weddings. He loved baptisms. Even daily Mass—it filled him with a sense of routine and peace that had always felt elusive to him with his parents owning a bar. But he hated giving last rites.

He knew it was important and helped ease people on their way out of this world. But when it was over, he always felt like he'd absorbed the person's panic and uncertainty. He didn't know where to put it.

The day after he and Sasha kissed, one of his parishioners passed away. The only time he didn't think about her in that twenty-four hours was when he was saying the words and just being there with a woman who hadn't missed Sunday Mass in four decades. He'd heard her confessions every week since he took over from the old pastor.

She was a good person, but she'd confessed every one of her uncharitable thoughts. And Patrick wasn't sure if she'd believed that she was free of sin before she'd died. He didn't know that he'd offered her an ounce of comfort or whether she was filled with guilt as she took her last breaths.

He didn't know what it was all for.

All he knew was that he would die with the sin of wanting Sasha on his soul. And he didn't know if it was enough to condemn him, but it was enough to make him question why he was still here. As a priest. In a church.

He wondered if he still had faith. If he'd ever had faith or if he had just wanted to hide from all of the hard things in life—falling in love, having his heart broken, investing enough in personal relationships to really have it matter.

He was about to pour himself a very large scotch when his phone rang. Dammit. He hoped it wasn't another emergency with a parishioner. He sighed when he realized that it was his brother. Chris probably just needed someone to hang out with, and that he could do. His brother didn't expect anything or project any of his bullshit on him because he really didn't dig deep enough to have any angst. Patrick wondered if he would be better off if he was more like him.

"Patrick." That one word from his brother sounded wrecked, and fear pricked at Patrick.

"What's wrong?"

"Dad fell." Patrick's heart sank. Their father wasn't the most open and loving, but he had always been there. He was the kind of guy who didn't say "I love you" very often but had all of your paperwork. If something was really wrong with him, Patrick wasn't going to be able to hide from his pain behind his collar. "He's okay, but we need to get him to the hospital to get him checked out."

"I'll be right there."

When Patrick got to their house, Chris had coaxed their dad—limping—out the front door and onto the stoop. Patrick jogged up the walk and grabbed their dad's other arm over his grumbling.

"I'm fine."

"I'm sure that's why you're limping."

His father grimaced. "I told this bozo not to call you."

"Well, he did one non-bozo thing and called me."

Chris snorted. "He was trying to change the light bulb at the top of the stairs." The very steep stairs that weren't up to any sort of code. He'd be calling Nolan & Sons—Jack's dad's company—to get a fix for that in the morning. Patrick's dad didn't like to take charity, but Sean Nolan was the only man cussed enough to get past Danny Dooley's front door when he was in a fit of pique.

By the time they'd loaded their father into Chris's car and gotten him checked out in the ER—nothing was broken, just a sprained ankle—Patrick was wrung out. He just wanted to go home and go to bed.

But after they got his Dad home and jointly carried him upstairs to his bedroom, he had to talk to Chris about how they were going to make sure their dad stayed home and in bed long enough to heal.

"Can you check on him tomorrow and cover at the bar?" Patrick asked.

Chris blanched. "I have a big case going to arbitration next week—"

Patrick didn't know why it was this time that he snapped, but it was. "Of fucking course."

"Dude," Chris said, like it was an affront to have to pitch in like a member of an actual family.

"You always have a big case." Patrick rubbed the spot between his eyebrows. "No wonder Bridget dumped you."

That was way pettier than he'd meant to be, but he was at his wit's end. His baby brother had shown up today, and he should be grateful. But all of the weight on his shoulders felt too heavy. His parishioners, his family, the fact that his feelings for Sasha weren't going away—he was ready to collapse under the weight of it.

The fact that his father had called Chris instead of him today was part of it. Danny looked at his lawyer son as a success. Meanwhile, he looked at Patrick like he was some sort of disappointment. The only person in the family who'd understood him—his mother—had died, and he was alone.

Other than Jack, who was too busy getting ready to welcome a baby right now to bother, he had no one whom he could turn to if he was in trouble, and he was always the person who had to bear other people's burdens. He'd willingly taken that on. And for the first time since he was a kid, he wished he could be as cavalier about other people's needs and feelings as his brother was. As his father always had been with his wife.

He wished he could be more like his brother and take what he wanted. He wished he could shirk all of his commitments and not even feel guilty about it. And when he thought about obligations he would shirk and things he wanted—it all coalesced into one thing.

Sasha.

"C'mon. You always do this. It's not like you have a swinging social life." Chris was such a dick.

"Shut up."

Chris laughed and walked toward the car, clicking the electric locks on his Tesla. "Let me know if you need me to pay any bills for Dooley's. I'll take it out of my mad money."

Patrick picked up his pace as he followed Chris. Their childhood home had a hedge right next to the walk that they used to try to push each other into when either one of them was unaware.

It wasn't kind or mature, but he couldn't really do anything about what he truly wanted. So, he shoved his brother into the hedge and then jogged to his rusted-out Toyota before Chris could retaliate.

CHAPTER TWENTY

WHEN SASHA RETURNED HOME after her haircut/boozy brunch with Hannah and Bridget, her sister's belongings were strewn all over the living room and several suitcases were precariously perched on pieces of furniture. She hoped this meant that her sister was either going back East or moving into her own place.

Although she'd appreciated her help with work in the past few weeks, it wasn't an ideal situation to teach her sister how to be an adult and have a real job. And now that Hannah was back in fighting form, they didn't really need help anymore.

Before Sasha could ask her myriad questions, Madison had her own. "What happened to your hair?" Madison asked as soon as Sasha walked through the door.

"I cut it." The night before, she'd hidden the chunk of hair that she'd cut off with a ponytail. Although she and her sister had grown closer over the past few weeks, Sasha wasn't ready to spill the beans on the fact that she'd been hooking up—in a manner—with a frocked priest. "Going somewhere?"

Madison's wide smile in response was alarming. For that matter, the way she was dressed, not in sweatpants but her former housewife uniform of jeans and high boots and a cashmere sweater, set off alarms as well. "I'm getting my own place."

"So, you're really going to leave Tucker?"

Madison nodded, and her grin got wider.

"And you feel good about that?"

Her sister just shrugged and kept folding clothes. "He called me last night and we had a long talk. It turns out that he was so bored with me that he could have died, too."

"Have you told Mom and Dad?" She wouldn't put it past her parents to threaten, cajole, or bribe any one of them into falling in line. Sasha just happened to have turned that around on them enough that they didn't bother to try very hard with her anymore.

"Not yet." Madison stopped folding and sat down. "Seeing Mother completely lose her shit made me scared of her. I feel like I understand you a lot better now."

"I think the point is that you understand yourself a lot better now," Sasha said. They'd made so much progress, and Sasha was filled with hope that her sister was actually turning a corner and about to make her life into what she wanted. Sasha thought Madison might stop caring about what other people thought a little bit more.

"I'm afraid. I just don't want to end up with nothing." Madison motioned around the room.

Then Sasha got angry. Her sister really thought she had nothing because she hadn't followed their mother's very precise playbook for success? Her sister didn't have any room to talk. "You think I have nothing?"

"Well—"

Sasha had her own business and was on her way to buying her

home from their parents. She would never deny that she'd been given a leg up in many ways by not having student loans to pay back and not having to worry about rent the first few years out of college, but her life was not frivolous, even though she planned parties.

She had friends who were more like family than her own family and a full life. Sasha didn't feel the need to run away because she felt empty—like Madison had. "The only thing I don't have that you do is a high-fiving, pleated-pant-wearing, soon-to-be-ex-husband who is only truly happy when he's playing golf with his boys."

"Tucker is not that bad. At least he wasn't. And I will definitely get married again." Madison crossed her arms. "You won't give anyone a chance. You have no one to come home to. You are truly alone."

Sasha only felt alone when she was with her family of origin. Hearing her sister denigrate the life she'd made on her own flipped a switch in her. She'd always thought she'd been bad or wrong because she didn't fit her family's mold. All of the tiny mental rebellions she'd tallied like a burn book against herself and castigated herself for—from her fantasies about Professor McDermott to her very real transgressions with Father Patrick—were just evidence that she'd never come up to snuff.

But maybe the fact that she could never quite fit the mold didn't mean that she was bad or wrong. Maybe it meant that the mold was wrong.

"I don't understand why you're so upset." Of course empathy would escape her sister. "I'm just telling you the truth."

Maybe it was the truth as Madison saw it. And perhaps they might have reached the limit of their common ground.

"I just want to see you happy," Madison said. Instead of telling her sister off, Sasha picked up one of Madison's blouses and started to help fold. She realized then that she was never going to see the world in the same way her sister did. And she might not see the world in the same way as Bridget or Hannah, but at least they saw *her.* Her family only cared about the version of her that fit with how they saw the world.

"I'm happy," Madison continued. And then she bit her bottom lip as though she was thinking about the next thing she was going to say. She hadn't done that before, so this must be a doozy. "It just took me seeing how miserable you are to realize it."

Miserable? Sasha knew she'd been mildly dissatisfied with life before, but she didn't think she was miserable. "I'm not miserable."

"You never seem satisfied with anything that you have."

Madison had a point there. She had started therapy for a reason. She'd been missing something that she couldn't pinpoint.

"So, me not being satisfied made you decide to be satisfied?"

"I guess."

She couldn't fault Madison for that. But she was going to have a lot to discuss with Pam next session.

PATRICK WAS NERVOUS ABOUT seeing Sasha again, but still he was disappointed when Hannah came into his office for a final meeting about the carnival.

It must have shown because Hannah smirked at him. "You were expecting to see someone else?"

He wondered what Sasha had told her best friend. He knew they were very close, but he'd also learned that Sasha was a bit of a vault even when it came to her friends. They were alike that way, smoothly gliding on the surface and not letting their friends in on how hard their feet were churning underneath the placid water. They were birds of a feather and kindred spirits.

Instead of probing deeper, he decided to take in the message sent by cutting off a strand of her hair—which Patrick wouldn't think about, even though it was still in his desk drawer—and sending her business partner in her stead.

"You're feeling better?"

Hannah certainly looked hale. "Yes. I'm very lucky that the bad morning sickness only lasted for the first trimester. It was like the fetus stopped trying to make me feel like shit once it knew we were in it for the long haul."

"Have you and Jack decided whether you're going to find out if it's a boy or a girl?"

"Nah, gender is a construct, and I know you're trying to change the subject."

"From what?" Playing dumb seemed to be his best option with Hannah. She seemed to be out for blood, and it probably wouldn't help. But he couldn't think of anything else.

"From the fact that you're toying with my best friend's emotions." Guilt hit Patrick in the guts when she said that. It was certainly how things would look, even though it hadn't been his intention.

"I never meant to—"

Hannah put up one hand. "It doesn't matter what you meant to do."

That was true. He hadn't intended to sin, but he'd done it anyway. And the thought that he'd hurt Sasha was even more torturous than having to live with violating his vows. She'd *told* him that they were not a thing when she'd walked out of the bar. But she'd kissed him, and he'd kissed her back.

She made him question everything. She terrified him.

His maudlin reverie was cut off by Hannah's sharp laugh. "You really like her, don't you?"

"Of course I like her." Patrick shouldn't really be discussing this with her. "She's my friend."

Hannah rolled her eyes at him. "Okay, if you're going to play it this way, I'm just going to have to lay it out."

Patrick could see why his best friend loved this woman. She didn't let him get away with anything. "If you hurt her anymore, if you lead her on and make her think you're leaving the priesthood for her only to chicken out like a fucking punk, I will make the fires of hell look like a damned picnic in the park."

"Noted."

Hannah nodded. "Now sign these contracts so that I can go home and defile my husband."

Patrick was jealous, but just looked at her. "I'm still a priest, you know."

"Yeah, like I care." Hannah smiled, and Patrick knew that she hadn't been bluffing about being more arduous than hellfire. "I like to see your collar in a wad."

The insinuation being that he shouldn't be wearing one anymore.

CHAPTER TWENTY-ONE

THE LAST PLACE THAT Patrick wanted to be was at the reception for Matt and Bridget's second wedding. He felt guilty about being relieved that they'd decided to get married at City Hall—Matt wasn't Catholic, and Bridget wasn't a churchgoer. But Patrick would have preferred to avoid the whole thing. Now that Jack and Hannah knew there was something going on, or something had gone on, he didn't doubt that all their friends knew there was more than a crush between the two of them.

He couldn't beg off, however, because Bridget would be deeply disappointed in him. He was genuinely happy that she'd found happiness after her toxic relationship with his brother. She was like family—sometimes more like family than his own—and he liked to think he was made of sterner stuff than making an excuse.

Plus, no matter what, he was going to have to see Sasha again. It was better if it was at a big public event rather than alone in his office. Or alone in the rectory. Or alone at Dooley's. Any of the places where he could forget that he wasn't allowed to touch her or kiss her or even want her.

He'd attempted to mentally prepare for seeing her again, but it had been foolish to even try. She looked even more ethereal with short hair that showed off her long neck. The new style should remind him of what she'd been willing to sacrifice to get away from him, but it instead made him contemplate the curve of her neck.

During the cocktail hour, he greeted the newlyweds and grabbed a beer. When he found a dark corner, he leaned back against the wall, hoping to blend into the lushly appointed furniture at the private club that Matt's parents had bought out for the night.

His eyes kept being drawn back to Sasha. He couldn't help it. She looked at home in the room—one where politicians had probably made backroom deals for a hundred years. This was a room he wouldn't ever be welcomed into, not unless he had the ambition to climb the Church's hierarchy. Bishop Rafferty was probably a member. Even his brother—who was absent from this event for obvious reasons—would be more at home in a room like this than Patrick was.

But Sasha laughed and smiled and seemed to know everyone. It made him feel like a miserable prick for wanting her. He could never give her this. Even if he left the Church, he didn't have a plan. Sasha was the kind of woman who wouldn't choose a man without a plan. She contained more multitudes than she usually let out, but she was a pragmatist.

And she didn't want him—not really and not for keeps.

Still, he kept willing her to look at him. She never did. And he decided to switch from beer to scotch.

SHE NOTICED HIM LOOKING at her, and it was very distracting. Trying to ignore him was the only thing keeping her sane right now, and he was making it impossible. An uncharitable part of her mind wished that he'd just stayed home, even if he had known Bridget his whole life.

When she felt his eyes on her, it just made her laugh louder and flirt more with everyone else. Maybe then he'd get the message that she'd moved on, even though she was really only trying and failing to move on.

He was even more handsome when he was brooding. Leaning back in an antique upholstered chair at one of the tables at the edge of the room, he looked disreputable—more like an old-timey gangster than a man of the cloth.

Hannah, who was still moving very quickly and silently for someone who was starting to pop an impressive belly, sidled up to her without her noticing. "Stop looking at him like that."

"I thought you didn't care that I was looking at him like that."

"I wouldn't care if you were looking at him like that if you were actually going to do anything about it, but both of you are too up your own asses to make a move. This is just torturing you both."

That's right, Hannah had gone to see Patrick because Sasha was too much of a chicken to be in a room with him after the kiss/scissors incident. "He seems tortured?"

"The man is a mess." Oddly, her best friend sounded delighted by that fact. "He's so forlorn that he doesn't know which way is up."

Sasha let herself glance at him then and met his gaze. It held for long moments, and she couldn't tear her eyes away from him. And he looked like he was trying to fill himself up with her, too.

"If he's so forlorn—if he wants me that much—why doesn't he come and get me?"

"Why don't you go and get him?"

"Because I'm a lady." Her automatic reply came out of conditioning rather than any real belief. When she thought about going after Patrick and telling him how she felt about him, her mother's voice cropped up in her head: *If a man wants you more than any of his other options, he'll let you know. If he doesn't, you know he doesn't want you.*

Efficiency was the name of the game when it came to her mother and courting rituals. Not quality.

"I seriously had no idea how fucked up you were before this." Hannah's words made Sasha finally break Patrick's gaze. "To think, I thought you had it all figured out when it came to dating."

"To be fair, I am very good at dating. I can always get a man to ask me on another date."

"I seem to remember a couple of proposals in there, too."

None of those had been from serious prospects—and one of them hadn't remembered proposing the next day. They didn't count.

Also, she hadn't been in love any of those times. "I might be good at dating, but I'm terrible at finding love."

"It still looks to me like you found it."

"I can't ask him to leave the priesthood."

"Why not?" Hannah put her hands on her hips. She was relentless when she sank her teeth into something, and Sasha had never been one of those things before. She wasn't the kind of friend who needed to be picked up and put back together. She was the kind of friend who did the picking up and putting back together. She wasn't entirely comfortable with the reversal.

"I don't know that I love him." Sasha laughed, and she sounded jaded, even in her own ears. "And I don't know that he loves me. How am I supposed to know if I can compete with God?"

"So you're refusing to even try?"

"What about him?" Sasha kept herself from pointing. "I think becoming a priest is making a pretty clear statement about how much he values romantic relationships."

"Come to think of it, becoming a priest is really the ultimate fuckboy move," Hannah said, sarcasm dripping from her voice. "Really says that he can't make a commitment."

"I think being pregnant has made you mean," Sasha said.

"Not being able to have champagne will do that to a girl."

Sasha threw up her hands and walked to the ladies' room. She didn't know what her hair was doing at any given moment now that it was short, and she had to make sure it wasn't standing on end after her frustrating conversation with Hannah.

It actually looked kind of cute, and it was easier to stay cool. She dawdled, though, washing her hands and buying time where she didn't have to be in the same room as Patrick.

But her time was up as soon as she walked out. He was leaning against the wood-paneled wall opposite the bathrooms.

"What are you doing here?" She sounded angry. And she was usually careful never to sound angry. She could be angry, but letting people know how she felt was not allowed. It was another thing that Finerghty women didn't do.

"I can go." Patrick held up his hands. "But I thought it would be good if we talked."

Sasha shook her head and wrapped her arms around her waist. "I think it's a bad idea."

"Oh, it's definitely a bad idea, but everything involving you and me is a bad idea."

"Then why are you suggesting it?"

He paused and then smiled so that one of his dimples popped. Jesus, he could clean up if he weren't a priest. And a rogue trail of jealousy hit her just thinking about it. He made her feel all the things at once—longing, anger, jealousy, happiness, lust.

"Because I can't help myself." His words sounded raw and vulnerable.

She couldn't help asking. "Are priests allowed to dance?"

SASHA WAS QUITE BRILLIANT, Patrick thought, as he led her on to the dance floor. If people gave him, in his collar, looks about them dancing together, he didn't notice. All he wanted to notice was how it felt to be able to touch her right now. To sway with her as the big band played music from a time that had long passed. To imagine that he wasn't who he was and was allowed to feel the things he felt when he was in the room with her. To wish that he could touch his mouth to hers again and again. Out loud and in public. To feel the heat of her body radiating toward him along with her palpable irritation.

He wanted to know the how and why of that irritation. She fascinated him endlessly, and he wasn't about to deny that he enjoyed the fact that he ruffled her normally unrufflable feathers.

"Is something bothering you, Sasha Finerghty?" He liked saying her name. Until that moment, he hadn't realized that he'd been saying it for a long time in his head, but getting to say it out loud was even more of a tattoo on his heart.

"What do you want from me, Father Patrick Dooley?"

Of course she asked the one question that he couldn't precisely answer. The answer wasn't simple. What he wanted from her was absolutely everything. But he wasn't in the position to ask anything of her right now.

So he gave her the only true answer he could give her in that moment. "I want to dance with you."

"That's not an answer." Her eyes held fire, but he knew she wasn't going to make a scene in front of all these people.

"I can't have what I want."

"Why not?" That was the question that had been in the back of his brain for weeks, and she'd just asked it. He also wondered why he couldn't just walk away.

"Because, believe it or not, I don't have all the answers."

"Oh, I would believe that." He loved it when she was biting like this. It felt truer than the flirtatious Sasha and the hyper-competent Sasha. It was the closest thing to the Sasha who had kissed him that he could have. "If you had all the answers, you wouldn't be keeping me on a string."

And then she made him mad, and he liked that feeling, too. Even with Ashley, he'd never liked fighting. It had always felt like it was the end of a relationship. It turned out that it had been when they finally told each other the truth.

As much as the fact that he didn't know what he was going to do about the problem of him being a priest, the terrifying idea of telling Sasha the truth about how messed up his feelings for her had made him was what stopped him from saying anything. "You're not the only one on a string."

She looked up at him and they stared each other down for a long moment. At the same time, they both realized that they were in a stalemate. Neither was going to be the one to put their heart on the line. He could see that about her, and she could see that about him. It was written all over her face.

If he told her how he felt about her now, and they broke up in six months because they weren't really compatible at all, he would feel like a fool. He would be in the same place he'd been in when he'd entered the seminary. If he didn't have Sasha, he didn't want anyone else. But he would have to ask to be laicized to figure it out.

"What do you want from me, Sasha?" He breathed out the words. She kept staring at him, but her mouth flattened. So many emotions crossed her face. She was not nearly as hard to read to him now. He wanted to coax her into giving him the answer that he wanted—"Leave with me. Choose me"—but she didn't.

She looked away and stepped as close as she could to his body without raising eyebrows. And, when they finished the dance, she moved away and didn't look at him for the rest of the night.

CHAPTER TWENTY-TWO

SITTING IN PAM'S OFFICE the next day, Sasha was no less confused than she had been over two months ago when she'd admitted her impure thoughts about Patrick to her therapist. Because of the fundraisers for St. Bart's and other work responsibilities, she hadn't been back since. She felt emotionally constipated, and the ensuing events hadn't clarified anything for her.

Even though Pam had been trained in Jungian analysis, she wasn't a therapist who sat and waited for the analysand to talk. Pam participated. Usually. Except for today. It was as though she'd smelled the turmoil on Sasha and wanted to smoke it out with silence.

Finally, after staring at one of Pam's very eclectic paintings for five minutes, Sasha asked, "How do you know if you're in love with someone?"

Pam sat back, raising her eyebrows as though she'd received a particularly juicy piece of gossip. "Is this about the priest?"

Sasha nodded. Even though she'd talked about this with Hannah and Bridget, and they hadn't judged her, she was still afraid to talk about it with Pam. Her therapist would see how she was judging herself for it all.

"My sister was here for a month."

"And how was that for you?"

Sasha shrugged. "It was—fine. She left her husband." Pam knew how much Sasha loathed her sisters' husbands. One of the reasons she'd started going to therapy was that she'd needed tools not to snipe at them at family holidays.

Another reason she'd started coming to therapy was so that she could be less messy. She'd thought that, if she knew herself better, she would have more control over her behavior. But sitting here in this room, exposing all of her dark thoughts, hadn't helped her tidy the inner workings of her mind. The deeper she went, the more complicated things were.

She sort of hated Pam for that right now.

"I think Madison and I are closer, though she still thinks it's kind of pathetic that I'm over thirty and alone."

Pam leaned forward, her brow furrowing in concern. The furrow reminded Sasha that she needed to make an appointment to re-up her Botox. She'd been furrowing a lot lately, and she wasn't going to allow her feelings for Patrick to condemn her both to hell and deep "elevens" lines.

"Do you think it's pathetic that you're thirty and alone? I want to hear more about that."

"No, I don't." And that was the truth. Sasha was grateful for the things she had—good health, a business, friends, a home that she would someday call her own. She was lucky. But she still wanted to know when she would stop longing for more. She wanted to stop longing for the kind of love that Hannah and Jack and Bridget and Matt had. Not everyone got that.

"I think maybe that I only want Father Patrick because I'll never have him." Sasha sighed. "Because I'll never have him, it's easy to pour all of my emotions and all of my longing into him."

Because she could never wake up with him, she would never have to smell his morning breath. She'd never have to negotiate bathroom time with him or argue about who needed to do the dishes. If he lived only in her fantasies, she would never have to figure out how to raise children with him. He would always be part man, part figment of her imagination.

"That could be. Tell me more about how you feel about him."

To do that, she had to tell Pam about everything that happened. By the time she'd poured it all out, their time was over. The whole time, her therapist was silent.

"Wow."

"That's it?"

Pam glanced at the clock but didn't chuck her out. "You have to tell him how you feel."

"Do I, though?" Why did she have to give Patrick something that he couldn't seem to give her?

"Yes. He has a whole lot more to lose than you do. I don't think that your feelings for him are like your other crushes on unavailable guys. I think what you feel for him is real. And it might not last. But it might be the thing that you've been looking for."

"He makes me feel chaotic inside." She was both drawn to him and hated how he made her feel.

"I think you just answered your own question."

"What question?"

"How does it feel to be in love?"

Fuck.

CHAPTER TWENTY-THREE

WALKING ALONG THE LAKEFRONT should feel romantic. The twinkling lights of the Chicago skyline, the Ferris wheel towering over the pier. The teenagers out past their curfew. The couples walking hand in hand, with eyes only for each other.

But all Sasha could feel was the stone in her gut. She felt incredibly guilty about stringing Nathan along. It hadn't felt wrong at the time, but she hadn't given this nice man the empathy that he deserved. Since her last session with Pam almost a week ago, Sasha had done nothing about Patrick. She hadn't called him or gone over to the church. She had no legitimate reason to, and she still wasn't sure what she would say to him.

When Nathan had called after his long road trip with the team, she'd jumped at the chance to go out with him. She'd wanted to see for herself whether her lack of feelings for him were more about her feelings for Patrick or whether they just didn't have any chemistry.

But it hadn't taken her even until the appetizers to realize that Nathan just wasn't the guy for her. It wouldn't have mattered if she'd never met Patrick Dooley. The idea that she was going to have to tell that to a very nice man who had been exceedingly patient with her and taken her out on nice dates, even though she'd never even let him feel her up, had ruined her meal.

It weighed her down more than cement shoes, and she doubted that she would feel more doom if Nathan was some mobster sent to execute a hit on her.

"Dinner was good." Nathan was trying, and that made it even worse. Dinner *was* great, but Sasha hadn't felt like herself. Before everything that had happened with Patrick, she would have been able to affix her charming personality and power through what might have been awkward emotional moments.

At the time, she'd felt like it was the only way to be. Now, though, the things she did to survive seemed not to fit anymore. The sinking feeling wasn't even the awkwardness. The conversation between her and Nathan had been stilted from the start. She could feel how much he liked her. It made him sputter and start, and it made her overcompensate.

She hated who she was with him. And she didn't need Pam to tell her that wasn't the best foundation for a long-lasting, mutually satisfying romantic relationship. It might have worked for her parents, but she wanted something different.

The problem was that she couldn't have the different thing she wanted. She dared not ask for it. Even if Patrick wanted to leave the priesthood for her, her family would never accept a laicized priest into the fold, even if leaving was ultimately his choice. The madness that had overtaken them would have to live inside her like a precious gem in her heart. Even if she should feel guilty about what they'd shared, she wouldn't give up the memory of the way he'd been with her for anything in the world.

She had to break up with Nathan.

In the middle of the walkway, she stopped and turned to him. It took him a few steps to realize that she was no longer next to him. Before saying anything, she looked him up and down. He really was handsome. Good-looking in a way that her mother wouldn't consider flashy and therefore dangerous. But she was repelled by his khaki pants and pressed shirt. His very appropriate and likely uncomfortable wingtip shoes. They felt like they came from a bygone era.

Sasha opened her mouth to speak, but Nathan beat her to the punch. "I have to tell you something."

Oh, this was a boon. If he'd picked up on her disquiet and decided to break up with her first, it would be ideal. Not that she'd been broken up with very often—at least not after this many dates—but not having to take on the onus of being the one who was too picky would be very nice. Her mother would still have something to say, but it would be a truncated period of sniping if Sasha was presumably licking her wounds.

"I haven't been honest with you." Nathan looked down as though he'd been caught with his hand in the cookie jar.

"Oh?" She cocked her head, and it struck her that it was her mother's technique for getting wayward children to tell the truth. That was something she could talk about with Pam later. Right now, it was time to get the information that may very well set her free from the self-abnegation springing from not being able to fall in love with a very good prospect.

"Don't be mad." He ran his fingers through his hair, messing it up. This was going to be good. "But I'm—I'm married."

That was the last thing Sasha had been expecting him to say. Married? She looked down at his left hand, noting that a tan line on his ring finger had not magically appeared there in the last few moments—like a secret decoder mark. "You're what?"

"Separated." That's what they all said. At least that's what they all said on Tinder.

Sasha couldn't help herself. A snort of laughter escaped her before she could tamp it down. Nathan looked at her with a wide, terrified gaze as though she was about to do the worst thing possible—become hysterical in public. "Did you decide to bring me down here to try to sell me the pier or dump me?"

Poor thing, he looked so confused. "What?"

"I mean, I'm pretty sure the city already owns everything over there." She didn't know why she felt anger, why her addiction to forbidden emotions only seemed to grow and never abate. But it wasn't so bad in this moment because she was mostly angry on behalf of Nathan's newly disclosed spouse. "You've spent the past three months trying to sell me something that belongs to someone else, haven't you?"

Nathan's face twisted, as though he were in a position to take exception with anything she had to say right now. "Wait a minute—"

Sasha wasn't finished. For the first time in weeks, at least since she'd first tasted Patrick's mouth, she was in a position of moral authority. She fully intended to relish it before resuming her fallen woman status. "We've been dating for months—you were out of town and texting me every day—and you're just telling me about your spouse now? The person you presumably stood before a priest and your family and God and promised till death do us part to?" She hadn't meant for her voice to rise quite so hysterically, but it did.

"You could have figured it out if you'd wanted to." Nathan's voice sounded as lame as his excuse. "You have Google, don't you?"

He had a point. Never once had Sasha thought about doing a simple web search on Nathan. She'd simply taken him at his word because he put on such a good face. And she honestly didn't really care all that much. She'd never really liked him.

"And I never tried to fuck you."

He had another point, although she wouldn't put it quite so crassly. She hadn't questioned the exceedingly gentlemanly way that he'd treated her because she was so thankful that she didn't have to close her eyes and think about a certain Catholic priest while Nathan pretended to know how to operate a clitoris. She really should give him more credit—he was married, after all—but there had to be a reason why he was separated.

"What is it about me that made you think I'd be totes cool with being your side bitch?" Nathan looked surprised to hear her curse at all, and that was a little bit more salt in the wound. She'd never been herself with him—secretly sarcastic and cutting. He'd only seen the carefully cultivated veneer she'd created for herself over decades.

"You should really watch your mouth."

It might not have been until that moment that Sasha understood why Hannah had lost it on so many of the guys who'd told her how she should talk or feel. Sasha had never behaved anything but perfectly, had never stretched the bounds of appropriate feminine behavior under the patriarchy. She hadn't even tested the fences before that night at Dooley's bar.

Although she'd always felt she was wrong for wanting to color outside the lines a bit, she only felt that way because she'd been living inside such a small plot of emotional land for so very long. So now, when she was just expressing her emotions in the most straightforward fashion possible—with profanity—she was shocking? That was fucked up.

"I'm not the one who's married. You should maybe watch where you're putting your mouth." Nathan had kissed her when they'd met outside the restaurant. Perhaps the fact that she'd never been to his home should have been a clue. Come to think of it, the fact that he hadn't been holding her hand for a romantic walk along the lakefront should have been another clue. Here she was, grateful that he hadn't tried to have sex with her, when he'd really just been trying not to break his marriage vows.

That thought imbued her with sympathy, and she no longer wanted to kick Nathan in the shins. She wanted to kick herself. She'd been dating long enough to know better. But she was still pissed that he'd thought she was the one to be made a fool of.

"I'm sorry. You were just so beautiful. And my wife hasn't even smiled in months." He looked dejected, but now Sasha was getting angry on behalf of his wife.

"Listen, I don't know what it's like inside your marriage." She knew a lot about what she didn't want a marriage to be in her own life, but she also knew there was a myriad of ways that people could be fucked up in their marriages. And she was also curious. "Why me?"

"You're just so sweet."

She snorted again. "You know nothing, Jon Snow."

Nathan looked as though he'd had a serious realization. "That's the thing. I don't understand half the things that come out of your mouth. But you're nice to me."

"And that made you think it was okay to date me for months before revealing that you're not just involved with someone else, but you have a wife?" Curiosity and anger were now engaging in a war of attrition inside her. She wanted to know what it was about her that attracted this kind of bullshit, but she was also sorely tempted to beat this man about the head with her purse.

"I just—" Determined to let him get his words out this time, she took a deep breath and waited for him to speak. "I thought if I could be with someone easy . . ."

"So I'm easy?" He was digging himself into a hole that Sasha would have to push him into if he didn't pull back real quick. "You know, I am sweet on the outside. But you remember those Everlasting Gobstopper candies that they used to have when we were really little?" She didn't let him answer. "They have sweet layers, but every so often you get a real sour one that you just have to power through." He nodded, apparently just then sensing the danger of his current situation. "You're about to hit a sour layer."

Nathan was silent for a long moment, and Sasha's anger ebbed. He'd only seen what she'd wanted him to see. That was the whole problem. The only man she felt like she could be herself with, who wanted her because of anything authentic, couldn't be with her. Maybe if she'd been more honest with Nathan, he'd want her for her. Doubtful. If he wanted someone who authentically wanted to smile at him, he should probably reconsider cheating on his wife.

"And I know that," Nathan said. "About date two I realized that you were just going through the motions."

"Why did you keep asking me out, then?"

"It felt nice for me to have your attention, even if it was temporary."

"That's really sad." She wouldn't have said that a month ago, and she was sort of surprised that it came out of her mouth now. She'd been raised to keep her mouth shut and judge silently. But that impulse had stunted her. In that moment, standing in the dark, surrounded by people and confronted with a man whom she didn't want, her body felt too small to hold all of the things she'd unleashed—anger, curiosity, and even compassion for Nathan.

"It's okay," she continued. Nathan really didn't deserve her absolution, but they'd all be going to hell if the only people who received it had to deserve it. "I used you."

"For what?"

"To maintain the illusion that I'm just a normal girl looking for a sweet and completely ordinary guy to marry her."

"Huh." Nathan didn't really seem to have the depth to process the fact that people had layers and motivations that conflicted with one another. He was simple. And she'd thought that would be safe. But it was the opposite.

What she wanted was something she couldn't have. And she thought it was maybe time to let herself want it and be open to the distinct possibility that she might not get it. But the wanting would still be worth it.

CHAPTER TWENTY-FOUR

PATRICK TRIED TO PRAY, but he was afraid it was no use. No one was listening. And he should know better. Although God could perform miracles—he really believed that—it wasn't like those miracles included a bleach rinse for every dirty thought he'd ever had about Sasha Finerghty.

No, God spoke in whispers—having doubts and then being able to help someone in a way that assuaged those doubts, finding something small and lost when feeling small and lost. Patrick tried to slow down and listen to the whispers. But nothing came.

In spite of the fact that he didn't feel as though he deserved to stand in front of his congregation that Sunday, he got up and did his duty. He put on his vestments and went out to do his job.

He stood at the altar and tried not to go through the rite of Mass by rote. Although the congregants could skate by on memorized ritual, Patrick tried not to. Even though it was a Buddhist concept, the idea of beginner's mind usually helped him center.

As soon as he looked out over the Sunday morning crowd and saw her, he knew that wasn't going to work today. He would have to block her out and rely on the years he'd been repeating the words and go through the motions.

He hated himself for how she pulled his intention. For years, everything had been tugged in the direction of God and duty and church. Now, it was only Sasha. He worshipped at the altar of the dimple in her left cheek, prayed novenas to the curve of her mouth. Her angelic visage was his North Star, and frankly it was fucked up.

Hadn't he given enough to the Church—to God—that he was exempt from temptation? Before she'd barnstormed into my life, he'd certainly thought so. Now, he didn't know which way was up.

Somehow, he got through the service. By some very small, inadequate miracle, he greeted parishioners as they filed out of the sanctuary. He did it because he didn't look at her. He couldn't expel her scent from his nostrils, but he was able to pretend that she wasn't the impetus of his fall from grace for a few minutes.

At least until she was in front of him—looking fresh and new.

Want washed over him, erasing any grace and sanity that he'd managed to scrape up since seeing her last. Beads of sweat popped up on his forehead. They matched his damp palms and the red he was sure had crept onto his neck.

Instead of shaking her hand—touching her would be deadly right now—he rubbed the back of his neck and dared to really allow himself to take her in.

That Nathan guy was really not smart. Anyone in their right mind—anyone who could—would marry this girl immediately and take her away from everything so that nothing bad could touch her again. Patrick had been fooled by her extreme competence and inherent grace when they'd first met. He hadn't seen the vulnerable, soft heart underneath all of that. But when she looked at him now, he couldn't help but notice that her dark eyes had an inherently delicate quality, not unlike the glass vases that his mother used to collect—the ones that his father broke in a rage right after her funeral.

He didn't know why he thought of that in this moment; maybe it was that there was something broken in Sasha's gaze as it met his that morning. When that registered with him, he forgot all concern for his equanimity and touched her arm. She started, and he dropped his hand.

They had still said nothing, but he felt as though they'd spoken for an hour. It was cruel, really, that they were so in tune. Some real Old Testament shit. He felt like Eve. She was the apple. The sensual, juicy apple that would be healthy for someone else to love. Not for him. He just had to keep repeating that to himself. It hadn't worked before, but he didn't have any other options.

"You cut your hair. Sorry I didn't mention it at the wedding." He might not know much, having grown up with only a brother, but the semiotics of hair were not lost on him. Something had happened, and all Patrick wanted to do was fix it. But it was not his job. When she didn't respond, he continued, "I shouldn't have said anything."

"It's okay that you noticed." She bit her lip and rubbed her palm over the ends of her shorn locks. She was still self-conscious about it.

He cleared his throat. "I like it."

Something changed in her face then, like it closed down for a split second and then came back online. She'd just successfully put distance between them even though neither of them had physically moved.

"Thank you." Her words echoed through the sanctuary, and he noticed then that it was empty. They were alone.

"Do you want to go for a walk?" If they were outside and he

was wearing his collar, he probably wouldn't try to touch her again. It might be enough to keep him from kissing her again.

"Can we sit in here?" She motioned to the back pew.

It was probably a great idea to be looking straight at an image of Jesus dying on the cross while he was with her, so he nodded and extended his arm.

The bench creaked when he sat down, and that was the only sound either of them made for a long beat. An awkward beat. It had Patrick bracing for bad news.

SASHA FLINCHED WHEN PATRICK looked at her. There was so much hope in his gaze. It was really too bad that she was going to have to dash both of their hopes. She'd shown up at St. Bart's that morning fully intending to beg Patrick to leave the church and be with her. After Friday night with Nathan, she knew that there was no one else for her.

Pam was right. A relationship wasn't worth anything unless it was totally naked. She had just been a little off on the kind of naked that Sasha needed. Well, she needed both kinds of naked, but the spiritual nudity that Sasha felt whenever Patrick looked at her clothed her skin in gold threads. Chills had gone up and down her spine when he'd looked at her the first time during Mass. And she'd felt herself dim as soon as he looked away.

She would have to get used to that feeling—the one of having stood in the light of his attention and then having that attention taken away forever. Because, although she had come here to beg him to be with her, something stopped her from wanting that.

She'd seen him say Mass plenty of times, mostly at weddings. But it wasn't until this morning—a totally ordinary Sunday—that she'd really seen how integral him being a priest was to the fact that she was totally in love with him.

Ironic and cruel it was that he was perfect saying the words and doing the things that had totally lost meaning for her years before. She might be lost and still searching, but Patrick was not. He was still on the path to a good and righteous life. And wanting him so much, loving him so much, was just a sign of how lost she truly was. Being a priest was so much a part of him that he totally got lost in it. She got totally lost in it even though she'd come here this morning to tell him how she felt.

And right now, sitting here, she didn't have an excuse to be here anymore. Everything for the carnival was set up. There was nothing left to do, and Nathan's team was still helping. Mostly because she'd threatened to tell his wife that he was seriously dating other women while they were still married. And he didn't want to disappoint God even more. She'd really laid it on thick.

Patrick would never think to be that devious or manipulative. He was too good. Too thoughtful.

It was too bad that he set her entire body on fire. Maybe it was him, but she had to start thinking that it was perhaps Jesus looking down at them, reminding her of how hot the fires of hell would be for eternity if she didn't stop this madness of an almost-affair with Patrick right now.

They looked at each other simultaneously. Patrick leaned down as though he were about to kiss her. Somehow—probably the little bit of grace from God she had left—she put a hand to his shoulder and turned her body away. He stiffened. Sasha allowed her palm to linger against his muscled shoulder. She would never, ever allow herself to touch him again, and the bad seed inside her—the one that had grown into an entire Venus flytrap just waiting to pull him in—needed to savor this last contact.

She breathed him in, the scent of incense mingling with the old-fashioned way he smelled. If she was never going to have him again, she needed to have him in her mind forever. If she was going to shut the door on what was between them, forever and ever, she was going to really milk her sacrifice for all it was worth.

"Thank you." That was the last thing she was expecting him to say. All these men in her life that she didn't want or couldn't have were out here surprising her. They had to stop doing that.

She dropped her hand, and they both looked forward. "No problem."

"What are you doing here?" He didn't sound angry or accusatory, but the words hit her like bullets to the heart all the same. Confusing, confounding man whom she understood perfectly all the same. He was hers in this way, and she would hoard that understanding all her life even if she couldn't touch him, smell him, even hold him for one night.

That thought filled her eyes with tears, and she looked down to her hands to try to blink them away. "I think it's best if I don't—don't see you again."

Out of the corner of her eye, she took in the way that Patrick's Adam's apple bobbed up and down. He didn't like what she'd just said, but he wasn't going to contradict her. "Why?"

She shouldn't tell him how she felt about him, and it was time to do the right thing. "They need you."

"More than you?"

Her need for him was bottomless and without end. But he couldn't know that. He needed to be of service, to be a conduit for

God. He needed more than just her—her small life, the parties, and the perfect place settings. It was her turn to nod. Only she hoped he wasn't noticing how weak her resolve was.

She tried to pull herself together. It wouldn't do for him to know how difficult this was for her. He would give his whole life up to make it so that she was okay. He wanted her now because she'd tempted him. She was Jezebel, but she had enough of a soul left to stop herself from causing him to fall.

She loved him too much to see him fall. Still, she couldn't actually say the words. "I think we're all set for the carnival next weekend."

Sasha could feel his incredulity without looking at his face. "That's what you came here to say?"

"What else would I be here to say?" Willful ignorance was one of the only tools in the Finerghty toolbox that she hadn't used with him. She'd always had a sneaking suspicion that he wouldn't let her get away with it. But she risked looking at him now, risked him seeing right through her. "There's nothing else I can say."

She choked on the words, desperately hoping that he would really understand. He stared at her for a long moment, and then looked down at his hands. She didn't risk that. If she let herself linger on the memories of him touching her, the ones she'd have to hoard forever, she wouldn't be able to leave. And she had to leave.

He let her off the hook with one word. "Okay."

Her heart was broken as she stood on shaky legs and walked out of the church. She'd never be able to come back.

CHAPTER TWENTY-FIVE

PATRICK USUALLY DIDN'T DRINK much while he was working behind the bar at Dooley's. His dad didn't have a rule about it, but it was more of an understanding. Tonight, he was pretty sure that his dad would comprehend his pain and why he wasn't just having a beer while keeping watch over the nearly empty bar.

He also didn't usually wear his collar while working. He only had to wear the collar when he was in public in his official capacity. Tonight, he was afraid that he would forget why he couldn't go after Sasha if he wore street clothes. There would be nothing keeping him from closing up and going to her, leaving it all behind.

When he'd become a priest, he'd thought he'd never get dumped or rejected in love again. He'd thought it was impossible. But nothing was going to shield him from the intensity of this heartbreak—not his vows to the Church or the ones he'd made to himself a decade ago.

He knew now that he couldn't keep his humanity in a box anymore, but he didn't know where to put it without Sasha. He wasn't narcissistic enough to have missed the fact that Sasha had seemed wrecked when she told him that they were over before they'd even had a legitimate beginning. But he was at a loss as to what had wrecked her. She had a spine of steel under her delicate exterior, and it had to be something huge if she was that shaken.

She'd cut off all her hair.

Despite his limited experience with women, he knew that was a big deal. It was symbolic and ritualistic. He loved her hair and cutting it off was a message. She was cutting him out.

He had no right to know why and no way to find out why, so he drank his scotch and rubbed the same worn spot on the bar clean while trying to pay attention to the two patrons deep in their cups in the back.

He couldn't have been more surprised when Sister Cortona walked in. She'd never visited Dooley's. He would've sworn that she didn't know where it was before she sat down at his father's bar and looked at him expectantly.

"You're not even going to offer a nun a beer?" She shook her head—which for once was not covered in a habit. "Kids these days."

Curiosity, if nothing else, spurred him to action. "What'll it be?"

"Dark lager. Not cheap shit."

Patrick had to laugh. She had great taste for a woman who'd taken a vow of poverty. He poured her a beer and took it back to her. And then he waited for her to tell him why she was there.

Luckily, she had more mercy on him than Sasha or his boss right now. "What the fuck are you doing?"

"I work here three nights a week." Patrick pretended to be obtuse, knowing it would rile her up. It was one of the only pleasures left to him, and he didn't intend to give it up. "I don't know what you mean."

"I don't have time for you and your stupid, wasted, pretty face to be obtuse." Sister Cortona took a long sip of her beer and relished it before working her ire back up and saying, "Why did you let that girl walk out on you?"

"Were you spying on us?" He'd tried to be careful after Sister Cortona had dressed him down for his crush on Sasha before, but his colleague didn't miss anything.

"Of course I was." She scoffed at him, and Patrick bristled. "You think I have anything better to do?"

"Well, you should be happy now." Patrick looked away, not able to sustain eye contact with her withering gaze. "Nothing's going to happen."

"You mean nothing's going to happen again?" Shit, she knew everything. "Why not?"

Patrick froze. He'd been calculating how he would explain himself if Sister Cortona brought his indiscretion up with the bishop. He was filled with shame at having to confess and repent— he'd never thought he'd be the guy who'd have strayed from his vows. In the scheme of things, what he'd done with Sasha was serious. Even though it was over, he felt as though his moral authority was completely gone. But without his vocation and without her, who was he? It was a question he hadn't wanted to answer a decade ago. And he didn't want to answer it now.

But the sister might not give him a choice. And maybe he should surrender to her superior wisdom. She was a hard-ass, but she'd never steered him wrong before. He wasn't getting any guidance from God, and he hadn't gotten up the courage to confess to his actual confessor, so maybe he should let Sister Cortona take on the visage of fate.

"Why not?" A few clarifying comments were probably in order first, though. "I'm a priest. We're not exactly allowed to run after women we're illicitly snogging and make grand gestures."

"I'm aware of that. Why didn't you go after her?" She was so matter-of-fact about something so confusing that Patrick thought he might be drunker than he actually was.

"I need you to explain to me what you mean like I'm one of the preschoolers."

Somehow she managed to look down on him, even though he was standing and she was sitting. "That's what I normally do." She took another sip of beer. "I swear to God, they let infants become priests. That's how fucking desperate they are."

"Want another beer?"

Sister Cortona nodded, and Patrick pulled her another pint. When he returned, she said, "I told you months ago that you should pursue her."

He nearly dropped the glass of beer on the bar in front of her. "You warned me to stay away from her."

"No, I didn't." She looked incredulous, and Patrick's frustration amped up about six points. It was almost refreshing after he'd walked around feeling dejected for three days.

"Yes. You did."

Sister Cortona took a deep breath. "I'm going to tell you a story."

"Really? Now?"

"You told me to talk to you like one of the preschoolers, and I guess we're having story time."

Patrick motioned for her to proceed.

"You know I wasn't always a nun." Honestly, Patrick had thought she'd come out of the womb with a habit, but he wasn't about to risk his neck by saying that. "Before that, I was a girl in love."

He couldn't picture her in love. "What does that have to do with me? You're now a nun, and—"

"I wish I wasn't."

Patrick's knees dropped. Hearing people's confessions for a decade about everything from bad thoughts to petty theft to marital infidelity had made him mostly impervious to shock about what would come out of people's mouths. But Sister Cortona had truly shocked him. "Okay . . ."

"If I had gone after her when she asked me to, I wouldn't be here trying to convince you not to make the same mistake that I made when I was just a wee lesbian." Patrick laughed. Their binge watch of *Derry Girls* had more significance now.

"But that was before you'd taken vows, right?"

"Yes, but it's the same. I was in love, but I was afraid. I was too afraid of disappointing my parents—the fucking homophobes they were, God rest their souls—to do what would have made me happy."

"You could leave and be happy now."

"She's married to a lovely woman and has three kids." Cortona shook her head. "You, however, have a chance to make a real life."

"I have a real life."

"Neither of us do."

"Then why do you stay?"

"I don't know. I'm still afraid. It's probably why I'm so mean. But, right now, I'm a nun so that I can make sure you don't waste your stupid, pretty face on getting fondled by septuagenarian widows until you're old and decrepit like me."

Patrick looked down. "I don't have anything to offer her."

"You have yourself. If you decide not to be a coward."

"That has never been enough."

"Then you don't see what I do." That was the nicest thing that Sister Cortona had ever said to him. It was bordering on mushy. That's probably why she felt the need to add, "But I'm starting to see why she dumped you."

"Are you going to tell the diocese about me and Sasha?" He might be considering asking to be laicized, but he was still afraid of causing a scandal. It might jeopardize the pre-K program.

"No. You are, when you tell the bishop that you're in love and intend to leave." Sister Cortona looked around the bar. "Nice place."

Patrick grokked that the subject was closed. He looked around, happy that he was in a familiar place. This was as much his home as the house he'd grown up in or the rectory.

"Are you going to stay?" Learning what he had that night, he was filled with concern for Sister Cortona. If she wasn't happy, she should leave. It was so simple when it was someone else.

But she blew out air. "I have to stay and break in the new dummy that they send to ruin the place."

"Do you ever think that it's beyond saving?"

"St. Bart's?" Patrick nodded, and she continued, "Every time you give me a hard time about the budget."

"What about the whole thing?" Maybe if priests and nuns couldn't have real lives, it wasn't worth it. A thing that held fetid, grotesque secrets and protected abusers for millennia had been the foundation of his life. He'd never questioned it. And the privilege in that made him feel dirty and ruined. It was only when he could no longer conform to the expectations he'd gladly taken on that he'd begun to question it.

She paused. "It exists and is going to continue to exist. I have no real power in the institution, but I do have power in people's lives. We feed the sick and minister to the poor, and I don't always agree with how we do it. Like all institutions, it is corrupt. If we lived in a utopia, there would be no reason for the Church to exist. It is ancient and broken. Like all ancient things. The institution itself is a false idol. But I also take comfort in the fact that it is ancient. There will be women after me who take vows and teach children and take care of the sick that no one else will touch."

Patrick understood what she was saying. Human beings were wired for ritual, and he'd found purpose in being the conduit for the ancient. In the liminal spaces—especially the ones between life and death—he felt purpose. He may have lost God, but he'd never lost the sense that being there to assure a family that their small one was never going to be alone, or a man dying too soon and away from his family that he would be welcomed into whatever came after, was important.

Could he give that up?

"You could give it up for her."

Patrick had almost forgotten that Sister Cortona was there, staring at him while he tried to process everything that he'd told her. "Are you a mind reader or something?"

She took another sip of beer. "Comes along with the habit."

"You're not wearing one."

"You ask too many questions."

And everything that she'd said to him was making him ask more. Before she'd walked into the bar, he'd felt hopeless—as bad as things had been after his mother's death. Watching Sasha step away from him was like watching his heart walk out of a room. He didn't know that he could survive it. He looked down at his third scotch of the night.

"Finish your drink and close up." Sister Cortona made a motion to his tumbler. "It won't do to have you dying before you make your escape."

THE NEXT AFTERNOON, PATRICK found himself staring at his mother's headstone in the Catholic cemetery near his father's house. The ground was wet from a midsummer storm, but he sat down anyway. The lilies he always picked up on his way to his mother's resting place were in his lap. For some reason, he didn't feel like giving them to her yet.

When his mother had gotten sick, he'd still been young enough that he hadn't gotten to know her as a person. As she wasted away, he'd been able to see her humanity slipping from her, but his personal pain had come from the fact that his *mother* was dying. His father may have been stingy with emotional support—thank you to toxic masculinity—but his mother had lavished both him and Chris with it.

He'd always known that he was loved, but he didn't know what else his mother had loved. Sometimes, when he closed his eyes, he could still smell the drug store shampoo that she'd used. He could remember being splayed on the couch, reading whatever adventure or fantasy series that he'd been into at the time while she sat across the room in her chair, reading novels or memoirs or poetry. He could see the light coming through the window and how it glinted off her hair.

Sitting here now, he wished he'd spent more time talking to her, figuring out why she got such comfort from religion and literature. He wished that he knew what formed her so that he would have some idea as to why she'd wanted him to become a priest. In a way, he now felt like he had when it became clear that his mother was dying. Except now, he was losing his faith along with the love he'd been willing to compromise that faith for.

He felt totally unmoored, and tears sprang to his eyes. He sat there, lost in thought for so long that he thought it might be growing dark when a shadow fell over him. Except he looked up, and it was his father, who was leaning on a cane and glowering at him.

"What are you doing here, boy?" His father squinted down at him. "Are you crying? She's been dead for well over a decade."

"You're here, too, you know," Patrick said. "And I'm not the one who's supposed to be resting flat on his back."

Patrick stood up so he could look his father in the eye, noticing that Danny had also brought lilies.

"I know that, but I never miss a visit." His father looked down at the beautifully etched stone. Like a good, morbid Irishwoman, his mother had picked out all of the accoutrements of death long before she'd gotten sick.

"I've missed too many visits of late," Patrick said. He didn't know how to broach the subject with his father, but he knew it was past time to avoid it. "Do you think we made her happy?"

Patrick's father looked at him as though he'd grown three heads all of the sudden. "Of course you made her happy. She was the happiest woman I ever knew. You should have heard her talk about you to her friends when they were playing cards."

"I always knew she loved me, but I always felt like maybe she wanted more. Like to have a job or that maybe she had a calling herself."

Danny chuckled. "She would have made a great priest, but she always said it was a good thing that the Church didn't allow women to become full-fledged members of the clergy."

These were more words than his father usually said in a whole week, so he didn't want to slow him down, but he needed more. "Why was that?"

"Well, she wouldn't have had you."

"Or Chris."

His father snorted. "Chris she could have taken or left. He was always a bit of a shit."

"But you are so much more proud of him than you are of me." Patrick knew that he had likely been their mother's favorite, but their father had always paid more attention to Chris.

"You're wrong there." The green eyes that Patrick shared with his father glinted, and the old man put one hand on Patrick's shoulder. He wasn't sure who that hand was meant to steady—perhaps it was both of them. "I am proud of the man you've become."

"But not that I'm a priest." When his father sighed heavily, Patrick pressed on. "I know that you had little use for religion either now or when I was growing up, but I just felt like it was the only thing I could do after Mom died."

Patrick left out the part about Ashley, because his father wouldn't get that. And it seemed silly now that he had these much bigger feelings for Sasha.

"Mostly, I just think that you're too selfless. You've given yourself away to people who barely notice or acknowledge you." His father shook his head and patted Patrick on the chest. "Your heart's too big to keep it for yourself."

"That was deeply poetic for a man of few words."

"How do you think I charmed your mother?" Danny ran a

hand over his silver beard. "It certainly wasn't this ugly mug. You can thank God you got your good looks from her."

"You wrote her poems?" He'd come here wishing that he'd known his mother better as a person, and maybe it was time to get to know his father better as well. "Can I read them?"

His father's face reddened. "Only some of them. Not the filthy ones."

Patrick laughed. "I don't need to read those."

"You tempted to write poems for that girl you brought to the bar?"

Patrick thought for a moment. Sasha didn't entice him to write poetry because she *was* poetry. The feelings he had for her were a song. The way his heart beat when she kissed him was a prayer. And the way he ached for her now that she'd rejected him was an answer. And, until that moment, when his father had revealed just a glimpse into his life, he'd thought he had to accept that answer. He'd come here to mourn Sasha, because it had felt right to do that sitting on bones.

But maybe the answer was to chase the poem down and try to change the answer to his prayers.

He didn't have words for his father just then, but he nodded.

"Thank goodness." Danny pulled Patrick in by the back of his neck for a hug. "If I was going to have to rely on your brother for grandchildren, I'd be in real trouble."

CHAPTER TWENTY-SIX

SASHA WAS DETERMINED TO avoid any close contact with Patrick at the carnival. And she was determined to make it a success, because she didn't want to have to come back to church grounds after this. Tonight wasn't breaking her new rule of not going inside the church because everything was outside.

Luckily, they were selling plenty of drink, game, and ride tickets, and they should meet their goal of saving the pre-K program tonight. She felt a pang when she realized that she wouldn't be able to say goodbye to Jemma or the kids. But it was too dangerous to be close to Patrick. She might well want him, but he was needed here. In the long run, she wouldn't be enough for him. She wasn't about to try to compete with God. She just had to keep telling herself that until the devil on her shoulder shut the fuck up.

That was all well and good until she laid eyes on him. He was smiling at something that Sister Cortona said, and her insides twisted at remembering what his smile had meant that one time for her. She should look away and focus on making sure that every-thing ran smoothly, but she couldn't tear her eyes away.

She stood in the middle of one of the walkways that they'd cre-ated between the game tents for such a long time that several people bumped into her. She didn't even do her usual thing of murmuring apologies. She sort of wondered why everyone wasn't looking at him, until she remembered that she was the only one in love with him.

Oh God. He wasn't just some guy she was hung up on. She was well and truly in love with him. And she'd just walked away.

The realization hit her so hard that she had to look away. Her hands itched for something to do. Anything that would take away the stabbing pain in her chest and the burning behind her eyes. Anything that would stop the tears that threatened from being noticed.

They needed to wait until she was alone.

That thought stopped her, too. She remembered the conversa-tions with Pam about feeling her feelings so that they could dissi-pate. Instead of running off to fix something or make something into a problem so she could fix it—the funnel cake station was a little catawampus—she ducked behind the ring-toss tent and stood there with her eyes closed.

She let the feelings rioting through her be for a long moment. Immediately, the intensity lessened. Yeah, she'd messed up, but she could make it right. Patrick might be a frocked priest, but he still had choices. He was still an adult.

As soon as she'd left Patrick sitting in the last pew of St. Bart's, she'd known that she'd made a huge mistake. Her best friend had told her as much when she'd recounted her and Patrick's conversa-tion the next day.

Hannah was right. Hannah was always right these days. Men left the priesthood all the time. They had from time immemorial. If he wanted to be with her, he could do that.

After the carnival was over, she was going to tell him how she felt and let the chips fall where they may. Instead of the dread and raw pain running through her body at the thought that she would have to live her life without him that she'd felt several emotions ago, she felt anticipation and the almost delicious fear that told her she was making the right/wrong choice.

That's how Hannah found her. "What are you doing? Communing with the nature spirits?"

"Yes, I'm calling on the Great Mother to bring me some of that good dick."

Her friend laughed, probably surprised to hear Sasha using crass and flippant language. "On sacred grounds, no less."

"I'm a changed woman," Sasha said, looking her friend in the eye, happy to see that she no longer seemed as though she was about to vomit. "How are you feeling?"

"Better." Hannah put her hand on her still ever-growing belly bump. "I barely have enough to complain to Jack about so that he brings home the good ice cream in contrition anymore."

"You're glowing."

"That's moisturizer." Hannah blushed, never able to just take a compliment. "Now, tell me about the D you're trying to catch. Is it Nathan?" Hannah lengthened the syllables of Nathan's name. She hadn't told Hannah about him being married. "Or Patrick?" She lengthened the syllables of his name even more, indicating her strong preference for the latter.

"Shhh." She might be ready to declare her feelings to Patrick, but she didn't think his whole congregation needed to know that she was about to steal their man. "The second one."

Hannah squeezed her fists in front of her face. "Yes!"

Jack walked up behind his wife and kissed her neck. "What are we celebrating?"

"Sasha's going to tell Patrick how she really feels like a grown-up." Hannah turned to him.

"Finally!" Jack, very dramatically, dropped to his knees as though he'd just scored a winning goal.

Sasha was shocked, though she shouldn't have been. Hannah and Jack told each other everything, after all. She *was* a little surprised that Jack wasn't upset that she was going to ruin his best friend's life. But, as it turned out, it wasn't a split decision in the Nolan-Mayfield household.

"Get up." Hannah looked at her husband as though he'd lost his mind. Just then, Sasha noticed that she didn't feel the stab of jealousy that she normally hated herself for when she looked at them. Maybe it was because what they had finally felt within reach. Or maybe somewhere along the way she'd let go of needing everything just so. Maybe, even if Patrick turned her down flat and decided to stay a priest, falling in love with him had changed something inside her.

Nah, it was probably just the therapy working.

There was a screech from the sound system that had them all swiveling their heads there. Over the speakers, Patrick's gravelly voice made a nervous-sounding noise. Sasha didn't hesitate to walk over to the area in front of the grandstand. She wasn't afraid of looking at Patrick anymore.

Hannah and Jack followed her.

Patrick stood alone on the small stage. Even from a hundred feet away, she could see Patrick's Adam's apple bounce a little in his throat, and he looked sweaty.

The fear she'd been feeling lost its deliciousness, and the sinking feeling returned.

PATRICK ALMOST DROPPED THE microphone when five hundred people looked at him—some from the congregation, but a lot of faces he didn't recognize.

Why had he thought this was a good idea?

Because Sasha would believe him if he declared himself in front of an audience. Because he had to explain himself to the people who'd put their spiritual lives in his hands for so long. Many of them had trusted him, and he couldn't help but feel that this was a betrayal of their trust. He wasn't going to be able to live up to the sacrament so he could face God, but he couldn't stay and look himself in the mirror in the morning for the rest of his life.

But he wasn't about to slink away in shame, either. Guilt would rest on his shoulders for what he was about to do—perhaps for the remainder of his days—but he had nothing to be ashamed of. He was in love, even though he'd never thought it would happen. It was undeniable, and it wasn't going away. His vocation had been enough for him for a long time. The people in the crowd had filled his life by giving him a purpose, but his purpose had changed. It had concentrated and focused on making one woman happy—if she would have him.

Hell, another wave of trepidation washed over him. What if she wasn't in love with him? What if she was in love with that other man?

He looked for her in the crowd, taking mere seconds to spot her. She stood alone, which gave him some relief, but she wasn't looking at him as though she was excited to hear what he had to say. By the same strange mechanism that connected them when they were close, he could feel her fear through the air. As though the breeze carried it to him, he felt it too.

He looked down for a moment, wondering if he should do this at all. But then he spied Sister Cortona out of the corner of his eye. Before he'd come up here, she'd let him know that the receipts from the carnival up until that moment had put them over the amount that they would need to keep the preschool program running. Then, she stood at the top of the stairs to the small stage. He would have to jump if he wanted to escape, which told him that he wasn't going to escape at all.

Instead of risking a twisted ankle from jumping off the stage and running, he cleared his throat and looked at everyone but Sasha. "Thank you for coming. As most of you in the congregation know, the pre-K program is the heart and soul of St. Bartholomew's parish. Without it, many area children, Catholic and not, wouldn't get the vital preparation they need to start kindergarten with children of more means around the city." He hesitated to mention God, who he was sure was readying his ticket to hell for what he would say later, but he had a role to live up to for the next few minutes. "Our joint calling as Catholics is to do good for one another. I'm happy to say that we'll be able to continue to do good for the kids in the area for at least another year. Thank you.

"I also want to thank you on a personal level, for being here for the past few years. I've tried to be the best priest I could for you. I want to thank you for being here, even though I've failed in so many ways." He was startled by the nervous laughter in the crowd.

Shit, they were probably expecting something much, much worse than what he was about to say.

"I—I'm leaving the priesthood." He'd spent the afternoon off on a meeting with the bishop, pleading his case to be laicized. It had taken hours, and a terribly embarrassing confession of all his sins. The bishop had wanted details, which really only strengthened Patrick's decision to leave the Church, even if Sasha turned him down flat. "The vocation that brought me here died." The nervous laughter hushed, and he met several disappointed gazes. "But not really—it just changed." He took one last deep breath before he said it, the mic shaking in his hand.

Before continuing, he sought out Sasha in the crowd again, relieved to find her still standing where she'd been before. He couldn't feel the fear anymore. In its place, he'd swear that he could feel hope.

"It changed because I'm in love with an amazing woman." The crowd went even more silent, but Patrick didn't balk. It was a shocking thing for most of them, and he hadn't been sure about announcing this in front of a crowd even moments before. "I wanted to tell you face-to-face, because I'm not ashamed. And I'm not leaving because I don't care about each and every one of you. Like I said, I just changed."

No one spoke. And, when he looked up, Sasha was no longer where he'd last seen her. A rock formed in his gut. Maybe he wasn't ashamed, but was she? If she didn't feel the same way about him that he felt about her, then maybe she'd run.

Fuck. He'd always prided himself on being wise, but what if he'd miscalculated this time when it was so important? Sister Cortona sniffed at him as he passed her on the way to the stairs leading from the stage, but it was oddly approving.

He wasn't sure what to do with himself. Should he go back to the rectory and pack his meager belongings? He could crash at the apartment above Dooley's for a while, but he would eventually need to figure out what to do with his life. Especially if the rest of his life wasn't going to include Sasha. He'd planned that a big part of his future would be owned by her. If she didn't want him, he didn't know what he'd do.

His head was down as he concentrated on putting one foot in front of another. As soon as he'd spoken, it was like all of the adrenaline that had allowed him to make his big reveal on stage had left his body, and he felt hollow and unmoored. Like someone had carved something vital out of him.

A decade ago, he'd become a priest to avoid feeling like this. He'd always been much more comfortable with empathy than with actually feeling emotions for himself. He'd almost forgotten how intense a heartbreak could be. He'd been numb for years, and coming back into the whole romance game had rocked him. All he could do was put one foot in front of the other.

He was so focused on avoiding eye contact with any angry parishioners that he crashed into someone. He reached out to steady the person and immediately realized whom he was touching. He looked up and the hollow feeling in his chest dissipated immediately. He was filled with her scent, with being able to touch her without his vocation in the way.

The rock in his stomach disappeared when she smiled at him. It was totally corny, but it was like the clouds parting after a string of particularly rainy days. The curve of her mouth made everything luminous.

"You love me?"

That was one of the drawbacks of announcing that you loved

somebody to a crowd instead of saying it to them alone. He'd never get to see the way that announcement made her feel when she first heard it. Instead, he'd have to say it again and again in the hope that it would delight her every time.

"More than anything." This time, when it was just her, he didn't struggle for the words to explain. "You're the missing puzzle piece. You're at least half of the pieces that I've been missing."

Thank God her smile got bigger. "I love you, too."

"I love you."

"We've already established that." She stepped closer to him, which made him wrap his arms around her. "And we've established that it's reciprocated."

"Do you have a plan for what to do next?"

A week ago, the twist in her smile—the one that said she definitely had a plan—would have worried him. Now, it filled him with hope.

CHAPTER TWENTY-SEVEN

SASHA HADN'T BEEN NERVOUS the first time she'd had sex. It was totally calculated, down to the instructions she would give that boyfriend. Plus, they'd done everything else, so P in V was hardly even momentous or important. She hadn't even thought very much of the notion of virginity, even though it had been very important to her mother.

She hadn't been nervous about any of the other times she'd had sex, either—mostly because it had never been exciting enough to get nervous about.

It had always been intended to get someone to like her or just to get off. Sasha had never had sex with the purpose of giving something to someone else before. That thought would make her feel sad if she wasn't about to have sex with Patrick Dooley—a man who loved her. A man who'd left the priesthood to be with her. They'd never kissed without it being a violation of his vows. They'd never touched without it being illicit and wrong.

For a split second after he'd told his whole congregation and almost all of the people they knew in the city of Chicago that he was in love with her, she was nervous that there wouldn't be the same intensity of feeling on her part if he wasn't forbidden. But that was gone when he'd literally run into her after leaving the stage. The way his face changed when he saw that it was her. The way his grip on her arms had tightened—as though he'd found a treasure and wasn't letting it go—reassured her at the same time that it lit up all her nerve endings.

When she'd taken his hand and led him to her car, the weight of it hit her all at once. It was only holding on to him that kept both of her feet attached to the ground. They hadn't talked about where they'd live or what he'd do. There was no road map, no plan. Never in her life had she gone into something momentous without any idea of where it would lead, and it should terrify her.

But no. As she started her car and pointed it toward her condo, she was nervous about getting naked with him, feeling the full weight of his body above her, waking up tomorrow with him next to her.

All they'd shared were some kisses and illicit groping. He knew more about her terrible family and hidden insecurities than he did about what got her off. It was so old-fashioned, almost courtly, and that felt ridiculous.

She'd wanted him to be hers and hers alone for so long that she felt giddy that it was actually going to happen. It was difficult to concentrate on navigating the traffic to her place, but she wasn't about to die before she got to fuck Patrick Dooley—unless that was going to be the punishment doled out for stealing him from God.

In that case, she could totally understand—he was one of a kind.

As they sat in bumper-to-bumper traffic on the Dan Ryan, she snuck a look at him. He smiled at her, looking almost goofy. "What the fuck are we doing, Patrick?"

He looked shocked to hear her say it, and then concern flashed over his features. Like he was worried about her kicking him out of the car on the freeway at this point. But then he said the perfect thing. "I have no idea what we're doing other than loving each other."

For some reason, that thought comforted her. The idea that she wasn't the only one who'd been taken apart and laid bare by their feelings for each other. She gave him another smile that she hoped didn't reveal how shaky she felt about this whole thing and then looked back at the road. "Where are we going to live?"

Patrick snorted. "I think they're going to kick me out of the rectory after that whole deal. I was thinking about moving into the apartment above Dooley's."

Sasha scrunched up her nose. That apartment was probably fine for a twenty-something just out of college, but there was no light. It seemed sad—not a place to start a new life. Patrick deserved to have light. It was fine, really, but Patrick deserved to live someplace beautiful.

Without thinking too hard, which would make her not say what she was about to say, she said, "How about my place?"

"Do you think it's too soon to move in together?" It was, but nothing about them being together was prudent or well plotted out.

"It's definitely too soon." But it didn't feel wrong. "But I've been dating the wrong guys for me, and you spent ten years doing the wrong thing for you. And I just think that we've wasted enough time doing what's right for everyone else, and I'm done wasting time. I think we're both done wasting time."

Patrick was silent for a long beat, and Sasha worried that he was going to turn her down flat. Everything about this made her feel as though her skin was flayed open. It was just so raw and real. She felt like she had been made partly of metal before falling in love with him. She'd gone through life like a robot. Nothing could get in, and she processed emotions like a computer instead of really feeling them. Now, everything had the potential to hurt, so everything did hurt. Even if it was anticipation. Joy hurt. She didn't want to imagine what him turning her down would do.

But then he tentatively reached over and grabbed her thigh, squeezing it as though he knew that she needed to be reassured. "I think you're right. We have a lot of time to make up for."

The way he lowered his tone about the second thing made her think that they wouldn't be leaving her bedroom, much less her condo, for the foreseeable future. Everything below her waist got hot and tight. Her toes curled in her shoes, and she had to brace herself from punching the gas.

"You can't say things like that when I'm driving."

"Noted." He moved his hand, and the lusty fog that had washed over her ebbed in part. The rest of it wouldn't ebb until they'd gotten back to her place, all their clothes were off, and they were lying in a sweaty pile of limbs for at least the fourth or fifth time.

"Seriously, what are we going to do?"

"You mean, what am I going to do for a job?"

That was one of her questions. She personally didn't care if he wanted to stay home and massage her feet every night, but she doubted that would make him happy. And him having some sort of plan might lessen the blow to her parents of her shacking up with a defrocked priest.

Not much, but a little.

"I was thinking of going back to school to become a therapist."

Sasha could see that right away. He'd be able to use his already existing skill set, and he'd look really hot in those sweaters with patches on the elbows. She was about to tell him to make a list of local graduate programs from her phone when they arrived.

As soon as she pulled into her parking space, he reached over her and unhooked her seat belt.

"Can we talk about that later?" he asked.

From the look in his eye, it would be much, much later.

PATRICK HADN'T EVEN GIVEN a whole lot of thought to what he and Sasha were about to do before Sasha had started prompting those thoughts a few months ago. He hadn't seen a naked woman outside of a piece of Renaissance art in well over a decade, and he was afraid that he'd forgotten everything he ever knew about sex.

His palms were sweaty, and he felt as though his heart could beat out of his chest at any moment. Probably so attractive to someone like Sasha, who could have anyone she wanted. Even though she'd said she was in love with him, he couldn't quite wrap his head around it.

No one had ever said that before and meant it. He'd never believed that anyone loved him, and he didn't know that he liked the feeling, even now. It was too much stimulation, almost. As they walked up to her second-floor place, he almost stopped on the stairs.

He loved her, and he was sure he wanted to be with her, but this was crazy. Maybe they should be moving things more slowly. But then his gaze caught on the sway of her ass as she made her way up the wooden stairs, and he thought that they had moved slowly enough for long enough.

She stopped at the top of the stairs, turned to unlock the door, and gave him a smile over her shoulder that told him that she had zero doubts about what they were about to do. He longed to kiss that pillow-soft mouth, and the sudden realization came over him that no one was stopping him.

He bounded up the last few steps and grabbed her shoulders. Her eyes widened in shock, and he realized that he was being awkward about this. Like they were in a car that was backfiring and jerking on the road. "Is this okay?" he asked. As soon as she nodded, he kissed her.

Even though they were standing in a hallway, where anyone could see, he didn't hold back. The freedom in being able to savor the taste of her, to run his palms down the bare skin of her arms. To hold both of her hands as she nervelessly dropped her keys to the ground. All of it was heady and powerful. If his feet hadn't been on the ground, he wouldn't know which way was up and which was down. He felt as though he were floating through the ether, and that this must be what heaven was like.

She moaned and opened her lips for him. He took advantage, raising one of his hands to the back of her head so that it wouldn't hurt her when he pressed her whole body with his. He couldn't get enough contact with her. He wanted to disappear inside her for days or months at a time. And yet, he knew that wouldn't be enough.

He dipped his knees and pressed her body higher, so that her breasts were pressed against his chest and her hips lined up with his. He couldn't stop the guttural sound he made. After spending all this time trying to avoid falling into her, the relief of being able to touch her if they both wanted, however they both wanted, was drugging.

He probably would have fucked her against the door if her downstairs neighbor hadn't come in. They might not have noticed that if said neighbor hadn't cleared their throat. But he wasn't embarrassed anymore. He didn't have to be. Sasha appeared to be shell-shocked by their kiss, so he bent down to grab her keys and let them both inside.

CHAPTER TWENTY-EIGHT

IF SASHA HAD ANY doubts about whether she and Patrick would have chemistry now that their love was no longer forbidden, Patrick's last kiss had extinguished them. The pure longing in every line of his body made her center ache. It made her feel like she'd walked out of one of those shampoo commercials where the women always sounded like the shampoo was giving them an orgasm.

Hell, she was surprised that she hadn't combusted against her front door, burning a hole in it instead of opening it like a civilized person. But nothing about how she felt about Patrick was civilized. And from the wild look on his face and the way his hair stood up in odd ways, indicating the path her fingers had taken, he didn't feel entirely civilized about her either.

As soon as he shut the door and stalked toward her, she put up a hand to stop him. He halted his approach immediately, and that warmed her. He was so in tune with her that she probably hadn't even needed to put the hand up. He would have done it as soon as he saw the concern on her face.

"Are we really doing this?" Sasha couldn't quite believe it. She'd just resigned herself to never having him—to never even seeing him again. And now he was all hers. He loved her, and he wanted to be with her.

He'd left God for her.

She felt powerful, like some ancient temptress. But all of those ancient temptresses had been punished for their wickedness.

"Only if you want to." He put his hands in his pockets, and he turned instantly from her lover to her friend again. "What's wrong?"

She wasn't sure she could sugarcoat it, even though her MO was sugarcoating things. "Are we going to be punished?" She took a step toward him; they were close enough to touch. "Is our being together wrong?"

Those were two questions that she really should have thought to ask herself before riding off into the sunset with him. Even if he wanted to go back, he couldn't. She'd permanently altered his life, and only now was she worrying about her soul.

Every insidious voice that had ever told her that her most natural impulses were bad and wrong and needed to be tamed rioted inside her.

Until he touched her face with his hand. It wasn't an explicitly sexual touch. But everything between them was imbued with that. She leaned into his palm, just quelling the urge to turn her face so that she could kiss his rough palm.

"Does it feel wrong to you?"

No, everything about being this close to him, having him in her home, loving him, felt right. "It feels too good. That's what I'm afraid of."

"I'm afraid, too."

"You are?"

He let out a short laugh. "Yeah, I'm terrified."

"Of what?" Even though he'd never said anything that had made him seem arrogant to her, she'd always put him on a pedestal—even though she was no longer religious, so many authority figures in her life had been priests that she'd elevated him in her head. The idea that he was scared right now brought him somewhat down to earth.

"I'm afraid of disappointing you." He would definitely do that if this worked out. But he'd *chosen* her. No one she'd ever been with had chosen her. They'd always left her. She'd never felt good enough. But Patrick did not expect her to be perfect. He'd witnessed her most sinful, wanton behavior. She'd let him see her most craven thoughts. But he was standing in front of her, giving her a tender look that told her he wanted nothing more than to be kissing her again right now. Instead, he continued talking, reassuring her. "I'm afraid that this won't last, and I'll be just as lost as I was the last time a woman I loved left me."

"I won't leave you." She knew that about herself, knew that it would rip her apart to leave Patrick because she'd felt hollow and empty when she did. "It almost killed me the last time."

His other hand joined the one on her face, cupping her chin and bringing her close. "I know that. I think I knew how you felt about me when you walked away, but I was too much of a dope to actually see it."

"You're not a dope—"

"No, I'm definitely a dope." He kissed her nose and sighed with satisfaction. "I've loved you for a long time. Maybe it was that night at the bake sale, when I almost kissed you."

"That was so hot—so wrong—but so hot."

"Shhh." Him making that sound sent a shiver down her spine

and made her center heat even more. "It wasn't wrong. Not even then."

"You are—were—a priest." Even though Catholicism wasn't for her, part of her still believed that there was something out there keeping track of all the wrong things everyone did and meting out punishment at the end.

"True story." He pulled her close, and she let him. Even if her soul was forever marred by how much she loved him, she wasn't strong enough to fight it anymore. "But I'm still a human being. We're consenting adults, and we fell in love. The only time I've felt like I was doing anything right in the past few months was when I was with you."

"Me too." She bit her lip, and the only reason she could say the next thing was that she wasn't looking him dead in the face. "But I've always wanted what I couldn't have. Always."

"So, you think that everything you want is bad?"

When he said it, it sounded ridiculous. "I'm so weird. Why do you love me?"

He pulled back and looked at her. "I love you because you're just the kind of weird that I need. I never had any problem sticking with my vow of chastity before because none of the women I met were you."

"Really?" Hearing him say the thing she almost never said out loud made her residual doubts disappear. After all this time lusting after Patrick, surely any god that actually existed would have struck her down if it was really wrong—or at least given her a bad bout of acne?

"Nothing in my life felt right until you walked into my office, ready to save the preschool."

"Nothing?"

"I was stuck. Bored. I didn't feel like I had a relationship with God anymore. It had gotten stale."

"Like a bad marriage?"

"Sort of?" He laughed.

"But everything is always forever with the Church—all the vows are forever."

"I don't know. Maybe that made sense when life was really short, but life is long. I don't regret becoming a priest. If I hadn't, maybe you and I wouldn't be together right now. If you only want what's forbidden, how else would I have gotten your attention?"

He had a point there. "Does that mean that you'll get sick of me after a decade?"

"Are you ever going to stop surprising me?" His voice was laced with humor, as though getting sick of her was preposterous.

"Probably not." If she had to resort to perpetually annoying him, she would do it for the sake of keeping things spicy. For now, she'd just have to keep him guessing with sex stuff. "I think I'd like to have sex now."

"Do we need to talk anything else out first?"

They had so much to talk about, but that could wait. They had time. Right now, she needed him to kiss her. She needed his clothes—the ones that still had church-smell on them—to come off. She needed to drink him in. It was the only way that she would feel like this was really real and really for keeps.

"I think we're done talking."

PATRICK HAD STUDIED ANTHROPOLOGY in undergrad. The concept of liminal spaces—the confusing and ungrounded feeling of being neither here nor there in the middle of a rite of passage—stuck with him. He'd thought about it every time he'd performed a wedding ceremony and the bride and groom had appeared nervous. He'd thought about it as he'd poured holy water over a baby's brow, anointed him with oil, and handed the child to godparents who seemed flabbergasted that someone was handing them a real human baby. He thought about liminal spaces when he was giving last rites, saying a funeral mass, or comforting a bereaved family.

After something ended and before something new, there was always the in-between. He felt as though he and Sasha were in a liminal space right now. He was no longer a priest. Sasha might know he loved her, but she didn't necessarily know that this was a forever thing.

They were no longer just friends, but they weren't yet lovers. Even this short time, the ride over and this conversation at her place, was too long to be in between.

So he kissed her again. He took her mouth in a way that was meant to tell her that he wanted her beyond all reason, that she belonged to him. And he let himself drink in the fact that she was finally his.

After an interminable moment, she opened her mouth to him, wrapped her arms around his neck, and pulled him closer. The kissed stretched out beyond their first kiss, the one she'd cut her hair off to get away from.

He plunged his hands into the short crop of hair, sifting through the strands with his fingers. He didn't know if he'd ever get used to the idea that he could touch her at will. She'd been forbidden to him for so long that he felt like a man who'd lived in poverty his whole life and won the lottery one day.

He didn't want to waste a moment of it, but he was paralyzed by the riches he now had at hand.

She was the one who broke the kiss. Her lips were swollen and looked even softer and more enticing. "Take my clothes off."

Her words brooked no discussion, so he reached around and unzipped the back of her dress. The way she looked at him, as though she was searching his face for doubts, didn't make him move faster. "Let me savor this."

One side of her mouth quirked up. "You've seen all the good bits."

"No." He shook his head as he pulled the sides of her dress to the front and yanked it down until her bra was revealed. It was lacy and wispy—her dark cherry nipples beaded up and pressed against it. Every inch of her made his mouth water. He bent down and sucked on one luscious tit through her bra. They were the perfect size and shape and he wanted to stay there forever. She gasped and held his head to her breast. With one hand, he pulled the rest of her dress off, leaving her in shoes and bra and panties.

He liked how it felt with her revealed to him, even though his vision was limited and her grip was so tight that he doubted that his scenery would change anytime soon. He felt as though he were drowning in her at the same time that he was learning her body.

He wondered if he would ever feel as though he had enough time with her. He let his hands wander because he was so impatient for her. He flicked her other nipple with the tips of his fingers, and her grip on his head slackened.

She let go of his hair and touched his neck and shoulders like she couldn't be quite sure that he was really there. She moved slowly, deliberately, as though she needed to memorize his body before consuming it. His mouth wandered farther down; his tongue dipped in her belly button.

And then he was on his knees in front of her. It felt sacrilegious, this worshipful feeling of completeness he felt staring at the core of her through innocent lace panties. But it didn't feel wrong. For the first time in a long time, he felt as though he were where he needed to be. He rubbed his nose against the soft skin of her gently curved belly and she shuddered. That she was just as affected by what was between them magnified the rightness in his spirit.

The atmosphere of rightness grew when he slipped his fingers in her panties and pulled them down, when he put his mouth on her center and kissed her there deeply. The smell of her made him so hard that he almost collapsed right there.

"Spread your legs, honey." She was honey, nectar, the only food he would ever crave. She spread her legs and he opened her, sucking her clit into his mouth. She cried out and held on to his shoulders as he kissed her. She made incoherent sounds that reached down and stroked him like a hand. He didn't stop, couldn't. When she came on his face, he was surprised he didn't join her because it was so intensely pleasurable to give her pleasure.

When it stopped, she knelt down in front of him.

The sounds that came out of Sasha's mouth made him feel like a god of sex. He felt raw and exposed, as if his parts were outside his skin, and he hadn't even been inside her. Fucking her was going to kill him, and he didn't care. He hated that they'd denied themselves this since they'd met years ago through their friends, but also knew that neither of them had been ready.

"I knew you were the one for me the moment that I saw you," she said, reaching out to touch his face. She looked flushed and debauched. He loved her so much that it hurt to stare at her too long. It hurt because she'd always been able to see inside him. She'd always admired him as a person, even when he didn't think he deserved admiration.

He only hoped that he could give that back to her. But neither of them had words in that moment, so he kissed her again. She worked the buttons free on his shirt, obviously feeling the same urgency that he was.

Once she'd pushed the shirt off his shoulders, he helped her by pulling off the sleeves so she could go for his belt, as though what was inside his pants was a Christmas present. He needed her to hurry up and wanted to slow things down at the same time.

"I don't want to fuck you on the living room rug," he said, putting a hand over her wrist to stop her from pulling him out of his trousers and boxers.

"You can be on the bottom if you're worried about giving me rug burn." It felt so weird to be talking about fucking her, to hear these words coming out of his own mouth.

It was weird, but also good.

They could do this.

He belonged to her.

This was real.

He kissed the base of her neck, causing a whole-body shiver. "You can have anything you want."

He knew her well enough to know that she wouldn't trust that she could have him. He knew that it would take a lot of time to believe that what they had wouldn't be ripped away from either of them. But Patrick lay down on her living room rug and tugged off his pants.

"I get to keep you." The best present she'd ever had.

"And I get to keep you." He smiled at her. "But you might not get to keep me for long if you don't get over here."

He was still wearing boxer briefs, so she climbed on top of him and pulled off his underwear. She fisted him in her hand and bent down to kiss him. His whole body shuddered. He put his hands in her hair, and she stilled for a moment, remembering the way that he used to look at her long hair and reliving the moment that she cut it off so that she would stop kissing him.

"Do you miss my hair?"

"No." He shook his head, and the tip of his nose brushed hers. "Do you miss it?"

She pressed her lips together for a moment. He wanted to open his mouth to reassure her that he would find her sexy and desirable no matter what, but that wasn't important. How she felt about herself was.

"I don't."

He kissed her again. "I've missed you."

"We weren't apart that long," she teased.

"Every day without you feels like an eternity in the dark."

Her heart felt as though it was going to burst out of her chest. "You can't say things like that."

"I finally can, and I plan to as much as possible. Get used to it." He had a stupid grin on his face, so she kissed him again until he nudged her entrance with his cock.

"I have an IUD and had an STI test after my last friend-with-benefits ghosted me." She wanted just Patrick. "Do I need to find a condom?"

He shook his head. "If you're sure?"

"I'm sure."

It felt as though he'd been waiting to be inside her forever. He didn't feel more connected with her now; he'd always felt connected with her. Being inside her, moving with her in the common pursuit of pleasure was life-changing, though. Every thrust changed his cells and drove home the fact that the woman above him was his home.

Sex with Sasha was a religious experience. Patrick didn't admit that to himself lightly, but he understood why sex was part of rituals in ancient religions. He realized why the Church wanted to keep its priests from experiencing it and tightly control how laypeople expressed it. Turning sweaty, writhing flesh into something new. This would never be anything less than procreative with Sasha. They weren't making another human, but they were making their love manifest.

Despite the fact that he'd have a rug burn on his back and scratch marks from her fingernails, the memory of her moving over him, taking him inside her, looking at him with a curious mélange of lust and love on her face would never leave him. It might be the last thing he saw before he closed his eyes for the last time.

If he met his Maker and found out that he'd condemned himself by choosing her, he wouldn't change it. He would meet his fate with this memory of her at the front of his mind.

He found her clit and tried to mimic the way she'd touched herself in the bar that night. She moaned and started moving faster. And then he wasn't thinking. He was feeling, and then he was coming.

Her body collapsed on his, and his motivation to move from the rug vanished.

CHAPTER TWENTY-NINE

PATRICK WOKE UP DISORIENTED—as though he'd been dreaming that he'd been laicized and told his whole parish that he was in love with Sasha. And then had another dream that she'd brought him into her home and they'd had sex all night. It was real, but he didn't feel like he deserved to feel like he hadn't missed a beat, like this was where he'd always been and always belonged.

Sasha stirred next to him, and he lost his breath when she smiled at him. "Good morning."

He couldn't help but smile back. "Good morning to you."

"What should we do—"

Her statement was cut off when her mother—sober this time but with a slightly constipated expression on her face—and a tall man who looked like he dove into piles of money as a pastime walked into her room.

Sasha pulled up the covers so as not to flash her parents. "What are you doing here?"

"The last time I checked, we owned this house, where you are currently in bed—naked—with a priest."

Her mother looked like she had murder on her mind, but he was more concerned about his physical safety with respect to her father. He hadn't said anything, but he'd perked up when Moira had mentioned that he was a priest. A naked priest, who by all accounts had defiled his daughter.

"He's not a priest anymore," Sasha said. "And you only have a key for emergencies."

"Well, I'm not a frocked priest." Patrick was going to have to go into a lot of canon law to clear this up, but accuracy was important here.

"I'll say he's not a frocked priest." Her father rolled his eyes and walked out of the room.

Moira didn't budge. She crossed her arms. "You have a lot of explaining to do, young lady."

It was never a good scene when "young lady" started getting thrown around. He'd counseled enough families dealing with misanthropic teen behavior to know that "young lady" was a harbinger of doom. Not to even get into the fact that Sasha was an adult.

But he didn't know what to do because he didn't know what he should do. Should he say something to her mother, who was totally out of line and crossing all boundaries, or let Sasha handle it herself?

They were both still sitting under the covers. Both still naked.

Sasha pointed at her mother. "Would you get out so that we can get dressed?" When her mother didn't move, she added, "Please."

Her mother didn't respond verbally, but walked out of the room, her heels clicking against the wooden floor. As soon as she left the room, Sasha shot out of bed and closed the door behind her. He didn't even get to enjoy the view because she pulled on a robe immediately.

When she turned to him, he couldn't help the probably dumb-looking smile on his face when she couldn't help checking him out. It made him glad that he'd been very physically active in the name of health for the last decade. He was happy she liked to look at him.

But that happiness was short-lived. Apparently, she remembered that her parents were out in the other room and had caught them naked in bed.

"Why do they have keys?" He had keys to his father's house and his brother's apartment for safety reasons. But he would never use them without permission and prior warning—especially in Chris's case. He never knew what he would find.

Sasha looked down and crossed her arms. He didn't want to risk his new relationship by saying it, but she looked like her mother when she did that. "Well, technically, they do own the place."

That made what they'd done the night before seem dirtier and somehow more illicit. Like they were teenagers, and he'd snuck into her room last night. He didn't hate that thought, and he realized he might have a more subversive streak than he'd previously thought. Or maybe that was just Sasha's influence on him.

They'd still crossed a boundary by entering their daughter's home at—he glanced at his watch on the bedside table—eight in the morning on a Sunday. "Okay—"

"Listen, I need you to let me do the talking." Sasha started pacing in front of the door as he got out of bed and looked for something to put on. Shit. All of his clothes were strewn around the apartment. And those were the only clothes he had until he packed up his things at the rectory.

Sasha noticed his problem and found him another robe. It was pink and way too small, but the too-short baby-blue pajama pants she found him really added to the look.

"I'm not sure what their game is, and we don't have time to talk strategy, so I'm going to need you to pay close attention to the words coming out of my mouth, and closer attention to the look on my face. I'll try to position us so that I can signal you if you're saying too much or too little. But if Moira heads for the liquor cabinet, all bets are off."

Patrick was totally bewildered. His family wasn't chock-full of talkers, but there were no mixed messages, and he certainly had never needed to strategize in order to get out of a conversation with them alive.

"Is it always like this with your family?"

She gave him a pointed look that said he was obviously new here. "You need to pick this up quick. I'm sorry about it, but it's just part of the package."

He stepped closer to her then and gave her a hug. She stood there stiffly for a moment. "We don't have time for this."

Instead of letting her go, he rubbed up and down her back until she relaxed. "I just want to help, and I obviously don't have the manual on your family, but I need you to let me help."

She pulled back and he looked down at her. Usually so put-together and competent, she looked lost. "I'm glad you're here, and I'd hoped that you wouldn't have to deal with them for a while."

"Are you ashamed of—this?"

Their whole relationship was so locked up in the taboo of how it had started and how she got off on it that he wondered for a moment if it had only been about the sex. Maybe, now that he was free to be with her, she'd decide that he wasn't a good bet. He'd known that was a risk going in, but she was worth it.

She was still worth it.

"No, I'm not." She was firm on that, and relief washed through him. "But my parents might be, and I don't want to sugarcoat that for you."

"I'm willing to stand up for us if you are."

"I am." She sighed. "But I just don't want to put you through this."

He wanted to tell her that he would suffer any number of indignities in order to be with her. He wanted to tell her that he loved her more than he'd ever loved anything in life. He wanted to tell her that he would do anything to ensure that she'd be happy—even let her go. But they didn't have time for that.

She turned and took his hand and walked them out of the room and into the fire.

CHAPTER THIRTY

PATRICK'S HAND WAS THE only thing holding her back from running out of her apartment screaming in nothing but a cotton robe. His warmth at her back was the only thing keeping her from being a shivering mess.

Her parents catching her and Patrick the way they had was a worst-case scenario. They liked to pretend that all their daughters were virgins until well after they were married. Her mother—who had always referred to sex in the extreme and rare circumstances that it came up with disdain—did not understand why all young women seemed intent on "ruining themselves" before marriage.

"I hope that you have a good explanation for this." Her mother wasn't going to cut her any slack at all. Disappointing, but good to know. And she'd made an error by making the opening salvo. Moira was losing her touch.

"I don't see how any of this is your business." Sasha was happy to see that Patrick had positioned himself across the island next to the coffee pot. He was even making coffee—four cups, so smart.

"Well, you live under our roof." Her mother was really rolling out all of the clichés today.

"You mean his roof, right?" She pointed at her father. "You don't own anything for yourself."

"Is this going to turn into you lecturing me on how you're so different from me and your sisters again because you earn your own money?" Sasha had the uncomfortable realization that she sounded just like her mother when she was being shitty and sarcastic. "We gave you the money to start your business, you know."

"I do know that, and I'm grateful." Sasha truly did feel thankful that her parents could afford to help her. She knew that without their help, she would have struggled to start her own business and keep it open over the past few years. "But I've paid you back, and now it's mine. And, maybe Daddy didn't tell you, but I've been paying him for this condo in installments, so it's technically my roof."

Her dad turned around and winked at her. It filled her with strength until her mother said, "Well, I never agreed to that, so any agreement you have with him is null and void."

Sasha looked at her father, who hadn't said anything as usual. When he said, "Happy wife, happy life," it was incredibly sinister, because the only thing that made her mother happy was keeping her children under her thumb. "We didn't sign anything."

He was right. Unlike the business loan that he'd given her, they hadn't signed anything with respect to the house. And he wouldn't put up a fight if her mother wanted to take the place away from her.

She looked around. She loved her home and the memories she'd made inside it. After college, she and Hannah had moved in and gone to work together at a big event-planning firm in the Loop. The place she'd grown up wasn't home—this was.

"Coffee?" Sasha had to suppress a laugh at Patrick offering her parents coffee while wearing her pink robe and too-small pajama pants. Her parents looked shocked to see that he was still there. Sasha was so happy that he was.

"I don't think I owe you an explanation, but the long and short of it is that Patrick and I are in love. He left the priesthood, and we're together now."

Her dad made some grumbling noise, took a sip of coffee, and then his mumbling became less disapproving.

"It's a scandal." Apparently, her mother wasn't going to let this go. "I can't let this happen. How will I explain this?"

Patrick had moved to her side, and Sasha leaned into him even though it made her mother's nostrils flare. "I don't care how you explain this."

Right on cue, her mother ripped open the cabinet where Sasha kept liquor and pulled out a bottle of Bailey's. Patrick squeezed her waist, and it was a good thing because Sasha felt like she was going to crumble. She looked up at him, and he must have seen something disturbing because his brow furrowed. He couldn't comfort her now, though. They had to deal with her parents first.

"You barely even know Patrick. Just get to know him, and you'll realize how good he is for me."

Her mother, free pouring, said, "I don't need to know any more. Last time I was here trying to prevent one of my children from ruining their life, he was a priest working as a part-time bartender. Now he's your *boyfriend*?"

Boyfriend didn't seem like the right word for what Patrick was. He was everything.

Her mother didn't need to hear that, though. "Dad, can you do something? Why did you even come?"

"Your sister was concerned about you," her father said. Thanks, Madison. So much for solidarity. "She said that if we were so concerned about how you were doing and why you were still unmarried, we should visit you ourselves."

So, her sister hadn't betrayed her; she'd just been rather careless. Forgivable. "Why do you two still live in the Dark Ages? I don't have to get married, either."

She glanced up at Patrick then, and he winced. They hadn't really talked about getting married to each other. She didn't know exactly how that worked for laicized priests. Apparently, fornication hadn't been a big no-no for him, but she didn't know how he felt about anything else. All of that would have to wait until she'd gotten rid of her parents.

"You're shacked up with a priest." Her mother pointed at Patrick, as though she needed to be reminded. "That's something right out of *The Borgias*."

"Believe you me, I'm tempted to do some poisoning right now." Sasha looked pointedly at her mother's coffee cup, which Moira put down immediately.

"Just coffee. Poison-free," Patrick said with a smile.

Sasha looked over at her father again, and he seemed like he was trying very hard not to laugh. And then she caught the giggles but couldn't stop herself. Soon, she and her father were both laughing out loud while Patrick and her mother stared at them in horror and bemusement, respectively.

"Well, I never." Her mom was so pissed that it just made Sasha laugh harder. "Stephen, stop it this instant."

Her father stopped on a dime, and Sasha was able to gather herself then.

"If you don't end this immediately, then your father and I will have no choice but to cut you off," her mother declared. "You'll have fifteen days to vacate the premises, and we'll have our accountant call on you to audit your books on the business."

"Stop treating me like a business associate." The fact that her mother had come up with this plan to excise her from their lives so quickly made Sasha feel as though she was being stabbed. Unlike the tiny wounds she'd sustained all her life from her mother's barbs, these felt like great, gaping wounds. This was the thing that she'd spent most of her life trying to avoid. She felt hollow as tears formed in her eyes. She didn't want to let them fall, but she wasn't sure she could stop them. "You're my family."

Never had those words felt more untrue to her. Despite the fact that she'd been in therapy for literal years figuring out the ways her family had warped her and her worldview, she'd harbored some hope that they loved her and cared about her.

She'd chalked their controlling behavior and rigid standards up to wanting her to be happy. She'd thought that they'd just had no idea what would actually make her happy. Now that she'd figured it out—that being with Patrick would make her happy—she realized that they'd *only* ever cared about how things looked to outsiders. They would *never* care about whether she was content, only about whether her life made them look bad.

Stunned, she stared up at Patrick. His eyes were filled with anger and unshed tears. She felt as though she'd been torn open, and he was seeing all of her insides. At the same time, she felt like she didn't have to walk on broken eggshells around her parents. She could stop the bleeding.

And she had to take a stand now because there was a question behind the righteous anger in Patrick's gaze. He wasn't sure that she was going to choose him over her family. She wasn't sure where they would live or how her parents would try to fuck her business over, but she was sure about choosing him. She was sure about choosing love.

"Get out."

Her mother rolled her eyes. "Don't be difficult, Sasha. Just do what you're told; say goodbye. We have brunch reservations."

"I'm not going with you, and I'm not saying goodbye." When she said that, she felt the tension melt out of Patrick's body. "You can send accountants and kick me out of here. But if you do that, you know you'll never see me again."

"If family means that little to you—"

Sasha put her hand up. "You might be able to convince Marlena to cut me off, but that just means that she doesn't want to be my family. And, if you don't want to accept me as I am—imperfect, scandalous, insufficiently cowed into living under your stupid rules—then you're not my family. That's not what family does. It's not what it means."

"This is your fault." Moira pointed to Patrick. "Before this, she never would have defied me. I ought to report you to the archbishop."

Patrick snorted and held up both hands. "First of all, reporting me to the archbishop wouldn't do any good. I've asked for and received laicization and dispensation from my vows. I'm in love with your daughter, and I'm going to be with her in any capacity that she'll have me. Even if she won't marry me."

Sasha turned to her father. "You're just going to let her cut me out of your lives?"

Her father's face reddened. He was ashamed, but he wasn't going to do anything about it. In that moment, she felt sorry for him. He might have more money than he could ever spend, but he was sitting on a throne built of lies and shame. She wouldn't live that way anymore.

Despite everything, she still hoped that her mother would see how wrong she was. It was a faint hope, but she didn't want to be the person who lost that hope. "I think, before anyone says anything that can't be taken back, you should leave."

Her mother opened her mouth to speak, but her father took her arm to lead her out.

"I'll make sure to send you the keys and have the place professionally cleaned."

Her father nodded and turned away. When they made it out the front door, Sasha turned into Patrick's arms. Happy that he was there to catch her, because she was now working without a net.

PATRICK COULDN'T BELIEVE THAT she'd chosen him over her family. He'd taken a leap of faith leaving the Church, knowing that he could fall flat on his face if she didn't really want to be with him. He'd pushed that fear away, knowing that it was the right thing to do even if things didn't work out.

But things could really work out. She wanted them to work out, and that was half the battle. He promised himself that he wouldn't do anything to make her regret the decision to choose him over her family. That started when he held her as she cried.

When she stopped, he stepped away to get her fresh coffee, realizing when he was done pouring that he didn't know how she liked it. She sat down at the counter, and it was just like she was sitting down at the bar at Dooley's. That bit of familiarity in this completely new situation made him smile.

She looked at him and gave him a weak grin. "Just cream, two tablespoons."

"It's so weird that I know how you drink a cocktail but not a cup of coffee." He set down the cup in front of her and poured his own. He leaned over and kissed her forehead, not knowing if he'd ever be able to get used to that. The freedom of not having to watch what he did and trying to control how he thought was staggering.

"We have plenty of time to learn." She looked down. "When are we going to move into the apartment above Dooley's—"

"It's been vacant for a couple of months. We can move in whenever we want." He worried for a moment that she might be having doubts after that whole scene with her parents. The way she'd drawn a line in the sand had made him even more ready to start his life with her, but he knew that some of her assurance may have been adrenaline.

"I didn't mean what I said to them about marriage. You know that, right?"

"We don't have to make any decisions about that right now." He'd sort of skipped over the deciding-to-get-married part. He could live without it, but he knew for sure that he wanted her forever. He paused, not wanting to hurt her by making her talk about that terrible scene with her parents but wanting to make sure she knew that he was there for her. "Are you okay?"

She waved a hand but ran it through her hair, pushing it off her red, splotchy, still-gorgeous face. She was wrecked. "I'm fine."

"You don't have to be fine with me." He covered her free hand with his. "You don't have to be fine."

"Well, of course I'm not fine," she wailed. "My family is a mess, and that was the last thing I wanted you to see about me. Especially after you gave your whole life up to be with me."

Patrick didn't know what to say to that. He only knew that it broke his heart. He didn't believe that she'd tried to conceal how she was feeling about what had just happened for nefarious reasons. But this wasn't going to work if they weren't going to be real with each other. That's why his relationship with Ashley hadn't worked, and he wasn't willing to sacrifice his relationship with Sasha before it had a chance to really get started.

"So, you're not fine. What can we do to get you closer to fine?"

"Please don't sing the Indigo Girls." Her lips twitched, which was a good sign.

"No singing. Got it." He nodded.

"You didn't think I was going to stand up to them for a minute, did you?"

He stopped in his tracks. He didn't want to say anything, because this was about her and her feelings. But he'd had a sinking feeling in his gut when her parents had issued an ultimatum. He'd doubted for a few moments that she was actually going to choose him. "They're your family."

Sasha stood up then and said, "No. Hannah and Jack and Bridget and Matt and . . . you are my family."

"I come along with an idiot brother and no real-life plan." Maybe it was time to put all of his fears out on the table. "I feel like I'm not enough for you, that you wanted the guy who was a priest and leader. Now I don't have that, and I'm afraid that I won't be enough to make up for losing your family."

"They didn't love me unconditionally." She didn't hesitate. "You loved me enough to give up your vocation. And yeah, their money

272

has made a whole lot of things possible for me, but that doesn't mean that I need to live my life exactly the way they want me to for the rest of my life."

"Is your business going to be okay?" He really didn't want this to cost her her livelihood. For one thing, she was proud of it. For another, it would be bad if neither of them had jobs.

Sasha waved a hand. "It will be fine. Their accountant is not going to find anything irregular in our books, and I've paid my father back with interest. That was just posturing."

"That's good." A relief. "So what do we do now?"

"What do you mean?"

"I haven't had a free Sunday in years." His outfit wasn't the only thing that felt foreign.

Sasha had a wicked smirk when she said, "I guess I'm going to have to introduce you to the concept of brunch."

CHAPTER THIRTY-ONE

BOTTOMLESS MIMOSAS WOULD HAVE to wait for another day. When Sasha called Hannah and filled her in on the morning's events, she enlisted Jack, Matt, Bridget, and Kelly to come help them start packing up. For her part, Hannah came with food and drink and insistent instructions.

Patrick was surprised that everyone dropped whatever they'd planned to do that Sunday to help him and Sasha. It wasn't that he thought that any of their friends disapproved of him leaving the priesthood or of his relationship with Sasha. But he'd never allowed himself to count on other people to help him. He guessed that was something he would have to get used to as a layperson.

He was in Sasha's living room, boxing up her extensive stash of books—mostly romance—when Jack approached him. "I didn't think you would actually do it."

"Leave the Church?" Patrick turned to his best friend. "Or shack up with Sasha?"

Jack laughed and patted him on the back. "Either."

Patrick felt the need to explain himself. It wasn't that he felt guilty about anything other than leaving St. Bart's temporarily without a pastor, but he thought he'd been careful about hiding his feelings for Sasha when he actually hadn't been. He had never lied to Jack about that, but he hadn't been open with his friend either. And Jack had always come to him with his problems. "I'm sorry."

"What for?" Jack picked up a bookend and wrapped it. "I kind of feel bad that it took me as long as it did to realize how unhappy you were."

"I wasn't unhappy for a long time. And Sasha wasn't the only reason it was right for me to leave—but she was the catalyst."

Jack paused before asking, "What are you going to do for a job?"

"Other than bartending?" Not that it wasn't a noble profession. "I was thinking about going back to school to become a therapist."

The wait for Jack's answer was agonizing because he wanted his friend to approve of his plans. Vulnerability was weird, but he guessed he would have to get used to it, not being seen as an infallible messenger from God.

"Are you going to start charging me for our talks?"

Relief washed over him. "Never."

An hour later Bridget and Matt left. Fifteen minutes after that, his brother shocked everyone by showing up. With more snack food.

"Thanks for being here." Patrick wasn't about to make Chris squirm when he'd done something nice that wouldn't benefit him for the first time in forever.

"A former priest has told me for years that I'm a selfish asshole, so . . ." Chris sort of shrugged, and Patrick hugged him. The Dooleys weren't huggers, so Chris stiffened up before patting his brother on the back a few times. He cleared his throat. "Put me to work."

After Sasha sent Chris and Jack on a trip to her storage unit, Patrick found her and planted a kiss on the back of her neck. When he looked up, Hannah was watching him with a look on her face that he would characterize as scary. If he was scared of her. Which he was not.

"Stop with that look," Sasha said.

Hannah popped some cheese into her mouth. "What look?"

"The look that says you're about to warn Patrick about what you'll do to him if he hurts me. I almost scared him off well enough on my own, and I don't need your help."

"Well, he needs to know that you'll have help burying his body if it comes to that."

Patrick's heart warmed that Sasha had someone who was so on her side after seeing how her family treated her. He would always have her back, but it was good that he wasn't alone in that. Sasha deserved all the good things—and he wouldn't be alone in giving them to her.

He hugged her from behind and whispered in her ear, "I promise I won't make you have to 'Goodbye Earl' me."

Sasha laughed and he couldn't help kissing her, even with an audience. He couldn't even stop himself when Hannah huffed and said, "Now that's just so cute that it's gross," and walked away.

THE NEXT FEW WEEKS were a blur of activity. Sasha moved out of the condo where she'd lived for over a decade. It was bittersweet because she was moving in with a very hot man who loved her and had a decade of sex to make up for. She really couldn't complain.

Maybe it was all the sexing that softened her up enough to answer the phone when her mother called a week after the scene at the condo. Moira didn't apologize, of course. "Sorry" wasn't a word that fit very well in her vocabulary. She did, however, invite Sasha and Patrick to their house for Labor Day weekend. Sasha knew it was a huge thing for her mother to just gloss over all the choices that Sasha had made of late. But it wasn't quite enough yet.

Sasha declined, but said that she would keep Thanksgiving open. She wasn't quite ready to share Patrick with her family yet.

There was one wrinkle in their bliss, though, when they were unpacking in the second bedroom of the apartment above Dooley's that they were going to share. Sasha was pulling Patrick's books out of a box on the side of the room where they would be stored. She couldn't allow his books on philosophy and religion to mingle with her romance novels. It would be unseemly—for the romance novels. She wouldn't want Lisa Kleypas to be bored to death sitting next to Thomas Aquinas.

She pulled out one of Patrick's five bibles, and a hunk of hair fell out. She was holding it and trying to figure out if she needed to find a way to fake her own death—the only option if Patrick was some weird hair fetishist—when he walked in and blanched.

He took the hair from her hand and said, "This is not what it looks like."

"So, you don't collect weird strands of hair?"

He looked down at it. "This is your hair."

"From the time I cut it off? You kept it?" She didn't know if she was flattered or horrified.

"Yeah, it's gross and weird. I'm sorry." He looked so embarrassed. It was so adorable that she was less creeped out by it.

"It's some real Derek Craven shit."

"Who is Derek Craven? Is that one of your ex-boyfriends?"

As a priest, Patrick probably didn't read very many romance

novels. She had so much to teach him. "Derek Craven is not one of my ex-boyfriends, Patrick." She grabbed him by the upper arms. "I know that you've read all the important works by dead white guys, but if you don't read *Dreaming of You* immediately, we're going to have to break up."

She hoped that her sarcasm came across, and it must have because Patrick smirked. "That seems serious."

"Don't worry. I will have a whole reading list ready for you." She turned him around and pushed him toward her already color-coded bookshelf. "We'll start you on this one." She pulled out her dog-eared copy of one of the greatest romance novels of all time and put in his hands. "I think you'll particularly enjoy the talisman work in this."

He caught her off guard by pulling her into his arms and kissing her. She stopped assembling a romance curriculum in her head. When he pulled back, he said, "You're not upset about the hair. I kept it because—I don't know—it reminded me of you."

"It's very gross, but you're very handsome and good at sex and I love you. So, I guess it's sort of romantic."

"Good." He took his book of philosophy and put it on his side of the room. Away from Sasha's romance novels. She smiled at him.

"But can I throw it away now?" she asked. "I can always grow more."

CHAPTER THIRTY-TWO

HANNAH'S BABY SHOWER WAS an *event*. Her and Jack's wedding had been pretty great, if filled with drama. But this one was going to be drama free. All of their friends and family were there and happy, and there was no one there to have a massive fight that would preoccupy them for days.

Sasha had been deliberate and ruthless with seating arrangements. Hannah's mother needed to be seated far away from Molly Simpson and Sean Nolan, because Hannah's mom and Jack's mom were bound to start divvying up holidays with Baby Nolan before they were even born.

Hannah had agreed to talking any of their know-it-all mommy friends—who'd put up a fuss about a co-ed shower—into leaving an hour before the shower officially ended so that she could have one glass of the very good champagne that Bridget and Matt had contributed to the cause.

It didn't matter that they were all gathered at their usual gathering place—Dooley's—with people they usually saw. The space was transformed. When they'd finished decorating, Patrick had congratulated her very personally in his office in the back.

And the shower itself went off without a hitch. Sasha had nipped any stupid games in the bud, knowing that a thirty-eight-thousand-weeks-pregnant Hannah would punch anyone who put a perfectly good chocolate bar inside a diaper in the face.

In the few months since they'd moved in together, Sasha and Patrick had put any talk of their future on hold. Everything had moved so fast up to that point that they didn't want to rush. They'd agreed that they were both in it for keeps, but they hadn't really talked about marriage or kids. Sasha had always pictured kids in her future, but she could live without them if Patrick didn't want to be a parent.

Their relationship was enough for her.

Sometimes, like at big family events where everyone used to look to Patrick for some words of spiritual wisdom, she worried that Patrick missed being a priest.

And the nice thing about hanging out with her friends and their dudes was that the dudes helped with cleanup. Hannah and Sasha got to spend some time hanging out in one of the booths talking about nothing and everything like they didn't really have much time to do anymore.

"How are you feeling?" Thankfully, Hannah's pregnancy had been very normal after the first trimester, but she could not possibly be comfortable.

Hannah sighed and took another sip of her ob/gyn-sanctioned champagne. "Pretty good. I've been having some contractions, but my doctor said those were Braxton-Hicks. Fake ones."

"Are you ready to be a parent?" Sasha knew that Hannah had long-standing misgivings about her own maternal instincts. She didn't share the same doubts about her best friend. For one thing, Hannah was a lot softer than people thought she was when they first met her. For another, she was going to be a ferocious mama bear when it was called for. She'd pretty much mama-beared Sasha into doing a whole host of things that had changed her life.

Hannah looked over at her husband and smiled. "With him? Definitely. I never feel like I have to teach him how to be a functioning adult person. We fill in each other's weaknesses. I know that I have him as my backup, and so I feel like I can do anything."

"Yeah, he might be able to keep you from overthrowing the PTA when they make unreasonable demands."

Hannah gave her a skeptical look as she finished her glass of champagne. "You know that's happening. You'll have to whip support from the moms who think I'm dangerous to the status quo."

"I don't know if I'll ever be eligible to be a member of a PTA."

"Haven't you and Patrick talked about kids?" Coming from someone else, that question might be offensive. But this was her best friend—the person whom she'd confessed her deepest innermost thoughts to for over a decade. And Hannah wasn't going to judge her for her answer either way.

"Not yet." Sasha hesitated. One thing about being in a relationship with her best friend's husband's best friend was that anything she said tended to come back to her as a conversation. Most of the time, it was fine. This was big, important, life-changing stuff, though. "We're just taking things day by day."

Hannah grimaced, and that made Sasha doubt her approach. But while her best friend took charge and stormed the barricades whenever an issue needed to be addressed, Sasha tended to skirt around the issue and take bites off the edges until it was more manageable. Their differences made them wonderful business partners but sometimes caused them to get frustrated with each other.

"I mean, we have time, and things have been so good. I don't want him to start thinking of all the things he's missed out on by giving up the priesthood. Like—he probably didn't want children if he was going to go ahead and become a priest?"

Hannah grimaced again and touched her stomach. "No, it's probably fine that you haven't talked about this. I actually think that I'm having a real contraction. Like a real, real one."

Sasha stood up and yelled, "Jack!"

THERE WAS A QUESTION for a few minutes as to whether they would make it to the hospital before Hannah dropped a baby. However, she'd been adamant about having her baby in a hospital and not the "fucking floor of Dooley's bar," so they'd rushed her to the University of Chicago Hospital even though she'd looked like she was working harder to keep the baby in than push it out at that point.

Not that Patrick knew very much about the birthing of babies. But they'd made it with minutes to spare. And even though Hannah's birthing plan had provided for Sasha to be in the room with her and Jack, the hospital put the kibosh on it.

Until they had news that the baby and Hannah were both doing fine, Sasha was pacing so quickly that she'd likely wear a hole in the waiting room floor.

She was biting her thumbnail, like she did when she was very nervous. It was one of her very few tells.

"Do you want to maybe sit down?" Patrick asked, knowing that it wouldn't go over well.

He was right. She looked at him as though he'd grown a second skull. "Hannah could be bleeding out, and no one could be listening to her. She needs me to go ham on people sometimes."

"Jack is not going to let anything bad happen to her." Patrick knew that his best friend would burn the hospital down if they didn't take care of Hannah.

"Do you have any idea of the maternal mortality rates for women of color? Even controlled for education, income, and previous health status—it's bad." He should have gently suggested that Sasha stop reading every pregnancy article published for the past few months. Sasha was throwing her hands around and tears were now streaming down her face. He was failing at this. He stood up and caught her around the waist. She glared at him. "Yes, I read all those stories. All of them. That's why I was supposed to go in with her."

"I know you're scared."

"She's my family," Sasha said. She'd been upset the month before when her sister Madison had sent her a picture from their other sister's baby shower. But after she'd pulled herself together, it felt like she had turned a corner, until right now.

"I know." He hugged her tight, and some of the tension seemed to drain from her body. "But I know it's going to be all right."

Her "But how?" was muffled against his shirt.

"I just have faith."

"Well, I don't," she said, this time looking up at him. "I only have faith in things I can see and control."

"And that's why you're the only woman I could be with."

"Huh?"

"You see and control all the things that can be seen and controlled. And I have faith."

She opened her mouth to argue with him when Jack came in happily, with a big grin on his face. "She's perfect."

They both rushed over to their beaming friend. "How is Hannah?" Sasha demanded, and Patrick clapped Jack on the back.

"She's perfect, too." He wiped his face. "The doctor said that it couldn't have gone better. It was so fast, and she was so mad at how much it hurt. But they're fine. They're both fine. She punched me in the dick at one point, which I'm going to have to get checked out. But she and the baby are fine."

Jack looked down for a long moment, like he was collecting himself. Patrick's heart ached with happiness for his friend.

"Can we see them?" That was Sasha. She wasn't going to believe that they were really okay until she put her own eyes on them.

"Sure, yeah."

Jack led them down the hall to one of the private maternity suites. It had only taken so long for Jack to get out to them because everything had gone so fast that a room wasn't ready for them by the time the baby had been delivered and checked out.

"What's her name?" Jack and Hannah hadn't shared any of the names they were thinking of before the baby was born, though they'd had plenty of finger-pointing arguments about it at family dinners over the past few months.

Jack looked at him. "Grace."

And then it was Patrick's turn to tear up. That was his mother's name. "You didn't have to do that."

"I mean, it's probably not too late to change it if you want to use the name."

Patrick looked over at Sasha, who was holding baby Grace and fussing over Hannah, who looked tired but happy. She didn't seem to have heard what Jack had said.

He'd been meaning to broach the subject of their long-term future for quite some time, but Sasha had deftly avoided it. He didn't think that she was going to break up with him, but he respected the fact that she'd been through a lot—exerting strong boundaries with her family, moving in to a less luxurious apartment with an ex-priest, now bartender, keeping a business running while her partner was using a lot of energy making a human.

But looking at her holding a baby made him want to know where she was at with it all. Did she want a house, marriage, and a baby? Or was she totally cool with how things were?

Everything was good. But he wanted more than everything with her.

When they were leaving—having promised to bring sushi and the rest of the very good champagne—he decided that it was time. They were walking down the hall, and he had his arm looped around her shoulders. "What do you think of all that?"

"All of what?" Sasha looked exhausted and confused and he had a moment of doubt that this was the right time to discuss this. "We have to go pick up Jack and Hannah's dog from Bridget—"

"Having a baby. You know. Making a new person and trying not to fuck them up too much."

Sasha blew out a deep breath. "You make it sound so poetic."

He stopped in the dim, quiet hallway and turned her toward him. "You want poetry?"

"Always," she said, a wry smirk on her face.

"Well, here it is. There once was a priest from Nantucket—"

Sasha hit him on the chest. "I meant, like Yeats, not a dirty limerick."

"Have you met my father?"

"Yeah, he's a dirty-limerick type." Sasha winked at him.

"You'd be surprised." Patrick smirked, but then he said, "You are the rose that blossoms on my heart, but I'd like you to be the rose that blossoms with my ring on your finger and my baby in your belly. But only if you want that. I'll keep you in my heart in an apartment above a bar with a roof that leaks if that's the only way you'll have me."

"You want that?" He hated that she sounded even a little bit surprised. "We just haven't talked about it. Did you just decide?"

Patrick shook his head. "No, I didn't just decide. I probably knew that was what I really wanted the day I walked in to see you reading to a bunch of preschoolers."

"That would not have been the moment to tell me."

They'd had a long road ahead of them to get here. "No, it wouldn't have. I didn't know that loving and caring for another human being could be a higher calling than the one I had."

"Are you sure?" He wasn't sure what else he could do to get her to believe this, so he dropped down on both knees and pulled out the ring that he'd been carrying around in a pouch in his pocket.

"I was going to do this at dinner tonight, but then Grace showed up."

"Are you proposing?" Her question was loud enough they got a dirty look from a nurse. "Get up."

"Are you saying no?"

She hit him on the chest. "Of course not. I'm saying yes. Yes, to being your wife. Yes, to having babies. All of it."

"Then why are you curtailing the moment? You know how I feel about ritual."

She pulled him by the hand toward the hospital doors. "Yeah, but I want to be the rose that blossoms on places that would get us arrested in public right now."

"That's my best girl."

ACKNOWLEDGMENTS

First, I have to thank my editor, Kristine Swartz, for letting me write a rom-com about a Catholic priest, and my agent, Courtney Miller-Callihan, for selling it to her. I want to thank my mom for letting me watch *The Thorn Birds* in the early nineties, Phoebe Waller-Bridge for making hot priests a thing now, and Sierra Simone for defining the trope in romance novels.

I knew I had to write a book for Father Patrick as soon as he made it to the page in *Not the Girl You Marry*. A huge thank-you to the readers who e-mailed, texted, and DMed me, asking when Father Patrick's book would be out. I honestly might not have had the stones to write this book without you. Thank you for allowing me to be as wild, creative, and vulnerable as I can bear to be. It's truly the honor of my life that my words have made you feel seen.

Sarah MacLean always encourages me to "take the finger," and I hope I did her proud. Kate Clayborn—thank you for talking me through writing a slow-burn romance on the train ride from New York in the summer of 2019. I want to thank Kennedy Ryan for reminding me—through her friendship and her books—that it's good to try big, hard things.

I wrote this book during a wild time in the United States and the world, and I'm not sure I would have been able to get through it without my friends. Adriana Anders, Alexis Daria, Adriana Herrera, LaQuette, Tracey Livesay, Alexa Martin, Katee Robert, Naima Simone, Nisha Sharma, Joanna Shupe, and the Wicked Wallflowers (Jenny Nordbak and Sarah Hawley and the entire Coven) really got me through. I adore you all, and I can't wait to hug each and every one of you again.

Finally, thank you to Brittney (@litandknits) for naming Madison's husband "Tucker"—it's truly the best/worst frat boy name.

USA Today bestselling author **Andie J. Christopher** writes edgy, funny, sexy contemporary romance featuring heat, humor, and dirty-talking heroes that make readers sweat. A graduate of the University of Notre Dame and Stanford Law School, she grew up in a family of voracious readers, and picked up her first romance novel at age twelve when she'd finished reading everything else in her grandmother's house. It was love at first read. It wasn't too long before she started writing her own stories—her first heroine drank Campari and drove an Alfa Romeo up a winding road to a minor royal's estate in Spain. Andie lives in the Nation's Capital with a French Bulldog, a stockpile of Campari, and way too many books.

CONNECT ONLINE

AndieJChristopher.com
🐦 AuthorAndieJ
📷 AuthorAndieJ
📘 AuthorAndieJ1

Ready to find
your next great read?

Let us help.

Visit prh.com/nextread

Penguin
Random
House